Also By Cathryn Grant

NOVELS

The Demise of the Soccer Moms ♦ Buried by Debt
The Suburban Abyss ♦ The Hallelujah Horror Show
Getting Ahead ♦ Faceless
An Affair With God ♦ She's Listening

THE ALEXANDRA MALLORY PSYCHOLOGICAL SUSPENSE SERIES

The Woman In the Mirror ♦ The Woman In the Water
The Woman In the Painting ♦ The Woman In the Window
The Woman In the Bar ♦ The Woman In the Bedroom
The Woman In the Dark ♦ The Woman In the Cellar
The Woman In the Photograph ♦ The Woman In the Storm

THE HAUNTED SHIP TRILOGY

Alone On the Beach ♦ Slipping Away From the Beach
Haunting the Beach

NOVELLAS

Madison Keith Ghost Story Series
Chances Are

SHORT FICTION

Reduction in Force ♦ Maternal Instinct
Flash Fiction For the Cocktail Hour
The 12 Days of Xmas

Cathryn Grant

MADISON KEITH

Ghost Story Collection - Volume 4

UGLY TRUTH
BELOVED GHOSTS

DC
Published by D2C Perspectives

About Madison Keith

Both the living and the dead like to reveal their secrets to Madison. As the administrative assistant in the basement office of a suburban church, she gets plenty of opportunity to hear from both. Through it all, Madison offers up a steady stream of opinions on everything from the subject of religion and ghosts to finding a soul mate.

MADISON KEITH GHOST STORY COLLECTIONS

VOLUME 1
>Fatal Cut, Shallow Water, Unholy Child

VOLUME 2
>Stone Cold, Deadly Streets, Lonely Ghosts

VOLUME 3
>Last Chance, Eaten Alive, Empty Home

VOLUME 4
>Ugly Truth, Beloved Ghosts

Cathryn Grant

UGLY TRUTH

A Suburban Noir Ghost Story

D2C
Published by D2C Perspectives

One

FROM THE FIRST day I started working at Central Avenue Church, I hated the basement area that stretched from the rear door of the front office to the restrooms at the back corner. Even in the middle of the day, it was a scary place when I was alone down there beneath the sanctuary floor.

The room was about two thousand square feet. The ceiling was only twelve feet high — too low for a room that size — so even though it was a large space, it felt claustrophobic. The floor was dark green linoleum tile from the fifties, laid on top of a concrete slab, causing an echo even when I wasn't wearing shoes with particularly hard heels.

The first door to the right of the main office led to a conference room. A bit further along that side was Pastor Kate's office. At the rear was an alcove with doors to the men's and women's restrooms, and at the left side of the basement was an office that hadn't been used as long as

I'd worked there. A few large closets along that same wall contained folding chairs, tables, and gardening tools.

Even when the conference room door and Kate's office door were open, the space was gloomy. The room wasn't designed very well, and the lights were operated from the alcove outside the restrooms, so I was forced to walk all the way across in the dark. Sometimes, when I sat in the church office, all I could feel was that vast empty space behind the side wall, waiting.

It was the second week of July. I'd been home from Marin County and my failed effort to find out more about my parents' murder for almost two weeks. Every day of those two weeks, my brain felt like it was floating in some kind of thick liquid that prevented it from doing anything more than what was required for survival — eat, sleep, work. Pastor Joe hadn't said a word about my trip, and I was glad. Kate had been on vacation when I returned, and I was half glad about that too. I had no idea what to say about what had happened, what I *wanted* to say about it, and I had no idea what my next step should be. Part of me was just waiting to hear from Detective Smith, telling me that interviewing my aunt and uncle again had turned the investigation in a new direction.

Pastor Joe and Pastor Kate take Mondays off, since they work all weekend, but just before lunch, Kate had stopped by the office. She'd been holding a small bowl with two goldfish. One was pure orange and the other was white with orange splotches. She laughed nervously, and placed the bowl on my desk. "I won these at a carnival yesterday, and Cherie is constantly circling the table, meowing and plotting her attack. Is there any chance you'd like to have them?"

The two fish hung motionless in the water, staring at me with bulging eyes as if they were assessing my qualifications. I wasn't sure how I felt about fish. I'd never thought about it. Aquariums full of exotic, silent creatures are fascinating, but so expensive and so much work. Goldfish would be easy, but less fascinating, for sure.

She smiled again, more of a grin this time. "If it's an imposition, just say so."

"No, they're cute."

She was still smiling, looking very anxious. I was either her last resort, or her only resort, for taking guardianship of the fish.

"Why did you enter a contest to win fish if you didn't want them?"

"I thought it would be fun. I thought Cherie wouldn't notice. I guess I underestimated the power of the food chain. If you don't want them, I can ask Joe."

The fish with the orange splotches darted to the surface of the water. It opened and closed its mouth several times. "No, I'll take them. Is it hungry?"

"Probably." She pulled a tin of fish food out of her purse and put it on the desk. "Thanks. Sorry I don't have time to talk. I need to go shopping and pay bills and get my yard weeded before the week slams into me."

"We'll talk tomorrow," I said.

After she left, I put the bowl on the counter behind

my desk so I wouldn't accidentally knock it over. I went upstairs to the kitchen and got a roll of plastic wrap to cover the bowl, and a pan to put on the floor of my car to keep the bowl steady while I drove home. I planned to feed them, but the phones began ringing non-stop and I had to finish the edits for the newsletter that day if I was going to proofread it and make the mid-week deadline. I completely forgot about the fish.

At nine-thirty that night, I was doing yoga on my living room floor and I remembered the fish. The poor little creatures, not knowing where they lived, drifting in the dark silence of the church office. I suppose they could have survived until morning, but as I moved to each new pose, I kept seeing that white and orange fish, opening its mouth, trapped in its glass bowl, incapable of getting food without my help.

Without finishing my yoga routine, I rolled up my mat, put on flip-flops, and drove back to the church. I parked in the gravel strip out front, went up the stairs and along the path that curves through the rose bushes and leads to the stairs that go down to the basement offices beneath the sanctuary. There were small, dim lights along the garden, and there was a light on outside the church office that's always turned on when the last person leaves.

I unlocked the door, went inside the main office, flicked on the light, and closed and locked the door behind me. The fish were swimming madly. I wondered if they'd been doing that all evening or if the light made them excited that someone had come to rescue them from starvation and loneliness. I went over to the counter and opened the can of food. I put a pinch in the bowl and they immediately sucked all of it up, leaving the surface of the water almost completely clear.

Then, the worst thing happened. I realized I'd left home so fast, I hadn't peed, and now I had to. Desperately. Frantically. Irrationally. It was a twenty-minute drive from the church to my condo, and I doubted I could make it home. I thought about going upstairs and unlocking the restrooms in the classroom wing or using the restrooms at the back of the fellowship hall, but then I told myself I was being silly. The basement wasn't all that much darker at night than it was during the day, and I was alone in the building half the time during work. So what if I'd once encountered an angry ghost near the restrooms? So what if I'd seen several ghosts at the church? It wasn't as if they terrified me. I think I was more scared of living threats than those from beyond the grave. In some ways, I wasn't even sure what scared me about that basement. It was just big and empty and dark. Maybe there were more ghosts than I'd realized and I was half aware of their presence every time I walked through there alone.

I took a deep breath, sprinkled one more pinch of food in the fishbowl, and went to the door leading to the basement. I opened it and stepped into the darkness. I scurried across the hall too fast, and about halfway into the room, I stepped on the back of my left flip-flop with my right foot. I stumbled and fell. My knees slammed into that hard concrete-topped linoleum tile. I cried out, but of course no one but the fish heard me.

For a minute or so, I sat on the floor in the darkness, rubbing my hipbone with one hand and my knee with the other. The ache was tremendous and I wasn't sure I'd be able to stand up. But the darkness ate at my spine, creeping closer, growing thicker, draping itself over my head and around my shoulders.

Before I saw it, I felt it. Another presence. I started to cry. I was so fresh from the experience of hoping for my parents' presence in the home where I'd grown up, I couldn't believe a spirit that was a total stranger was contacting me again. While my parents' spirits remained hidden, a murdered stranger's ghost had appeared, and now this. It was so unfair. Someone out there — whether it was god or the universe or superior beings on another planet — something was mocking me. I know that was a hugely egotistical way to look at things, to assume I was so important that the whole universe was focused on making me suffer, as if there weren't seven billion other people with their own suffering, but that's how I felt.

Slowly, the space in front of me turned from darkness into a pale yellow. A shapeless, sexless figure appeared. It wasn't anything like a human form with visible appendages, more like the vague suggestion of a head with the entire body draped in a shroud. The place where its feet should have been touched the floor, but it still wavered slightly, as if it couldn't quite get its footing.

After several minutes. A red gash appeared on the

neck. It spread like a split opening in the ground. Then, thick, dark drops of blood oozed out. The blood ran down the front of the figure. It seemed to pool on the floor, although I wasn't about to creep forward and put my fingers out to confirm that impression. I inched back, afraid the blood would splash on me.

The blood continued to flow, so much blood I wondered how there could be any left. Surely it was more blood than was contained in a human body, although maybe it just seemed that way because I was mesmerized by the steady progress. It didn't let up or gush more rapidly. It seemed as if I sat there for half an hour, but it couldn't have been that long because I needed to pee and I wouldn't have lasted.

I got onto my hands and knees and stood slowly. The thing remained where it was.

"What do you want?" I said softly.

There was silence.

I took a few steps to the right, hoping I could make my way to the restroom without the thing following me, without it getting upset and doing something to hurt me. I took a few more steps, limping from the pain in my hip and knee. I hoped I hadn't done something to seriously hurt myself, that it was just a violent bruising that would fade like any other bruise.

"Did you trip me?" This wasn't really fair because I was pretty sure I'd stepped on my flip-flop, but it seemed somewhat coincidental that I'd fallen at that time, in that spot, and then the thing appeared.

It moved closer.

My body felt lighter, almost insubstantial. At least the need to use the restroom subsided as I felt myself withering, as if all the moisture had been sucked out of me. "Do you want something?" I spoke quite loudly this time.

"Pastor Joe," the thing whispered, so softly that if I'd cleared my throat or taken another step, I wouldn't have heard.

"What about him?"

"Pastor Joe."

"Yes?"

"Joe."

"Are you looking for him?" I folded my arms and tucked my hands between my ribs and upper arms. They were so cold, so dry, it seemed as if they were going to turn to dust.

"Joe."

"What do you want?"

"He hurt his flock."

"How?"

"He was so wrong." The whisper was softer, and I suddenly realized the blood had stopped flowing. The red gash in the neck area had turned black. The figure seemed smaller and thinner now. Wispier. "So wrong. So wrong. So wrong."

"Wrong about what?"

Now it was even more faint, somewhat brittle, as if it too was being drained of moisture. Maybe losing all the blood had left nothing.

I stood there for several more minutes and it faded into the darkness. I couldn't spend any more time standing around. I limped to the alcove, turned on the lights that filled the entire, cavernous room, and ducked into the women's restroom.

When I came out, I was reluctant to turn off the lights and repeat the journey. I decided to leave them on. I'd get to work early to turn them off and no one would know they'd been burning through electricity all night. It wasn't that I didn't want to see the ghost again. I didn't want to trip and fall, whether it was my own clumsiness or the ghost that caused it, my whole left side ached.

I reached the office without seeing it or feeling anything out of the ordinary. I went into the office and shut the basement door. I tore off a piece of plastic wrap from the roll I'd left on the counter. I covered the fishbowl and used an exact-o knife in my drawer to make a few slits in the plastic. I tucked the food container behind the waist of my yoga pants. I carried the pan under my arm and held the fishbowl with two hands. The water sloshed as I limped to the door. I held the bowl in one hand, turned out the light, and went outside. I hobbled slowly along the path to the bottom of the stairs and made my way slowly to the top.

By the time I got to my car, my hands were damp from water sloshing up and leaking out beneath the plastic wrap. I put the pan on the passenger side floor and placed the bowl in it. I got a sweatshirt out of the trunk and wedged it around the bowl to keep it as steady as possible.

On the drive home, I began to regret leaving the lights on and not waiting to see if the ghost returned. What could it mean that Joe was hurting his flock? What was he so wrong about, aside from his disdain for the unexplained supernatural?

Two

THE NEXT MORNING, I arrived early so I could check out the basement before Joe and Kate showed up. I dropped my stuff on my desk and went into the basement area. It was as scary as always, even at eight a.m., even with the lights still on. The shadowy corners provided hiding places where someone could be watching me. I went to the alcove and turned out the lights then returned to the center of the room. I stood quietly, listening to my breath echo off the low ceiling. I closed my eyes. Nothing felt out of the ordinary.

I opened my eyes, half expecting to see the yellow figure, but I was alone.

I heard the outer door to the main office open and close, followed by the sound of someone pulling the carafe off the coffee maker stand. I walked across the basement and went into the office.

Kate stood in front of the coffee stand, holding the pot while she shrugged two shoulder bags onto the floor beside her feet.

I took the carafe out of her hand. "I'll make coffee."

"Thanks." She heaved the bags back onto her shoulder where they pulled at her black sleeveless top so her bra strap slipped out. "Sorry I was in such a rush yesterday. How was your trip home? How was your weekend?"

"An uneventful weekend. JD and I went to the beach Sunday." I raised the carafe in her direction. "Let me take care of this."

I went back into the basement.

When I returned to the office, her bags were gone, and she was sitting in one of the armchairs facing my desk.

"How did the fish do?"

I dumped coffee grounds into a paper filter and stuck it in the basket. I poured the water into the coffee maker, put the carafe in place, and flipped the switch on. "They seem fine."

"Good."

"I forgot to bring them home. I had to drive back here last night and pick them up."

"I'm sure they would have survived one night."

"They were hungry, so I was glad I did."

"Well thanks again for taking them off my hands. I don't know what I was thinking." She pushed her hair off her face, and ran her fingertip down the center of her nose. She looked at her finger, inspecting it for excess makeup.

The coffee pot gurgled and the aroma filled the office.

"Promise you won't give me a hard time if I tell you something?" I'd planned to tell JD about the ghost first, but now that Kate was sitting right in front of me, I couldn't resist the urge to talk about it. And really, since it had appeared fifteen feet from her office door, she was likely to be more interested than JD. Even more so because it was possibly someone she knew.

"About your trip back home?"

"No, I'll tell you that over lunch . . . or sometime . . . maybe."

She crossed her arms and looked at me as if she couldn't make up her mind whether to be annoyed at my evasiveness or hurt that I wouldn't tell her all the details. She was already hurt that I'd refused to tell her how my parents died. Maybe I should tell all of them everything. Standing there, waiting to tell Kate about the ghost in the basement, and waiting for the coffee to finish brewing, it suddenly seemed ridiculous that I was so secretive.

All this time I'd been so good at hiding my life from people I worked with. Hiding it from almost everyone I knew. It's not like the whole world wants to know your life story and your wounds, but I went out of my way to evade the most casual questions. I had no idea why. Right that minute, waiting for the coffee, like I'd done a thousand times before, I had an abrupt change of heart. Maybe I was worn out from all the things that happened when I was in Marin County. Maybe I just didn't care if they felt pity for me, or viewed me differently, or treated me differently. Maybe it was maturity, or the look on Kate's face that said she really was a friend, and what kind of friendship is it when you refuse to tell someone about a major part of your life? An event that shaped your entire view of the world, an event that drives you back home like some other force has taken over your will and your body.

"I came back for the fish about 9:30. And when I got here, I . . ."

Kate stood. "I need caffeine for this."

"It's not quite done."

"Then hold on. Because I know what you're going to say."

"No you don't."

"I think I do."

I smiled.

She grimaced and stepped up close. The last few drops of coffee trickled into the pot and the machine beeped that it was ready to serve. She filled a mug and handed it to me, filled one for herself, and returned to the chair. She blew on her coffee and took a tiny sip, pursing her lips as if that would keep the steaming hot liquid from burning them.

"So I came into the office and gave the fish a bit of food and then I had to pee."

She took another sip of coffee and put the mug on the table between the chairs. "And you saw a ghost."

"Do you know about it?"

"I don't know about any ghost haunting the basement, but I know you."

"I don't see ghosts every day."

"Did you see one in Novato?"

"Yes."

She laughed.

"But how did you know I saw one last night?"

"The way you started the conversation."

"I guess that was obvious."

She nodded.

"Have you ever felt anything, heard anything in the basement?" I said.

"Just my own nervous thoughts." She crossed her legs and studied the toe of her red cowboy boot. It seemed like awfully warm weather for boots, but the basement stays cool and maybe she was planning to stay late, or go directly to an air-conditioned place after work.

I waited, hoping she'd ask me about the ghost, but she only seemed to want to investigate her boot. She seemed to have forgotten about her coffee. I wished she'd start talking. It was impulsive to blurt it out so suddenly. I should have waited, should have suggested eating lunch together, which we probably would anyway, and told her then, when there was more time. Joe was likely to show up any minute.

"Do you want to know what it looked like?"

"Not really."

I went to my desk chair and sat down. The room felt cold. I drank some coffee and turned to face my computer. Thinking she would give me a hard time had been the wrong thing to worry about. It looked like she didn't care at all. The silence continued. I turned to face her and leaned my elbows on my desk. "Why don't you want to know about it?"

"It's tiring."

"Tiring?"

"The tension between you and Joe. Knowing that anything you saw means there's some kind of problem that's going to get stirred up. Hoping you'll stay away at night, and that will be the last of it. So many reasons."

I sipped my coffee. The coffee pot made a hissing sound like it wasn't quite finished after all. Outside a dog started barking.

"Okay, then. I guess I should get to work," I said.

"No. You can tell me. That's how I feel on one level, but now of course you've made me crazy curious."

The problem was, now I wasn't as enthused. I felt like I was forcing her to listen.

From the corner of my eye, I saw a shadow pass in front of the drapes covering the large window behind my desk. It was Pastor Joe, so now the story wasn't going to get told. I felt like the ghost was trapped inside me, bubbling and pressing and needing another person to help me make sense of what it looked like, and the confusing things it had said about Joe.

The door opened and Joe stepped inside. He greeted us and went immediately to the coffee pot. One thing the three of us have in common is we're all a bunch of caffeine addicts. First thing in the morning that pot is gurgling and filling the room with the aroma of strong coffee. Every few hours, one of us is making a fresh pot, and it seems like we're always walking around with a mug of steaming coffee in our hands, like it's an additional appendage.

After he'd filled his mug, Joe turned to me. "Any messages?"

I hadn't checked the answering machine. I'd been there for over twenty minutes, and it's not like I'm in trouble for not writing them down immediately, but his next question would be what were we talking about, or not talking about, that caused me to skip the first step of my routine. He can be quite nosey.

He looked past me at the glowing number on the machine. "It looks like there are two."

"I haven't gotten to them yet."

He shrugged. He walked to the phone stand on the other side of my computer and pressed the play button. I grabbed the message pad to write down the details. It's not like he's a tyrant about messages, not like he can't write down his own phone numbers, but I felt sort of bad that I was more interested in getting Kate's input on a ghost than doing my job during working hours.

Both callers were asking about the Vacation Bible School coming up in August. Kate was in charge, but Joe remained where he was and listened anyway. Then he went and sat in the other armchair.

After several minutes of silence, Joe asked Kate how

many kids she thought they'd have for the Vacation Bible School this year, and whether she had enough volunteer teachers. For fifteen minutes or more, they went on about staffing and the schedule, as if whether to have snacks after the first hour or wait closer to lunch was the most important decision they'd make all week. While they were talking, both of them got up and refilled their coffee mugs.

I turned to the computer and opened my email. I didn't want to sit staring at them when I had nothing to contribute to the conversation. Even though my phone was still buried in my bag, I heard it bling with a text message.

As if he'd heard it too, and it changed the directions of his thoughts, Joe turned toward me. His face shifted into a fatherly smile. Not that I can describe precisely what a fatherly smile looks like, I've forgotten my father's face, except in photographs. But that's what I felt. I looked away for a moment, and wrapped my hands tightly around my coffee mug. It wasn't as warm as I'd hoped. I got up and went to the coffee stand.

"I never heard about your visit home," he said.

"It was good."

He nodded, but neither one of them spoke.

After a moment or two, he said, "Just *good?*"

"I saw my aunt and uncle, had dinner with them. I met a . . ."

Silence again. I scrambled through my head, searching for a way to finish that sentence without mentioning ghosts or murder. Nothing came to mind, and I decided murder was better than ghosts, at least in Joe's view.

"You met . . ." Joe prompted.

"I met a woman who was part of a murder investigation."

"How did that happen? I thought you wanted to visit your childhood home and spend time with your relatives?"

This was why I was glad he hadn't asked about the trip, until now. I love Joe, as a friend, I guess you could say. I surely don't see him as a father figure, although he seems to see himself that way. Of course, he thinks he's everyone's father, because of his job. He acts as if he's Kate's father or wiser older brother. Although she and I haven't discussed it, I can see her skin turn bright red next to that white-blonde hair, dismissing his unasked for advice, or his dictates about how things are going to be, when it's something related to her area of responsibility. I don't think he intends to be superior, he's trying to be helpful, but more often than not, people don't want help and advice. Even when they ask for it, quite often they secretly hope you'll ask right back what they think, so they can proceed as planned.

"It's a long story," I said. I half turned to my computer and put the mug down by the mouse.

"I have some free time."

Without looking at them, I said, "I was taking a walk." I hated the lie. Hated myself for even thinking of a lie. My lips froze as if something inside me was trying to stop me from piling more lies, or half-truths, on top of it.

Joe laughed. "Are you going to make us pull it out of you one sentence at a time?"

Kate said nothing. I think she knew where this was going.

I turned toward them. "I met a woman who was sobbing. She told me her neighbor had been murdered. Later, I found out the woman I met was the killer. The dead woman had been her lover."

Kate stood. She looked at me with a steady gaze. She knew those few simple sentences covered over a huge number of things I hadn't mentioned, and it was likely that if there was a murder, and the murderer was identified when I was around, there was something not human involved. She refilled her mug and started toward the doorway to the basement.

"Where are you going?" Joe said.

"To work."

"Madison's talking."

"Well, *Dad*, I have work to do, and Madison seems a little reluctant to tell us much about it, so it's probably good if we all get busy."

Joe smiled. I couldn't tell if he recognized her sarcasm, or was so pleased with her calling him *Dad*, he didn't really care.

Suddenly, just like earlier, I wondered why I was hiding the fact I'd seen a ghost. Why did I hide anything here? It seemed there was something about this church, something about working there that had made me more and more hesitant to say what was on my mind. I'd always been secretive about my parents' murders, but on every other topic, I said what I thought, usually without actually giving it much thought. I don't know if I was changing because I'd been told to stop talking about ghosts, or if the whole place had an atmosphere of hiding the truth. There'd certainly been enough of that over the past few years. I suppose all people hide parts of their lives, but at the church, maybe because of the supposed bond of all being one big happy family, secrets bred like fruit flies.

Kate remained in the doorway, looking at me. I could tell she wondered what I was going to do and I think she was really hoping I would keep my thoughts to myself.

I scooted the chair close to my desk, leaned my elbows on it, and propped my chin in my hands. My hair, which I hadn't braided or clipped up that morning, fell across my shoulders and arms, and brushed against the desk. It partially covered the sides of my face. I straightened my back to make it fall away from my cheeks. "I saw my aunt and uncle twice, and I visited the house where I grew up. But I spent a lot of the trip at the place where this girl was stabbed. I saw her ghost several times, and I couldn't seem to keep myself away."

Part of me felt like he'd baited me. He asked about my trip, and when I stumbled, he pushed. I guess it's not fair to say I was baited, but something about it felt like it had spiraled out of control before I could even blink.

He stood up. I felt the coldness coming off him. "If you mention ghosts again," he said, "we should probably discuss you finding another job." He went into his office and closed the door.

Kate raised her eyebrows and stared at me. Her eyes looked as hurt as I felt. She backed out of the doorway and clumped across the basement to her office, her cowboy boots echoing through the whole building.

I stared at the armchairs. Two minutes ago, the two of them had been sitting there blabbering on about Vacation Bible School schedules, and now I might not have a job, unless I was going to become even more adept at keeping secrets. The room felt completely empty of human life. Even the coffee pot was sputtering — as empty as the room. I went over and turned it off.

I worked on the mail-merge to get the newsletter ready to go out to all the church members, then checked the calendar to see if there were other upcoming events I needed to send notices for separately from the newsletter. My fingertips were numb, my whole body, really. My brain felt like it was floating inside my skull. The thick coating I'd experienced the past two weeks returned, clogging all my nerves so thoughts couldn't make their way around.

The phone started ringing every few minutes, more of the same questions about the Bible School. Since Kate was there, I transferred all of those to her, but even having those brief conversations did nothing to puncture the numb, disconnected feeling.

It makes sense that the pastor of a church that believes there are two destinations for the human soul after death wouldn't be interested in entertaining the idea of ghosts and an alternate realm. And it wasn't as if he'd fired me on the spot, but I'd rarely talked to church members about my experiences. Just to him and Kate, most of the time. And Joe's wife, Cindee. So I didn't understand what the big deal was. I wondered what he'd think if I mentioned a ghost was once again staking out its territory at the church itself.

Once the newsletter was on its way and the phone had calmed down. I took the coffee carafe into the basement, headed toward the restroom to rinse it and fill it with water for a fresh pot. I walked slowly past Kate's partially closed door, hoping she'd call me into her office and beg to hear about the ghost making its home right outside her door. Not a sound came from her office.

As I was returning with the full carafe, I thought I saw a glimmer of yellow in the corner opposite from her office. The handle of the carafe, heavy with water, shook in my hand. I put my other hand under the bottom to steady it. I glanced behind me, took a few steps closer to that side of the building, and then decided it was just a lingering impression on the backs of my eyes from the night before. But right then, I determined I'd come back to find out more about it.

I walked toward the center of the basement, again moving slowly, hoping Kate would call out to me. She didn't and I returned to the main office and started a fresh pot of coffee.

FOR THE REST of the morning, I fiddled around,

trying to look busy. Joe's door remained shut, Kate didn't come out to the front office, and the coffee pot was still full of dark liquid at quarter to twelve. I was so bored, I wondered if I should start looking to see what other jobs I might be interested in, and qualified for. The problem was, my computer screen faced the open area of the office, so anything displayed there was immediately visible when Kate walked through the basement door. And although it wasn't directly in Joe's line of sight, he'd definitely notice if I scrambled to change screens before he came up to the edge of my desk.

It was so quiet, I heard birds rustling in the ivy outside on the opposite side of the path. They weren't tweeting, just digging around for bugs and seeds. I pulled my phone out of my bag, thinking I'd use it to visit one of the online job sites. It couldn't hurt. If Joe came out, he'd assume I was playing a game or messaging someone. If he thought I wasn't doing my job, I didn't much care. Obviously my actual job performance was less troubling to him than the fact that I'd seen a few ghosts. As if I had a choice in the matter.

He'd never accused me, well only slightly accused me, of making it up. He didn't flat out call me a liar, but he didn't believe me. So didn't that mean he thought I was liar, he just didn't have the courage to say the word? I really wondered sometimes what he was thinking. When I was first hired, he seemed to really like me, but recently he'd been very boss-like, except when he was trying to be fatherly. He'd hired me because he wanted someone who wasn't part of the church, someone who wouldn't be tempted to share confidential things that are overheard in the office — conversations like he and Kate discussing the highly sensitive issue of when to serve snacks to children. If I wasn't a church member, didn't it make sense I'd have different beliefs? Not that my inclination to see ghosts is a belief. But maybe I see them because I'm not all locked down to the world being a certain way, where there's no room for things that don't make sense, things that are contradictory or confusing. I think anything can happen, and maybe if you think that way, anything *can* happen.

When I unlocked my phone, I saw the text that had come in earlier.

JD: *Dinner at Mezcal tonight? And I'll stay over?*

I texted back: *Sure. I thought you were working.*

JD: *Switched schedules for Ben's anniversary.*

I texted back: :)

I closed the text window and opened a web page. I typed monster.com, but before the page loaded, I heard Kate's boots in the basement. I locked my phone and placed it on the desk just as she walked through the door.

"Want to go out for lunch?" she said.

For some reason, I glanced at Joe's door. Still closed. Usually, he would have been out for at least two coffee refills by that time.

"It smells like stale coffee," Kate said.

"It's been sitting there all morning."

She walked over and turned it off. With her back

toward me, she said, "What do you feel like eating?"

Her voice sounded slightly off, maybe a little nervous, which is unusual for Kate. She's always sure of what she's saying, what she's thinking, what her plans are. The only time she's ever been nervous was when she saw a ghost, and she got over that quickly enough.

She turned to face me. She looked worried.

WE WENT TO a bar and grill that emphasizes the grill at lunch and the bar in the evenings. It was dark for a lunch place, with chocolate-colored paneling, forest green chairs, glossy dark brown tables, brass light fixtures, and a brass pole running along the front of the bar. It's one of those places that tries to offer something for everyone — burgers and tacos, Chinese salad and egg rolls, steak and pasta, vegetarian and gluten-free. The result is decent enough food but nothing that's remarkable. Kate likes it because they have fast service and she can eat whatever she's in the mood for without spending time up front trying to decide where to go. I'm picky about being in the mood for a particular kind of food on a particular day, but I'd still rather go to a place that does one thing better than everyone else.

Kate ordered a salad with prawns and beets and I ordered a burger with fries. When the food arrived, she pointed out that someday I wouldn't be able to eat food like that without gaining weight, and also pointed out, with extra emphasis, that it wasn't very good for me.

I stuffed a French fry into my mouth and sipped the

iced latte I'd ordered. Lots of things aren't good for me
— smoking, beef, keeping secrets, and probably the
amount of coffee I consume. When I'm forty, I'll worry
about all of that, like Kate does.

She cut a beet into tiny pieces and ate one. "Tell me
about your ghost."

"I don't have a ghost."

She rolled her eyes.

"Which one?"

"The one in the basement," she said.

"Do you have an idea who it might be?"

"How would I know that?"

"Maybe because you heard someone was killed down
there? You've felt something odd?" I smiled. "You saw it
yourself? It could be a lot of reasons. Earlier, you acted
like you were afraid of what I'd say, and now it seems like
you're . . . I don't know . . . intense about it."

She pulled the tail off a prawn and sucked the flesh
out of the shell. She laid the tail on the edge of her plate.
"I feel uncomfortable talking about it at the church."

"Because of Joe."

"Not just that. I'm there to teach people certain
truths, and I feel like I'm betraying my calling."

"Really?"

She nodded, but kept her eyes averted from mine.

I decided not to push her. She sounded honest,
almost vulnerable. "But also because of Joe," I said.

"I don't like what he said to you."

"Thank you."

"He doesn't always handle things well."

"It's funny you would say that."

"Why?"

"This thing I saw, this ghost, it mentioned Joe."

She put down her fork. "Maybe I should have ordered a glass of wine." She smiled but her face had the same uneasy expression she'd had earlier.

"It was yellow. And it was bleeding."

"Do ghosts bleed?"

"It had a gash in the neck area, and red stuff was coming out. I assumed it was blood. I thought it pooled on the floor, but then when the spirit disappeared, there was nothing."

The restaurant was filling. People were talking loudly. I raised my voice a bit. "It, the ghost, said Joe had hurt his flock."

Kate glanced to each side, like she was worried someone we knew was sitting there taking notes. She turned back and put her finger to her lips.

"No one cares what we're talking about."

"You never know."

"It's noisy. I was afraid you wouldn't hear me."

"I can hear you just fine." She stabbed a tomato. It dangled off her fork, the pulpy center pulling apart from the skin and the inside edge. "Joe would never do anything to hurt the people he cares for. Never. That's an ugly accusation."

"I'm just telling you what it said." I lifted the bun off my burger and rearranged the pickles so they were more evenly spaced. I put the bun back in place and took a bite. The whole pickle came out, slapping against my lower lip. I poked it into my mouth. "*Was* someone killed down there?"

"Not that I know of."

"I wonder if Joe knows."

"Well you certainly can't ask him, so it doesn't matter."

"If I were him, I'd want to know about ghosts haunting my church."

"You're not him. And he doesn't think anyone is haunting anything, so there's nothing to know."

"So he thinks I'm a liar?"

She sighed. "Who knows what he thinks."

"Maybe I could ask Cindee."

"Probably not a good idea." She plucked the tail off another prawn, then she worked her way across the plate, removing all the tails. She gathered them up and piled them on her bread plate.

"You've never felt anything weird down there?"

"It always feels weird down there. It's too cold and it's dark, even with the lights on. It always feels like someone is in the corner watching you."

"I know. I feel that way too. Maybe this ghost has been there for a while."

"It's paranoia. Not a ghost."

"You don't know that," I said.

"Well I don't think it's any weirder than any other basement. And I've never heard of anyone being killed down there."

"Maybe it wasn't murder, maybe something else happened. And then that person died and they chose the basement for their haunting."

"They choose the places they haunt?"

"I don't know. I'm learning about them as I go."

"Look." She put down her fork and leaned forward slightly. "I'll fight for you, defend you. I know you're not crazy or lying. But you have to stop talking about this at the church."

"I have to know who it is. I have to know . . ."

"You don't have to know. Leave it alone."

"I can't. There's no way you can ask other people about anyone who died there? Or about anything bad that happened in the basement, maybe before you started working there?"

"No. I really think, for once, you should try to forget about it."

"Or else I'll lose my job?"

"I don't think that will happen. And I said, I'll fight for you, but you're deliberately antagonizing him and you have to stop."

We finished our lunch and I think she assumed I was going to let it go, or maybe she just hoped I would. I think she knew me better than that.

Three

TWO DAYS LATER, I was at my desk, alone in the office, entering expenses into the budget tracker. Outside, I could hear the lawn mower as the gardener worked on the patch of lawn at the center of the garden. Kate was at Costco getting supplies for the Vacation Bible School, and Joe was making hospital visits. A woman had given birth the night before, another woman had been in a somewhat serious car accident, two men were recuperating from hip replacement surgery at different hospitals on opposite sides of the county, and a woman was going in for a mastectomy — Joe would be gone most of the day.

Despite all my complaints about Joe being rigid, he can be very comforting, and although I'd never seen him visit someone in the hospital, I'd overheard him on the phone enough to know that he was a good listener. He isn't one of those people who tries to tell you how you should be feeling. I'd even heard people scream out their pain to him and he let them carry on, giving them a place to clean out all that gunk, pouring it into his ears like he was a human garbage disposal.

A few months earlier, I'd walked into his office, thinking he was finished with his phone call because it was so quiet in there. I needed to ask him a question about a flyer for the senior citizens' lunch. He was holding the phone away from his ear, tugging on one hair in his beard that was a little longer than the others. His eyes were closed and his head was tilted up, as if he would have been gazing at the ceiling, if his eyes were open. A woman was screaming about how unfair life was. Standing a few feet from his desk, I could hear her voice through the receiver. She raged about how badly god had treated her. She shouted that she had faith, and that was supposed to mean she'd be taken care of, that her life would be blessed. Her voice was a roar, as unfiltered and raw as any ghost I'd ever heard. Joe just listened. He let her go on, uninterrupted. He tugged that single hair and let her vent all of her bad feelings onto him.

I returned to my desk, and when he finally spoke, his voice was low, so I couldn't hear what he said. There'd been something very tender about his expression, and the tone of his voice when he responded to her.

The lawnmower stopped. I was breathing in the quiet when a shadow passed by the drapes behind my desk. Those drapes are always closed, which kind of defeats the purpose of a large window, but if the drapes are open it would get too bright and I wouldn't be able to see the computer screen.

The door opened and Cindee stepped into the office. She greeted me and walked to the armchair closest to Joe's office door and flopped down. She swung her purse up and around, landing it on the seat of the other chair. She grinned. "What's new?"

"Not much."

"I spent all morning getting my classroom ready for VBS."

"How's it decorated?"

"There's a huge construction paper tree that covers an entire wall. Each day, the kids will cut out a paper apple and print the Bible verse they memorized. They'll hang their apple on the tree. The thing that took the longest was cutting out two hundred leaves."

"Wow. That's very thorough. But it sounds cute. Remind me what age group you have?"

"Six and seven."

"That'll be fun."

"I miss having kids that age." She sat up straighter and pushed her hair behind her shoulders.

"Teenagers can be fun, in their own way," I said.

She laughed. "Most of the time. How was your trip home?"

"Fine."

"And?"

"It was fine."

"That's all?"

After Kate's lecture about ghosts, there were very few things I could tell Cindee about the trip without stepping over that line. I guess I could have mentioned my aunt and uncle, but there were only a few things I could say on that topic without mentioning my parents' murder. I couldn't tell her about the detective, couldn't tell her about Karen's ghost, couldn't tell her about getting into the house and feeling lost and alone. I guess I could have told her that last part.

"You look like you're sorting through a filing cabinet, trying to decide what one piece of paper you can pull out and show me," she said.

I smiled.

"Did you meet the owners of your parents' house?"

"Yes."

"And did they let you look around?"

"Not inside, well, I . . ."

"What?"

"They aren't the owners. Renters are living there — a couple — about my age. But the landlord let us look around." I wondered why I hadn't mentioned that to Kate. Maybe she didn't ask the right questions, or didn't ask detailed questions, like Cindee was prone to.

"Do you feel like you got some closure?"

"It didn't feel the same as I remembered."

"Going back to a place that used to be yours is hard. It's never the same."

"Maybe."

She crossed her legs and tugged her jeans to arrange the seam along the side of her leg. Once again I wondered why I was working so hard to keep information from all of them. It required a lot of effort. It made my head ache — all of these things pressing on the inside of my skull. What did it matter? So what if they looked at me differently once they knew about my parents. So what if they pitied me. Why was that so horrible? They probably already looked at me differently because I was so private. Maybe it didn't matter so much anymore, with my parents dead for so long. With the investigation stale and stalled.

"And I heard you had something weird happen while you were there."

I crossed my legs and arms, twisting myself into a coil.

"What's wrong?" she said.

"I'm not supposed to talk about it."

"Since when?"

"Since Joe made it clear I better keep my thoughts and my *experiences* to myself."

"You sound very upset. Don't be angry at him, he's just . . ."

"You don't need to explain."

"You two have a good relationship, I don't want to see that change. If you're angry at each other, it will poison the atmosphere."

"That's not my fault."

"Please don't be angry at him."

"Are you trying to be the peacemaker?"

"Maybe. A little."

"It won't work."

"Try to understand where he's coming from."

"I know exactly where he's coming from."

"Where's that?"

"He thinks I'm making up stories, or imagining things."

"You . . ."

"And he doesn't want anything contrary to your doctrine being talked about. Ever. Which is kind of funny since he hired me *because* I wasn't a member of the church. So you'd think he would expect me to have different views."

"You sound like you hate him." She looked like she was about to cry. I wondered if trying to smooth things between us was her idea, or he'd suggested it.

"I don't hate him. But maybe he's right, maybe I should look for another job. I can't help what happens to me. I see ghosts. In fact, I saw one . . ."

She uncrossed her legs and sat up straighter. She glanced at the door.

"He's making hospital visits."

"I know."

"He has a long list."

"You can't quit. He wasn't serious."

"I think he was. And I think you know that, isn't that why you're here?"

"He's a good guy."

"Yes, he is. But ghosts seem to want to reveal themselves to me, and I can't do anything about that. It's become a rather large part of my life, for whatever reason, and I feel like I have to consider every word I say." Speaking it out loud made me feel a little guilty. Joe's attitude toward ghosts wasn't the only reason I was careful with what I said. I was just more aware of it because of my recent trip home — talking to Detective Smith, visiting my aunt and uncle. Between that and the ghosts, my whole life was now littered with things I couldn't, or didn't want to, say.

Cindee was quiet, and as I waited for her to say something, I wondered whether Joe would be more understanding of the ghosts if he knew about my parents being murdered. On the other hand, he might think I was so damaged by their horrible deaths that I was imagining ghosts as a way of coping, unable to let go of my loss. Cindee had already guessed that I'd hoped to see my parents' ghosts when I visited my old house. What she didn't know, was how likely it was that their ghosts were lingering because of their unsolved murders.

"You don't have to watch everything you say. If you could just not tell him about your supernatural experiences."

"In this case, it involves him. But I guess he doesn't want to know that."

"How can a ghost in Marin County have anything to do with Joe?"

"Joe knows I saw a ghost in Marin County. He doesn't know I saw one in the basement a few nights ago."

She uncrossed her legs. She was wearing high-heeled sandals and her ankles leaned toward each other so the bones were touching. "You aren't serious."

"You know I am."

"Here?"

"It's not the first time."

"I know, but it's so . . . I thought we were done with that. I can't . . ."

"You thought that couldn't possibly happen here again."

She smiled half-heartedly.

"The ghost I saw mentioned Joe."

She folded her arms and grabbed her elbows as if she was cold. I thought I saw her shiver slightly but she must have caught herself because it only lasted half a second.

I waited for her to ask what the ghost had said. Maybe she was too busy deciding whether to believe me, knowing I wasn't a liar or crazy, but not able to really believe. She wanted to, with a small part of her, but another part of her did not want to think about things that contradicted her view of the world. She definitely did not want to create a chasm between her and Joe.

"You heard something speak?"

"Yes."

"How do you know you weren't overhearing a few gossiping biddies? We have several of them here, you know."

"It was ten at night."

"What day was this?"

"Monday."

"That's the night the women's book club meets."

"They were gone. The parking strip was empty when

I got here." It was possible there had been cars in the parking lot on the far side of the other buildings. I didn't look, but I know I was alone in the basement, and I was quite confident they were all gone because the place had a deserted feeling about it.

"You saw a ghost and it spoke to you."

"Yes. It was pale . . ."

She closed her eyes. "I don't need to hear what it looked like."

"Why not?"

"It's not important."

"It is to me."

"What did it say? Something bad?"

"Why would you think that?"

"Because you wanted to stall by talking about how it looked."

"It said Joe was hurting his flock."

She looked like I'd slapped her. Her face turned dark red and her upper lip trembled. She shifted in the chair. For a moment, I thought she was going to stand up and walk out.

"I'm sorry. You asked."

"You brought it up first. He's a good man."

For the most part, as far as I'd known him, I agreed with her. But I couldn't ignore that the ghost seemed to know something I didn't. It might know things even Cindee didn't know. It's not like she followed him around at work all the time. I gave her what I hoped was a gentle smile.

"You're not agreeing with me?" she said.

"I don't know him like you do."

"Are you really that angry at him? So angry you can't acknowledge he's a good man?"

"I'm upset. And I can't ignore what this thing told me."

"That's not fair. You've worked with him for a long time now. How can you judge him? Over something you don't even know?"

"I'm not judging. I just don't know much about him, except what I observe here."

"That's cold."

"It's the truth. I'm not saying he's a bad person, just not gushing over how good he is."

"What else did it say?"

"That's all."

"You're going to stop trusting him, and think badly of him because a *ghost* told you one tiny piece of something and didn't bother to elaborate? Do you realize how that sounds?"

"It happens like that a lot. Their stories dribble out," I said.

"It's not fair."

"Are you going to tell him?"

"No! And I don't want you to either."

"Trust me, I'm not."

"Did you mention it to Kate?"

"Yes."

"Why? Why would you do that?"

"Because Kate's the only person here who believes

my experiences! She's the only person here that I can talk to. Joe is basically calling me a liar. And fine, if he doesn't want me to talk about ghosts I've seen at other places, I suppose I can live with that, but when I see one here, I'd think you, and he, would want to understand what's going on."

She stood up. She was breathing hard, as if she'd just run three miles. Her face was still red, adding to the effect of just completing a run. She pushed her hair back, then twisted it around and tried to tuck it up in a bun, but it collapsed around her shoulders. She went to the door and opened it. "I need to get some air." She went outside.

When the door closed, I heard nothing. Her shadow didn't pass behind the curtains, so I assumed she was standing just outside the door, leaning against it, maybe.

I thought back over the conversation and tried to figure out how we'd ended up where we were. I was being a little unfair, refusing to tell them anything about me and my life, but oh so happy to disrupt theirs. I didn't have to tell Cindee about the ghost. I could have waited until I had more information, but she pushed me — saying he wasn't serious about me looking for another job. She was wrong. I wondered if I was trying to hurt Joe because he'd been so disrespectful toward me. I didn't think I was, but sometimes you do things, and you're not even sure what's underneath it all.

After what seemed like fifteen minutes, although it probably only seemed that way because I was watching the door, doing nothing, the door opened and Cindee stepped back inside. I could tell she'd been crying. It struck me that she seemed very upset for not even being sure she believed ghosts existed. Even though she argued, she seemed to be taking this one's word about her husband. Possibly, she knew what the ghost was referring to after all.

She settled in the chair facing me. "So."

I smiled. "So."

"Were you scared when you saw this thing? Why didn't you run out of the room before it started speaking?"

"I'm not sure. I usually don't run, though. I guess curiosity trumps fear."

"So you were scared?"

"Not really. I wouldn't call it scared, maybe anxious. Nervous."

"And why would you believe this thing? This thing, this being, whatever, that's making you anxious and nervous? Why would you believe it, some non-thing, over a man you work for and trust and know? A man who's treated you very well? Why?"

"You make it sound like I'm betraying him, that I'm listening to gossip."

"Isn't it the same thing?"

"I don't think so."

"Some *thing* you don't even know undermines your boss and you take it at face value?"

"So you believe that I saw it? That it spoke to me?"

"I don't know what to believe. It's very compelling

when you're so insistent. I don't believe people's spirits come back from the dead, but I guess I don't think you're lying. It's possible you're hallucinating."

"You think I'm crazy?"

She shifted in the chair, glanced at the coffee pot, and then at some point on the wall behind me. Without looking at me she said, "I told you I don't know what to think. You're very convincing."

"Do you know what the spirit was talking about? How he might have hurt his flock?"

"No!" She blinked rapidly and her face, which had returned to its normal color, developed two perfectly round red spots right over her cheekbones. "He would never . . ."

"Maybe he doesn't realize he's hurting them. It could be something he's not aware of."

"That's ridiculous. He would never hurt one of his parishioners. He would never hurt a human being at all."

"Except me."

"What does that mean?"

"He's hurting me. By calling me a liar."

"He never called you a liar."

"Come on. He doesn't have to. He says ghosts don't exist and I'm not allowed to talk about them. What would you call it?"

"He's not trying to hurt you. He's trying to stand up for what he believes. For what he knows to be true."

"He doesn't know what's true."

"The word of God reveals the truth."

I stared at her. I didn't say anything. I watched her eyes shift to the right. Whether she was checking on the door, still worried he'd walk in at the wrong moment, or too afraid to look directly at me, I wasn't sure.

"I guess you really don't believe the word of God," she said.

"I'm open to possibilities. Unlike Joe. I've never trashed his experiences . . . with praying or whatever."

"He doesn't . . ."

"Yes, he does."

She stood. "I don't know what to say to you."

"Do you know of anything he's done to hurt the people who look up to him? Trust him?"

"I'm offended you would even ask that question."

I let her words hang in the air, hoping she'd noticed how I might be equally offended, and hurt. She hadn't responded to that, not really, except to fling the Bible at me.

"I don't want to fight with you," she said after a while.

"Neither do I."

"Will you please put those thoughts of him out of your mind? And give him the benefit of the doubt?"

"I can't put it out of my mind."

"What if you never see it again? You'll just be mistrustful of him forever? Never let it go?" She picked up her purse. "I'm sad that things are like this between us. I wanted to hear how your visit home was."

"It seems like you want me to cut Joe all this slack, but he doesn't cut me any."

"Not true. Look at all the time off he's given you — Australia, going to your old home . . ."

"I mean me, as a person."

"He likes you, Madison. And he thinks you do a good job. He's always commenting on how cheerful you are, how you make people feel welcome. That you're sharp and get things done and never make mistakes."

"But none of that matters if I say the word *ghost*."

"I think you should be careful about where you're headed with all of this."

"I'm not headed anywhere. I came into the office to get my goldfish and this thing appeared to me and was pretty specific."

"Don't go starting trouble when you don't have anything to base it on."

I looked at her. Did she think she was my mother? Maybe she was too lost in always being the Mom to her four daughters. But just because she knew my mother was gone, she didn't get to take on that job. This is what's so weird about working in a church. In what other job would you have your boss's wife showing up and being your friend one minute, and your pseudo-mother the next, and something else entirely, maybe almost a partial boss herself the minute after that?

I didn't want her to leave angry, and I don't think she wanted to, because she kept lingering near the door. She touched the knob every minute or so, but didn't actually put her hand around it and turn it.

Ghosts are real. I've seen them and heard them. Yes,

they can be scary and creepy, but they've told me true things that helped bring them peace of mind, hopefully eternal peace. You'd think a minister would be supportive of that.

She spoke softly. "I should get going."

"Bye."

She looked at me, waiting for me to say more. When I didn't, she opened the door and walked out.

AFTER WORK, I decided on the spur of the moment to drive to Half Moon Bay to see JD. Even if I had to wait a few hours for his shift to end, I needed to see him. I always needed to see him, but right then, I needed to talk face-to-face about what happened with Cindee. I didn't want to explain it on the phone when he was on his way home from work. Most of all, I needed him to hold me while he listened. Staying up until he got off work at two in the morning, then driving back from the coast early in the morning was going to make me very tired for my job, but I didn't care. I also needed to be as far away as I could get from that church and their ghosts and their close-minded staff.

I went home first and packed a bag. I ate a cheese sandwich, fed the fish, fed the birds, and changed their water.

While I drove to the coast, I thought mostly about the stubbornness of Joe and Cindee. I used to think she was more open than he was. She'd always seemed like she was on the fence regarding the subject of ghosts. But either he'd moved her over to his viewpoint, or told her she had to get behind him no matter what she thought. As I turned onto Highway One heading north, I started thinking about the members of the church. Except for brief encounters in the church office, or a little small talk before business meetings when I was there to take notes, I didn't really know any of them beyond saying *hello* and *good-bye* and *how's your summer going?* For the first time, it occurred to me to wonder whether any of them had ever seen a ghost. If more than half the people in the United States believe in ghosts, it was likely at least a few of the church members harbored secret views. It was possible some of them had seen and heard and felt things that weren't discussed during Sunday morning services.

There was no one I knew well enough to ask, and if it got back to Joe, I'd definitely be out of work. It was probably a good idea to put concentrated effort into seeing what other job opportunities were out there, but before I even considered making that kind of move, I needed to find out more about the latest ghost.

I stopped by The Distillery to surprise JD, and after a quick kiss, I went to his condo.

The sun was down and it was cold. I made a pot of coffee, filled a mug, put on my sweatshirt and Ugg boots, and went out onto the balcony. His balcony looks out over a wooded area that's quite peaceful. Even though mine looks into a green belt, his is better, more secluded. When it's sunny and clear, a thin strip of the bay is visible through the trees.

It was colder than I'd realized. I went back inside, and grabbed the afghan off the chair in his living room. I settled into one of the Adirondack chairs and took a sip of coffee. I thought back over all the things I'd learned about Joe since I started working at the church. At first we got along great. He was so easy to work for, friendly and all of that, and he still was, but in the beginning he hadn't been so controlling.

Kate would say he always tended toward controlling. Even though she's a pastor, he's definitely the lead guy. Still, they're colleagues and they each have distinct areas of responsibility, so the fact that he often insisted on having the final word irritated her. With me, though, the whole problem of control was about the ghosts.

With the warm coffee mug in my hands and the afghan wrapped around me, I was feeling cozy, and I'd started to regret drawing such a hard line with Cindee. If I'd stayed calm, and listened to her instead of spouting off right away, I might have gotten some information about what Joe had said about me. I also might have had some clue about what the ghost was saying. Refusing to echo her statement that he was a good man blew my chance. I'd have to go back to the church at night and see whether the spirit appeared a second time.

As I swallowed the last of my coffee, I decided I'd do that on Saturday night. Friday nights there was a weekly youth event in the fellowship hall. Besides, after staying up most of the night, I'd want to go to bed early on Friday. I couldn't wait around for a ghost if I were crashed on the floor in total exhaustion.

When JD arrived home, I was asleep in the chair. He woke me with a kiss, silly as that sounds. He sat in the chair next to me, not needing an afghan or even a sweatshirt. His voice was strong and soothing in the darkness. "What made you decide to come over?"

"I had an argument with Cindee."

"About what?"

"That ghost I saw."

"You told her about it?"

"Yes."

"You told her what it said?"

"Yes."

"I'm not sure that was a good idea."

"Why?"

"Not a good idea to get in the middle of anyone's marriage, especially theirs."

"How am I in the middle of their marriage?"

"By telling a guy's wife something negative about him. She's going to defend him to the death."

"I guess that's what happened. I didn't think it through, and the conversation got away from me."

"As they so often do."

I laughed.

"What made you tell her?"

"It was sort of her fault. She came by the office when Joe wasn't there. It was obvious she wanted to be the peacemaker between Joe and me. We were talking about ghosts and Joe's rules for not mentioning them, and it sort of popped out."

"What are you going to do now?" He scooted his chair closer to mine.

I turned my chair toward his and put my lower legs on his lap. "I'm thinking I should seriously start looking for another job."

"Really?"

"It's only a matter of time, don't you think?"

"Probably." He stood. "Let's go to bed. It's cold out here."

I smiled into the darkness. I guess he needed an afghan after all. We went inside and closed the glass door. I rinsed my mug and we got ready for bed.

When we were lying in the darkness with our arms and legs twisted around each other, he said, "Are you planning to look for a job over here? They can be hard to find, but it's not impossible."

"I haven't planned that far. Even thinking about changing jobs feels weird. I'd miss Kate, for sure. If I'm working over here, it seems harder to go back to school at some point."

He didn't say anything. And what I didn't say was — *What about your idea of moving to Marin County and renting my childhood home? Maybe that would be a good place to find a job.* Later. I'd mention that later. I wondered if he was thinking about it in the silence, or if he'd forgotten about it. He isn't one to forget things, so maybe he'd deliberately put it out of his head.

I heard his breathing change, announcing he'd fallen

asleep. That was unusual for him. When he gets off work he's wired up from all the activity and social interaction, not like my job where I sit around all day, and half the time I'm by myself. It usually takes him a few hours to wind down.

Before I did anything about changing jobs, I needed to find out more. First, I'd see if the ghost showed up again. Second, I'd see if it had anything new to say. And third, if it was still cryptic, I might have a look around Joe's office.

That was a really bad thing to even think about, much less plan for, but my days there were numbered, so I didn't have a lot to lose. It might be illegal and unethical — it was definitely unethical — but so was hurting your flock so badly the dead were coming back to do something about it.

Four

I WENT TO the church at twelve-thirty in the morning on Saturday. Actually, that would make it Sunday, but it still felt like Saturday night. I dropped my bag on my desk and opened the door into the dark basement. I walked to the center of the room and stood there, feeling like an idiot. A slightly nervous, mildly scared idiot, waiting for a ghost to make her appearance. If I screamed, even someone walking around the garden up at the street level wouldn't hear me, much less someone in a neighboring house, hundreds of yards away, deep asleep in the middle of the night. If she didn't show up, I was just a silly girl thinking she had some special connection with the supernatural world.

After what seemed like forever, I pulled my phone out of my pocket and checked the time. Twelve-forty-two. I sighed. I yawned. I wished I had coffee, but making a pot was not the way to entice a ghost. At least it didn't seem like the right approach. Maybe if it were a coffee-loving ghost, it would have been the perfect lure. I laughed softly.

I stood there for another five or ten minutes, my mind wandering over nothing. I started to doubt what I'd seen. My legs ached from standing in one position on hard linoleum over concrete.

Finally, I went outside and smoked a cigarette, but I put it out after fix or six puffs.

I went back inside the main office and sat in one of the armchairs and looked at my desk, picturing myself sitting there working. I rarely saw the office from that direction, and could probably count the number of times I'd sat in one of those chairs.

Although I was waiting for her to appear, hoping she'd speak to me, I knew that on a deeper level, I had a less admirable reason for being there. Once the idea had been planted, it grew into a compulsion and I knew I was going to do it, even though it was so wrong. It was the perfect time to look around Joe's office. In fact, if I was honest, that was part of why I was sitting just outside his door. There was no deluding myself into thinking there was any justification. It was on the ghost to tell me more, if she really wanted closure or vengeance or anything at all. It wasn't my responsibility to "help", yet that was what I was planning to do.

I listened to the silence.

The entire building was blanketed in that thick quiet that's partially soothing but also frightening in some way that I can't explain.

I dozed off for a few minutes, and when I woke, I stood up without thinking, almost as if I were sleep-walking. I went to Joe's door, took my keys out of my pocket, and unlocked it. I turned on the light and closed the door, locking it behind me. I'm not sure why I did that. If someone came in, I couldn't escape being discovered. I suppose if someone who wasn't Joe or Kate showed up, I could wait it out and leave them thinking Joe had carelessly left the light on. Joe, Kate, the janitor, and I are the only ones with keys to his office.

The wall behind Joe's desk, and the one adjacent to it, are occupied by floor-to-ceiling bookcases. The wall opposite his desk has a window with a couch in front of it. The drapes were closed, of course. Near the fourth wall are two armchairs. Above the chairs are some paintings by various members of the church — a large one of the ocean, one of a child holding a puppy, and one of a woman in a meadow. They're amateurish, except for the ocean. Whenever I focused on those paintings, I wondered what Joe would do if ten or fifteen more people wanted him to hang their artwork. He'd quickly run out of space and then how would he choose? Maybe he assumed that anyone who made such a request was a little off balance, and he wasn't worried about there being that many needy artists in his congregation.

I stood there, overcome for a moment by what I was planning to do. Even though I'm not under the same religious rules as Joe and the members of his church, there's an innate or nurtured knowledge that you don't go through other people's things without their permission. And yet, that's done all the time when someone dies. In many cases, most cases, permission is given through the dead one's will, but not always. And maybe not to all the people who wind up going through their things. But you definitely don't do it to the living, and even more definitely not to your boss.

Trying to put myself back in the semi-sleepwalking state I'd felt earlier, I went to his desk and sat down. I opened the top drawer. It was quite tidy — pens lined up, a few sticky pads in a stack, a tray of paperclips, some coins in their own little dish, loose keys in another dish, and a few greeting cards. I pulled out the greeting cards. They were all for his birthday and none of them said anything beyond what a wonderful, wonderful guy he was and how he deserved the very best blessings throughout the year. It almost made me gag. I put them back.

His side drawers had more office stuff, notes from some sermons, and other uninteresting stuff. The bottom drawer contained hanging files. They didn't have the plastic labels attached, but there were manilla file folders inside each one. Each manilla folder had the subject written on the tab in Joe's block printing.

Shockingly, after his tidy top drawer, and the stripped down appearance of his desktop, the files were not in any kind of order that I could figure out. I wondered if they were priority order. If so, his priorities were a bit odd. The first folder had a few lists of sermon topics, the second was stuffed with business meeting notes, and the third contained several applications from people who had applied to be the administrative assistant before I was hired. Maybe that was a new priority — he was looking back through his files for a replacement for me.

That thought was a bit of a shock. I stopped looking for a few minutes. I'd assumed that unless I really threw down the gauntlet regarding ghosts, my position was secure. I'd thought he'd continue to warn me until I sensed that the next warning would be the last. Maybe I'd failed to sense it as strongly as I should have, and I'd already reached the last warning. Or maybe it had been on his mind for a while. Or, maybe it meant nothing at all. The files were just badly organized.

I leaned back in his chair and tried to picture myself working somewhere else. No images came to mind.

After a few minutes, I knelt on the floor and returned to the files with all seriousness. Toward the back, I found seven manilla folders with handwritten notes from counseling sessions. I sat back on my heels. Even though that's what I knew I'd been searching for, I hesitated. I still had a chance to only partially betray his trust, if partial betrayal is even possible.

Only the first names appeared on the tabs of the folders, but still . . . It seemed a betrayal on his part that the notes weren't locked up, and that he took notes at all. Pieces of people's lives were captured in a drawer, vulnerable to others if Joe died suddenly. Things people were so afraid to talk about they could only go to their minister, were exposed and available to travel somewhere they didn't belong.

They hadn't given me permission to know their stories, but *I* knew I could trust myself to keep their secrets. I rationalized my next move by thinking about the anonymity of a first name. Thousands, tens of thousands of people, shared first names. Surely I knew some of them from seeing them come into the office, and so I had seen their full names at some point in time when I scheduled the appointments, but I'd never remember, never be able to connect all the names and faces. I'd force myself to forget.

The first set of notes was for a woman named Jenna. I read about her husband's addiction to porn and her pathetic attempts to try to lure him away. I felt sick to my stomach, seeing into an invisible woman's heart. I was amazed that she'd shared it all with her minister. Somehow I didn't think of a minister as someone you'd want to talk to about your sex life, but then, I wouldn't talk to anyone about my sex life, period. I wondered what advice Joe gave her. That wasn't in the notes.

I read about a woman who'd lost her child to leukemia.

I read about a couple whose twenty-year-old son was living on the streets, using crystal meth, and how the wife couldn't stop giving him money because she didn't want him to starve, and the husband was angry and wanted to cut him off.

It seemed as if their voices were crying out to me, because nothing was ever really resolved. There was probably temporary relief from talking to someone, unloading feelings out of your head and into another person's head, but what else was there? Joe couldn't fix any of that stuff. He could give an opinion about how they might approach it, but why was his opinion more valid than anyone else's?

As I read more, my heart softened toward Joe. He had to carry a lot on his shoulders, hearing these stories, not really able to do anything at all to help. All he could do was listen.

Then I realized these might be people he was currently seeing. I was pretty sure I was looking for something that had happened a while ago. I put the folders back and turned to the filing cabinet tucked between his desk and the bookcase. The top drawer was completely full of folders bearing first names. I was horrified at all the problems. I yawned. It was going to take a long time to dig through all those notes, and the more I did it, the worse I'd feel. I shivered. I zipped my hoodie but was still shaking, my hands dry and crinkly from touching all that paper, and my fingertips almost numb. It seemed as if the room was getting colder. I pulled on my hood and tugged the cord to tighten it around my face. The shivering stopped, but my fingers were still cold and stiff.

I pulled out a stack of ten files and began reading. I wasn't sure what I was looking for. I had a vague idea of some kind of untimely, harrowing, guilt-laden death, but was that going to be recorded in the notes? If someone talked to Joe and later took his own life, it wouldn't be recorded there. And if someone committed murder, would Joe write that in his notes? But didn't he have a responsibility to report something like that? Even if it wasn't a law, surely it was required by his faith.

I read stories of abortion and adultery, eating disorders and violent tempers. There was so much pain, I could hardly bear it. As I read, I started to wonder what Joe would say if I told him the secret from my life. What would his advice be regarding my aunt and uncle? What would he tell me to do with Detective Smith? Would he advise me to find a way to lease my childhood home, or to let it all go, as people are so fond of saying, as if that's so very easy — to just *Let go.*

It took me two hours to skim through all the notes. I was surprised I hadn't gotten tired and fallen asleep, but I suppose the adrenaline of sneaking through his office, breaking every rule of human integrity, the chill in the air, and the pain in the stories, were keeping me alert.

I put everything back in the file and sat in his chair again. I tipped it back so I could look at the ceiling instead of those dull paintings right at eye level. That didn't last for long because the fluorescent lights made my eyes ache. I closed them and I think I fell asleep for a few minutes, but it was that weird kind of sleep where you feel like you're awake and noticing what's going on around you, but when you wake you aren't sure what state you were in.

The office had become even colder. It was summer and it felt as if I was standing on top of a snow-covered mountain. I hugged myself and tried to keep my teeth from rattling against each other. Part of me wanted to go into the basement area and see if the ghost appeared, but the other part of me was suddenly scared. It really is scary seeing these things. Each one is frightening in a new way, and forcing myself to go looking for that fright was not what I wanted to be doing at three o'clock in the morning. And if the ghost thought Joe betrayed her, maybe she'd now feel the same about me, having observed me reading about her life in his files. I wanted to be home in my cozy bed, listening to my birds fuss and coo, even better, wrapped up in JD's arms.

If I didn't hurry, soon it would be light and then I'd have other problems, like someone showing up early for Sunday services. I stood and pushed the chair close to the desk. I stared at it for a few minutes, trying to remember exactly how it had been positioned when I came in. I hoped Joe wasn't so precise he remembered the exact position he left his chair in every day when he locked his office door. I finally decided to leave it pushed in, trusting that my gut was telling me that's how I'd found it. I went to the door, opened it, and turned out the light.

As I turned to step into the main office, something breathed on my neck. The chill that ran down my spine was bitter, sub-zero cold, immobilizing me so I couldn't move my feet. As if I had no control over my body, I felt drawn back into the office, my feet dragging across the carpet by some other force than my own muscles and bones. Once I was standing in the center of the office, the door slammed closed and I was in complete darkness. Not even the light over my desk seeped through the gap at the bottom of the door. I cried softly, suddenly angry at myself for being so casual about my fear.

The pale yellow figure appeared in front of me, so close I could touch it, if I wanted to. The red gash was still at its throat, but no blood was pouring out as it had before.

I stood trembling, waiting for it to speak or do something, hoping it wouldn't continue to move my body according to its will. "Who are you?"

"He's betrayed them. Every single one of them." The voice was thin and inhuman, like the wind in a canyon.

"How?"

"He doesn't belong here. He has no right."

"Who did he betray? What did he do?"

The creature began to wail, so loud my ears felt like they were bleeding. I covered them with my hands but it didn't do any good. I stuffed my fingertips inside, and the sound was only slightly dulled. It penetrated my skull, wrapped itself around the inside of my head as if wire were being twisted around my brain, pulling tighter until it, too, was bleeding.

I began to cry. "Please stop. Stop! Please. You're hurting me. I can't stand it." I continued begging it to stop that awful sound. I wondered how long I could bear it. I tried moving back to the door, but my legs and feet failed to respond.

After what seemed like hours, the sound began to

fade. It was still there, but bearable. "Are you going to let me know how I can help?"

The wailing continued. After several more minutes, words began to take shape again. "I lost my daughter because of him. Lost her forever. Forever."

"She died?"

"To me, she died to me."

"What do you mean?" I shouted, trying to make myself heard about the awful sound, as the intensity grew again.

"He betrayed me."

"I don't understand."

"The pain is too much. I want to take it all back, every word. But it's too late. He needs to know what he's done."

"What's your name? Why are you here?"

Would it keep me captive until daylight, or would it take me with it? I longed for JD. I hadn't even told him I was coming here, he would have no idea what had happened to me. I started sobbing. "Please let me go. Tell me what you want from me."

The words faded and the piercing sound grew stronger. I put my hands to my ears again, expecting to find blood coming out of them. There was nothing, just icy cold flesh.

The yellow form glowed in front of me, the gash crossing the entire throat area, if you could call it a throat, since the shape of anything resembling a head was vague and watery. I tried to lower myself to the floor, hoping to curl up in a ball and protect my ears, but my body refused to cooperate with that as well. I bent over, crouching slightly, closing my eyes. At least I had control of my eyelids, and my hands and arms. After a while, the sound faded again. When I opened my eyes, the thing was gone. The room was still unbearably cold and my ears continued to ache as if a large needle had been inserted in each one. I touched them again, still expecting blood to accompany the pain, but there was nothing.

I moved toward the door, my feet sluggish as if I'd been sitting on them and all the feeling had gone away. Finally I reached it and turned the knob. I looked at my hands, still convinced I should see blood.

After staring at my fingertips for a few minutes, I closed the door, and locked it. I grabbed my bag off my desk, went outside, and ran to my car, my ears throbbing with each step.

At home, I crawled into bed and wrapped the comforter around my head, trying to soothe my ears. The pain wasn't nearly as great, but they still ached. I was worried something had been damaged, but how would I know? I decided if they didn't feel better when I woke up, I'd go to the ER.

I no longer felt guilty for snooping through personal notes. I was too scared and hurting too much to think much about what I'd done. I hadn't learned anything useful, and lying in bed, I wasn't sure why I'd thought I would. There was no way to tie that spirit to anything I'd read. It was so vague in its accusation, it could be anyone.

My dreams were filled with a pale yellow spirit but it

was bathed in utter silence, turning the dream into a nightmare where the sharp, painful cries had destroyed my hearing and all I would know for the rest of my life was silence.

When I woke, I was sweating, which was a nice change from the bitter cold. My parakeets were chirping. Hearing them, made me start to cry softly. All the pain was gone.

Five

WHEN I FINALLY got out of bed at eleven, there were four text messages from JD. I called him while I changed the birdcage liner, gave them completely fresh water, refilled their seed containers, hung up a treat, and fed the fish. JD didn't ask why it had taken me so long to call after all the messages, and I decided it was better to tell him about my crime and the ghost in person.

He said there was an Art and Wine festival in downtown San Jose, and asked whether I agreed that would be a relaxing way to spend the afternoon. Even though the wine wasn't interesting to me, I love art, and they always have fantastic food at those street fairs and festivals.

Twenty minutes later, the doorbell rang. I was just out of the shower, my hair sopping wet on my back. I folded it up in a towel and pulled on my dress. As I trotted to the stairs, I heard JD's key in the lock.

When I reached the first floor, he wrapped his arms

around me. He put his hand on the towel, steadying it on my head and we kissed. "I took a gamble that you'd want me to come over. I was halfway here when you finally called."

I laughed and kissed his nose. "It's not really a gamble."

He patted my turban. "Late start?"

"I'll tell you about it after we get going."

I took his bag upstairs. He went into the living room and watched part of a golf tournament while I dried my hair. Before I went back down, I took my cigarettes out onto the balcony. I lit one and leaned on the railing, trying to think how I was going to explain what I'd done, under what set of ethics I thought it was okay to dig through my boss's personal papers.

With the sun gleaming overhead and the pale blue sky, I wondered again why it had seemed like the thing to do. It was so wrong, and I couldn't understand how I'd justified it to myself. I hadn't, actually. But I'd ignored my feelings and gone with my compulsion to get information. Now, I felt as if I'd been driven by something outside of myself. Or was that just more rationalizing?

I blew out a thin, lazy stream of smoke and thought about the whole evening. It wasn't as if I'd argued myself into it, or excused myself. It was like a hard knot inside my chest that made me feel like I had to do it, like I had no choice. Then I thought about how I hadn't been able to move my feet or legs while the spirit was in Joe's office, piercing my eardrums, and tearing at my brain. Was it possible that when I'd seen the ghost the first time, it had done something to the inside of me that compelled me to go looking at other people's secrets? I shivered, despite the sun on my bare arms. I put out the cigarette and went downstairs.

Since it was already early afternoon, we had to walk six blocks from our parking spot to the closed-off streets where tents were lined up on both sides. JD got a wrist band and two tickets that would allow him two locally brewed beers.

We wandered past paintings and photographs and handmade jewelry, holding hands and not really talking, just enjoying each other's touch and the sun and the music and the intoxicating smells — cooking beef, garlic, and popcorn. At least those were the smells I noticed. Spices and the irresistible aroma of fried artichoke hearts and sizzling potstickers mixed with the other foods, making me feel as if I hadn't eaten breakfast. Ghosts and betrayal faded to the back of my mind.

After an hour, our feet were hot and tired. We found a booth selling Thai shish kebobs, jasmine rice, and cabbage salad with peanuts and sesame dressing. After we ordered our food, JD got a beer, and I went into a coffee shop for an iced latte. We found a table half a block from the stage where a band was playing Mexican music. The tunes managed to stir up feelings of happiness and created an urge to sing along with them, even though we couldn't.

Just as I was about to tell him what I'd done, he said, "Have you heard anything from Detective Smith?"

I shook my head and pulled a piece of beef off the skewer. I bit it in half. "I don't think he was planning to get in touch with me."

"So what are you going to do?"

"I'm not sure."

"How come you haven't mentioned it?"

"I thought you were sick of hearing me talk about it."

"Maybe a little, but not really."

"I guess I'm trying to sort it out." I thought for a minute, trying to decide if that was true. It was always hovering at the back of my mind, but the ghost in the church basement had pushed it to a far corner.

"Okay." He took a long swallow of beer, and glanced over his shoulder. "I don't suppose we can smoke."

"Only if we give up our table."

He took another sip of beer. "We need to quit."

"I know."

We smiled at each other.

"Tomorrow," he said.

"Definitely."

"I'm sort of curious about what's going through your head."

I took his hand, lifted it toward me, and kissed his knuckles. "When I figure out what's in my head, you'll be the first to know."

"I just don't want you to spring something on me and not give me time to think it through."

"What would I spring on you?"

"Going back up there, moving up there."

"That wouldn't be sudden. You know I've thought about it."

"But I don't know what you've thought *lately*."

"Okay. What I've thought is I don't think I'd want to try to rent that house. Even though I appreciate you suggesting the idea. It would be too sad and too weird. Besides, the more I think about it, I think Jan was rude, so eager to get rid of Kevin and Gwen. Just because she doesn't get to snoop in their lives, they make her nervous? I don't want a landlord like that."

"Good point."

"So yes, I want to go back up there and stay for a while. I want to see if I can convince Gwen and Kevin, mostly Kevin, I guess, to let me inside the house when they're not there. I don't feel like that's completely out of the realm of possibility. It's not like they said they'd get a restraining order if I came back. And there's my aunt and uncle."

"You'd stay with them?"

"No. Maybe. That's actually a good idea I hadn't thought of."

"I thought you were angry with them."

"Yes, but they're part of this, so maybe there's no way around it." I smiled and picked up the last shish kebob. I pulled off a piece of beef and held it out toward JD's lips. He opened his mouth and I popped it inside.

"Clearly you have been thinking a lot about it. Just not

telling me." He looked slightly hurt. I wasn't sure if he was teasing or not.

"I tell you everything."

"Everything?"

"Do you tell me every single thing?" I said.

"Almost."

"What haven't you told me?"

"That I'm sick of driving back and forth to each other's place. And I'm ready for a job change. And I wonder . . ."

"There's no surfing in Marin County," I said.

"It's not that far from the ocean."

"More than ten minutes."

"I'd survive."

"You'd do that?"

"Would you?"

"It's a big step."

"It is."

"I've always had the idea I should resolve my past before I plan the future."

"I know. But sometimes the past can't be resolved."

"Don't say that." I spoke softly, not as angrily as I would have a few weeks earlier. I'm not sure why. Maybe I was just tired of everything, tired of trying so hard. Maybe it was the ghost. She really scared me. It made me think a little bit about all the good things in my life. Waking up to my singing birds and a beautiful day that I take for granted most of the time, and then thinking about how much I love JD, and how amazing he is . . . I just wondered if I didn't have to feel like I was fighting the whole world all the time.

"You sound different," he said. "Calmer."

"That doesn't mean I'm giving up."

He laughed. "I never in a million years thought you were giving up. On anything." He stood. "I really want a smoke."

We scooped up our trash and carried it to the extra cans placed along the street for the festival. We headed toward the bandstand, then skirted around it and out onto a four-lane road. The train station was on the opposite side. We crossed the street and found a bench on the sidewalk outside the station.

JD lit my cigarette and then his. We smoked quietly for a few minutes, watching the traffic, which I know is a strange way to enjoy a summer afternoon when there's an art festival a hundred yards away, but we could still hear the band, and sometimes it's fun watching people in cars, seeing their expressions and gestures, not knowing what they're talking about. Maybe it's a little like watching ghosts. You have no idea what they're saying and you have to try to guess. It's probably easier with ghosts than with people sealed silently inside of cars.

"I guess I want it to be over," I said.

He put his arm around me. I leaned my head on his shoulder, then sat up so I could take a puff on my cigarette.

"I know you do," he said.

"But it's a giant glass wall."

"More like brick, since you can't see what's on the other side."

"Yeah."

"I don't understand why all these ghosts track me down, and my parents' . . ."

He squeezed my shoulder. "Maybe you want it too much. You said the ghosts come to you because you're open. Maybe wanting it so bad, hounding the detective, trying to get into that house, it's the opposite of being open."

"That's a good point, actually. Except I don't know how to be different. I can't go up there and not try to talk to Detective Smith. And I for sure wouldn't see them if I didn't try to get in the house."

"How do you know?"

A car drove past with a huge Doberman Pinscher in the back seat. His head was out the window, ears flapping, and his mouth wide open as if he was grinning at the world. You don't think of Doberman Pinschers as the most gleeful dogs in the world, but this dog looked wild with happiness.

"I tried too hard last night, but the ghost still showed up."

"Oh?"

"Yeah, I was going to tell you about that."

"You went to the church at night?"

I nodded. I knew I should blurt out what I'd been doing, but something held me back. Maybe the same thing that first propelled me, without really questioning, into Joe's files, and then rooted my feet to the floor.

We continued smoking. When we were both nearing the end, we walked to the covered area and found a large concrete ashtray filled with sand. We put out our cigarettes and crossed back to the festival side of the street. We turned right and walked up two blocks to a section we hadn't looked at yet. The first booth near the corner was filled with pottery. We stood for a while, touching the soft beautiful surfaces. They weren't high gloss, just a smooth silky finish that made you want to press your cheek up against it.

JD bought me a small grayish blue bowl. After the artist wrapped it up, we continued walking.

"So what made you go to the church? Looking for the ghost, I assume?"

"Sort of. That's why even though what you said about being open to ghosts makes sense, it's not like I never put forth any effort to hunt them down."

"What do you mean, *sort of?*"

Leave it to him to ignore my wondering and my wanting to go back to talking about *why, why, why* my parents' ghosts have never come to *me*, and zero in on my quiet little hint that there was more to what happened than I'd said so far. "I did something bad."

He stopped walking. "Should I be sitting down?"

"Maybe."

We walked to the end of the street, holding hands, and sat on the curb. I put the wrapped bowl between my feet. "I looked in Joe's office to see if he had any notes from counseling sessions that might give me an idea about the ghost and what she's upset about."

"Shit."

"I know!"

He pulled his knees up higher and pressed his face into them, holding this head as if he thought it was going to fall off. In a muffled voice he said, "Why would you do that?"

"Right now, I don't know. Because it seems stupid and I can't imagine what I thought I was going to find. But the weird thing is . . ."

"It's not just stupid in that sense."

"Yes, I know. It's wrong. Illegal and unethical and all the other *ills* and *uns* you can think of. Immoral, maybe."

"Do you want to get fired?"

"No. I guess I thought I owed it to the other people who are my employers. Joe's my boss, but really, I work for the whole church. And if he's doing something bad, and if he hurt people enough that a ghost appeared to try to fix it, shouldn't I do whatever is necessary?"

"What if it's not telling the truth?"

"Why would anyone lie, after they're dead?"

"I can think of several reasons."

"Such as?"

"I don't know. But I will!"

"Can I explain what happened?"

He lifted his head. His face didn't look as disgusted as his voice had sounded, which made me feel better. I mean, I know I totally did the wrong thing, and I know it was far worse than going into my old neighbor's house after he died. And I know it was betraying Joe and the people I was supposedly doing it for. Even if they never found out that I knew their secrets.

"Do you still love me?"

He wrapped his arms around me. "Of course I do. Why would you ask that? I'm just . . . I think I'm mostly shocked."

My foot nudged the wrapped bowl and it toppled on its side. I wriggled out and grabbed it, then went back to hugging him.

After a few minutes, he let go of me. He pulled out his cigarettes, offered one to me, and lit them both.

"I decided I *had* to look. It had crossed my mind, and I felt bad about even considering it, but when I talked to Cindee, she tried too hard to defend him. And Kate was a little defensive too. I felt like I was the one the ghost came to because I was the only one who wouldn't get all supportive and excusing him no matter what. And then I thought if he betrayed his whole flock, as she said the first time, or hurt them, then maybe . . ." I took a drag on my cigarette, realizing that believing a betrayal would be documented in notes was absurd. What had I been thinking? For some reason, I just thought there would be something tied to all the counseling he does.

"And?"

"I honestly don't know. It doesn't make sense when I tell you. So let me explain the rest."

"Okay."

"I was leaving the office and I'd just turned out the light, when this force pulled me back inside. The door closed and I couldn't move my feet. I couldn't see the light from the main office under the door. It was unbearably cold and there was this sound that was so loud and so intense I thought my ears were bleeding." I told him the rest of what happened, but not that I now wondered if the ghost had somehow, without me knowing, compelled me to do something I wouldn't normally do. I wanted to see if JD saw it that way. If he did, I'd feel much better. I hoped he wouldn't think I had doubtful morals.

We sat quietly, smoking. Watching the flip-flops and sandals and athletic shoes and boots of people walking by, as if the whole world had shrunk to feet and ankle bones and lower legs.

"Then what?"

"It just screamed, it carried on about Joe's betrayal and how he took away her daughter."

"But how is that betraying an entire church of people?"

"I'm not sure. I haven't really thought through it much."

"So you think this thing can control your movements?"

"I know it can!" I waited, imagining myself crossing my fingers. But that was all he said.

We put out our cigarettes and stood.

"Ready to head home?"

I nodded.

As we walked, he said, "What are you going to do now?"

"I don't know." And I meant that about everything — my job, the ghost pointing a finger at Joe, looking through private notes, my parents' ghosts, my aunt and uncle, and talking to the detective again to see if I could persuade him to let me know what my aunt and uncle told him, if anything. I didn't know what I would do about any of those things.

JD LEFT EARLY on Monday to go surfing with his friends and I went to work.

That evening it cooled off a bit, so I spent two hours cleaning the condo and trying not to think. I let the birds out so they could fly around my bedroom while I took their cage onto the back deck and hosed it off. There was still a patch of sun on the edge of the deck, so I left the cage to dry for an hour. I put the fish in a serving bowl, washed out their bowl, put in fresh water, and dropped in the liquid that purified tap water so it was more life-affirming for them.

By the time the birds were snug in their home again and the bathrooms were sparkling white, I was starving. I made a salad out of shredded carrots and avocado and turkey. I took it outside so I could eat and watch the sun go down.

While I'd been cleaning, my mind had been semi-blank — focused on scrubbing and vacuuming, enjoying the movement and watching all the dust slide away. It made me feel calm, like I was floating outside of myself, watching.

As soon as I started eating, my brain began munching on all the things I'd talked about with JD — all the things wrong in my life. Not wrong, I guess, but unfinished. I decided to make a list. I thought it might help me focus on one thing at a time so I wasn't half-dizzy, my head spinning in circles, racing faster and faster, until I felt I was on one of those rides that spins so fast you can't see, and each car is spinning independently of the main mechanism, which is spinning. As if that's not enough, the arms for each car fling you out and yank you back around until you're laughing so hard you're almost crying and wondering if your brain has spun right out of your skull.

I left my salad half eaten and got out a little notebook with a red cover. I wrote down:

Church ghost

Joe's betrayal

Cindee

Detective Smith

Gloria and Paul

New job

Moving to Marin County

Living with JD

Parents' ghosts

Seeing it written down made me realize that the easiest item on the list was to call Detective Smith, which

I did immediately, even though it was almost eight in the evening. Of course, I got his voice mail. After I left a message, I finished my salad and washed the plate and went into the living room. I surfed the web on my iPad and then laid down. I fell into a pleasant, dreamless sleep.

The phone rang just as I was drifting back to consciousness. It was Detective Smith. I was shocked that he'd called me back so quickly and so late.

"Hi," I said.

"Madison?"

"Yes."

"Detective Smith."

"I know."

"Do you have a minute?"

"Yes." My heart started beating hard. Thudding like one of my birds was trapped inside my chest, beating its wings against my bones, desperate to escape.

"Sorry I haven't called. But I talked to your aunt and uncle."

"Okay."

"I learned the breakdown in their relationship with your parents wasn't about borrowing money."

"I didn't think so."

"Your parents suggested to Gloria that she had a drinking problem. Gloria was offended. And hurt, I guess."

"So they lied to you. I already knew that."

"Yes."

"How did she explain her lie?"

"She said it was too painful."

"Well doesn't that mean they might have lied about other things?"

"Not that I've been able to determine."

"Why would she lie, and make my parents look bad?"

"I don't think she was trying to make them look bad. She was upset. She felt it was personal and an unfair accusation and so she made up a story."

I pulled my legs onto the couch and sat in a lotus position to try to clear my head and keep from crying with frustration. "And you believe all that?"

"Why wouldn't I?"

"Because she lied! She could be lying now."

"It's nothing material regarding the case. There's nothing to suggest they killed your parents or had anything to do with it."

"But there's still something not right."

"That may be, but not related to the case." He let out a huge sigh.

"How do you know?" My voice was shrill.

"Madison. Calm down. I'm telling you what I know and what we've learned. As a courtesy. If you're going to get hysterical, I'm going to hang up."

"I'm not hysterical."

"Fine. We questioned them, there's nothing there. They made up a story because she was embarrassed. It happens."

"I just don't . . ."

"There's one other thing. It's minor though."

"What?"

"You didn't understand how your aunt and uncle showed up so soon after you found your parents' bodies. How they knew."

"Yes?"

"You called them."

"I did?"

"And once I asked them about that, it came back to me. I hadn't made a note of it because it wasn't important to the investigation."

"I don't remember that."

"You were distraught."

"I hadn't seen them since I was a child. Why would I call them?"

"I can't answer that. But you obviously found the number, and knew enough about either your parents' will or the fact they were the only relatives. I don't really know."

"That's all?"

"I'm afraid so."

"Now what?"

"That's all."

"What do you mean?"

"You asked us to interview them, it seemed warranted and we talked to them. There's nothing that provides new leads or any indication of a suspect. Just like before."

"That can't be right."

"I'm sorry. I'm very sorry. I know you keep hoping for a different outcome."

"I just don't see how two people can be shot in their bed and no one saw anything, no one knows anything. They can just get wiped off the face of the earth and no one knows why."

"You realize, we could find out who and you still might not know why."

That was exactly what JD had said. Thinking of him, and how he'd said it so gently, was the only thing that kept me from screaming.

Detective Smith cleared his throat. "Another thing to think about is, sometimes, when people find out why, that doesn't provide any peace of mind."

"Why is that?"

"If it's a gang, or a random killing by a mentally ill person, it can be worse. It seems meaningless."

"It already seems meaningless."

"As I said before, I think you should find other ways to get some closure on this."

"How can you not work harder?" I whispered. "Talk to more people, go back over everything again and again and again. Until you get the answer. It wasn't a gang. My parents let them in the house!"

"I'm as frustrated and disappointed as you are."

"I don't think so."

"It's been a long time. People have moved, things change."

"Life moves on, right? As if they never existed."

"Don't torture yourself."

"I'm not. You are."

"That's not fair."

"I'll tell you what's not fair."

"I should go now," he said.

"So what are you going to do?"

"Nothing, right now."

"Well, you did nothing for quite a few years, so I guess everything is the same."

"Good-bye, Madison." He disconnected the call.

I threw my phone on the floor. Luckily it didn't crack.

Six

JOE WAS OUT of the office. On Sunday after church, he and Cindee had gone to a beach cottage north of San Francisco for three nights.

I knew Kate and I would be alone on Tuesday, but I wasn't about to tell her what I'd done, so I couldn't really mention that I'd seen the ghost again. There was no way to tell that story, and make her understand how terrifying it had been, without letting on that I was in Joe's office. And I wasn't going to lie, snooping was bad enough.

Late in the morning, I was typing up Joe's sermon notes. He handwrites his sermons, word for word, even though he doesn't preach from what he wrote. He does it to get the ideas in his head, then he makes a few notes from that. After he preaches, he adds more notes in the margins, putting in things he said that didn't come to mind until he was standing in the pulpit. I type up all the notes and revisions and file them. I wasn't sure what he was saving them for, but I could see how, if you'd put all that work into collecting your thoughts, you'd want to preserve them.

Suddenly, I lifted my fingers off the keys and put my hands in my lap. When I was a teenager, before my parents died, and especially after, I'd kept diaries. Where were they? The curiosity was so intense, I thought about abandoning work for the day, driving home, and emptying all my closets. I'd thought about those diaries on and off over the years, but not since I'd gone to see Gloria and Paul and found out they were ambivalent about being my guardians. Not since I found out they'd lied to the police. It wasn't as if I thought I'd written any secrets about Gloria and Paul, something that would give me insight into who they were and what they were really like back then, but still. Detective Smith said I'd called them when I found my parents' bodies. Why did I not remember that? Was it possible I'd written about it? But more importantly, those books were filled with my wounded, grief-stricken thoughts and feelings, alongside all my normal teenage thoughts. My whole life, and my mind, were distorted by the fact that my parents were not only dead, they'd been murdered in cold blood. And I don't think it's dramatic to say that, because that's what it was.

When I'd moved out to my own place, I'd packed everything and taken most of it with me, but there'd been a few boxes left behind. My first place had been a studio apartment, and I only had one closet. The attic in Gloria and Paul's house was huge, so it made sense to leave some things behind. I'd moved a few more times before I ended up buying the condo, and I'd forgotten all about those abandoned boxes. Did Gloria and Paul remember? Did they move my stuff when they bought their new house on the hill? Surely they wouldn't just toss something that belonged to me. Then I started worrying, now that I'd seen Gloria and Paul in a new, less flattering light, whether they'd read my diaries.

The minute that thought passed through my head, I started crying. I pushed my chair away from my desk. I got up and hurried through the basement, not thinking at all about how scary it was, only thinking of how fast I could get to the restroom before Kate saw me.

I looked in the bathroom mirror and cried harder. How could I have gone through the secret lives of so many people, betrayed Joe's trust, and now believe I had a right to be upset, worrying whether someone had read my thoughts? And it wasn't fair, because I didn't even know if Gloria and Paul had opened the boxes.

I turned on the faucet and splashed water on my face. The cold felt good on my inflamed skin, but it didn't stop the crying. I was sobbing, my nose running. I've always been a person who respects other people, who obeys the law, who tries to do what's right.

No matter how much Joe harassed me about ghosts, no matter how much he tried to stifle who I was, I had no right to betray him. Not just because he was my boss, but because he was another human being. I wasn't who I pretended to be, and I might as well be lying about everything. And all those people! They told him their most painful experiences, thinking they were safe. They had confidence that a man who had taken pledges before god would keep their secrets, protect their little hearts from even more pain, the pain of exposing things you don't want exposed.

I went into the stall and sat on the toilet, weak from crying. Even sitting down, it was hard to breathe.

After a few minutes, the sobbing began to subside, like it always does. Tears still ran down my face and my nose was completely clogged. I knew I was going to look hideous for at least half an hour. I wasn't sure how I was going to manage avoiding Kate's scrutiny while the swelling dissolved and the red faded away from my eyes and nose. It was nearly lunchtime.

Any minute, she would come out to the main office and suggest we head up to the kitchen together.

When I was breathing normally, I stood and unlocked the stall door.

Kate was standing by the sink. How had I not heard her come in? Was I crying that loudly, was I so lost inside the twists and turns of my own head that I was completely unaware of the presence of another human being?

Clearly I was.

"What's wrong?"

I stared at her.

She stepped toward me and wrapped her arms around me. Her thick body felt like a soft, comforting pillow. I wanted to lay my head on her shoulder, but resisted the temptation. Too bad I wasn't better at resisting other temptations.

She let go of me. "Tell me what's wrong. Please. Nothing happened with JD, did it?"

Her face looked like it was going to melt at the thought of something wrong between JD and me.

"No, we're fine. Everything is fine with us."

She looked at me, waiting.

"I really don't want to talk about it. I'm sorry. I'm sorry you heard me. I didn't mean to get hysterical."

"I thought someone died."

"I know. I guess a lot of things built up."

"We should go eat lunch." She went into the stall and pulled a bunch of toilet paper off the roll. She handed it to me.

I blew my nose. I dumped the toilet paper in the trash and turned on the faucet. I bent over and splashed more water on my face. It felt so calming, almost as soothing as thinking about what a good friend Kate had become. She started out a bit prickly when we first met. Maybe both of us started out prickly. And maybe that's why we'd become friends. I turned and smiled, even though my face looked like a wet dishrag.

As we walked across the basement, she said, "Why won't you tell me? You know you can trust me."

"I just can't talk about it." Tears started leaking out of my eyes. Luckily she couldn't see my face. I tried to breathe more slowly.

We locked the office door and went upstairs. By the

time she saw my face again, I had it back under control.

She heated her frozen Indian meal and I got out my cheese and tomato sandwich. Along with my sandwich, I'd brought a bag of dark, almost purple, Bing cherries. I'd packed a ton of them, so I dumped them into a bowl and put it in the center of the table for us to share. I got out another bowl for the pits.

Kate sat across from me. Steam rose off her cardboard food tray. She popped a cherry in her mouth, chewed, and spit the pit into her hand. She dropped it into the empty bowl. "I wonder if you're having a delayed reaction from the emotions of visiting the house where you grew up."

"Maybe. That could be part of it." It wasn't that at all, but it was possible that my effort to peek into the past had made me more unstable, so I didn't feel like I was completely making things up.

"I guess it wasn't what you'd hoped?"

"No. Not really."

"So your parents died at the same time? In a car accident?"

I put a cherry in my mouth and took a sip of water. I chewed slowly. I swallowed the fruit and sucked on the pit, letting my tongue work off the bits that were left until it was stripped smooth. Still, I continued to roll it around in my mouth. After all that time, and all that keeping things to myself, I suddenly knew I was going to tell her.

She waved her hand in front of my face. "Hello? Madison? You look like the pit got stuck in your throat.

Spit it out!"

I removed the pit and placed it in the bowl. "My parents were murdered."

She stared. Her face became even more pale than usual, the makeup seeming to fade in front of my eyes. "I don't know what to say."

"I know. That's why I don't usually tell people."

"I'm so, so sorry."

"Thank you."

"You were fifteen?"

I nodded.

"I can't begin to imagine . . . that's huge. How do you seem so . . . I don't know . . . centered, self-aware, something."

"Meditation. Yoga." I smiled.

"I'm sure that helps."

"Actually, lately, not so much."

"Why not?"

"When I went up there, I found out some bad things."

"What?"

"My aunt and uncle — Gloria and Paul — I lived with them. After."

Kate grimaced.

"I found out they didn't really want me, or something. I don't know. It's confusing.

"You poor thing."

"They weren't getting along with my parents, but they took me anyway. I never knew that." I ate another cherry, talking around the pit. "And I also tried to talk to the Detective on the case, to get him to interview Gloria and Paul again, since they lied about why they weren't on speaking terms with my parents."

"Wow."

"The detective called yesterday. He said Gloria admitted she'd lied, made some lame excuse about being embarrassed, and the detective just let it go. He's basically stopped looking for the killer."

"Why?"

"It's been so long, they talked to everyone, no leads, no evidence. Blah, blah, blah blah."

"Excuses."

"Exactly."

"Have you thought about hiring a private investigator?"

"No." I let the suggestion roll around in my head. "That's a good idea."

She shrugged and stabbed her food unnecessarily hard. After she'd eaten a few bites, a piece of rice clung to the corner of her mouth. Her tongue darted out and snapped it inside.

"The detective makes it sound like it's hopeless."

"Do you believe him?"

"I don't know. I'm not sure."

"Do you mind me asking how they were killed? I don't want to pry, or be gruesome. I just . . . I don't . . ."

"No, it's fine. They were shot. I found them."

"Oh my God!"

"They were in their bed, lying on their backs. They looked peaceful, I think. Or that's how I like to remember it. They just had bullet holes in their foreheads, it wasn't, you know . . ." I waved my hand around.

My gesture must have been wild, because Kate reached out and took hold of my wrist. She slowly lowered my arm to the table. She patted the back of my hand, then picked up the cherry bowl, and held it out to me.

I took a cherry. "Sorry, I get wound up . . ."

"Do *not* say that!"

"Sorry." I laughed.

She smiled. "I'm glad you can laugh."

"It's not like I'm depressed all the time, sitting around thinking about nothing but them."

"I know."

"I'm really quite happy."

"I know."

"But I wish the detective would try harder."

"Sure. I guess this is why you're so passionate about ghosts."

"I'm not passionate about them." I smiled. "And I don't think that's why. It's not really related."

"No? You wouldn't love to see your parents' ghosts and find out who killed them?"

"Okay, of course I would. But that's not how it started out. Ghosts had never entered my mind before I saw the first two."

"Well it's definitely related."

"Okay fine."

"Not just because of wanting to say good-bye to your parents. I think it's related because maybe the reason they come to you . . . I can't believe I'm saying this . . ." she smiled and looked down like she was embarrassed, although she didn't blush. She pressed on, "Maybe they come to you because you're passionate about finding out what they want and helping them find peace."

"Wouldn't anyone?"

"Maybe not. It's like you're a minister yourself."

"Oh, god. I don't think so." I laughed. "A minister to dead people?"

She smiled. "Just saying."

I finished the first half of my sandwich and drank most of my water. "Well lately I'm wondering if I should just let go. That's sort of what JD thinks, and it's definitely what the detective thinks."

"Don't." Her voice was hard. "Don't ever let go."

"What else can I do? The detective believes everything Gloria and Paul tell him. He's not interviewing anyone else. He has no ideas for pursuing new leads."

She looked at me and pushed her food tray aside. She pressed her forearms on the table. "Do not give up. I did that and it's a huge mistake."

"What do you mean?"

"I gave up on something important. And it was the biggest mistake of my life."

"What was that?"

Her eyes filled with tears. She ate a cherry and looked

toward the windows along the opposite wall from where we were sitting. There was nothing to see outside, just an empty corridor. Because of the angle of the covering, only a small sliver of the garden was visible from where we sat. She looked back at me.

"My little brother took off. When I was nineteen. I was away at college."

"Oh."

She coughed and blinked several times. She tipped her head up toward the ceiling. When she spoke, her voice was as thin and fragile as tissue paper. "He was fourteen."

"Do you know why?"

She shook her head. "That's part of what's so awful. I have no idea. For a long time, we were sure someone took him, but the police insisted he was definitely a runaway."

"How could they be so sure?"

"I have no idea. Like you said, blah, blah, blah. They have their statistics and all that, I guess. Anyway. I spent years looking for him. Years."

"Wow."

"Every weekend I went to San Francisco and walked around. I called his friends, I talked to his teachers. I went to other cities in the area. I actually did hire an investigator. And that doesn't mean they can't help, but in my case . . ."

"It didn't."

"No."

"I spent my vacations traveling to LA and Sacramento, up to Portland, Seattle. Everywhere I could afford to go."

"That sounds hard. He could have been anywhere."

"Yes." Her eyes filled with tears.

"And you didn't find him?"

"No. And I stopped looking. When I graduated from seminary, I decided to let it go as all the experts tell you to do."

"Well I guess eventually you have to."

"No, you don't."

"Then are you still looking for him?"

"He's dead."

"Oh, no." I felt the tears coming. What a couple of leaking faucets we were. Not that I wanted to make fun of us. We both had good reasons, very good reasons. And there's nothing wrong with crying, I just felt like that's all I'd been doing for the past hour or more, and now Kate was too. "How? How did you find out?"

"He overdosed." She swallowed. "He had a cell phone. Not a smartphone, so it wasn't locked. And it still had our home phone number in the contact list. That hurt almost more than anything. That he had it right there in his hand for years, and he never called. And I have no idea why. No idea what happened. And he died right in San Francisco, which was my original instinct. And I hate myself for giving up. I might have saved him."

"You can't save someone."

"Yes you can."

"I don't think so."

"I could have gotten help for him."

I decided to shut up. What did I know? I wouldn't want someone telling me how to feel and how things were. That's what bugged me about Joe. And here Kate was pouring out her soul to me and my first instinct was to argue with her and try to make her feel better. I was trying to wipe out her pain by saying she couldn't do anything, as if I could do anything at all to make her feel better and not beat up on herself.

We sat there eating cherries, neither of us talking. I wrapped up the other half of my sandwich. Slowly the heap of pits in the bowl grew larger. We kept eating until all the cherries were gone. When we were done, we sat there, both of us turned sideways, looking out the windows at nothing, lost in our own worlds of *why* and *what now?*

"Don't give up," she said.

"It's not like I can save my parents."

"I know. I didn't mean to make you feel bad, that way, but there's something awful about giving up. It's like you're giving up on good things. You just can't give up. You can't."

"What should I do? I'm not sure I can afford a private investigator."

"Tell the detective you want to review the files."

"They let you do that?"

"I don't know, but it's an idea. And they should. It's your parents! And if you push hard enough, you can do a lot of things that *they* don't *allow*."

"I never thought of that either. I feel kind of stupid

that you have all these suggestions two minutes after I told you."

"It's because I have a fresh perspective. It's all new to me, you've been thinking about it over and over for years."

We stood, as if by agreement. I carried the bowls into the kitchen, dumped the pits, and washed out the bowls. Kate picked up a towel and dried them.

"You could ask them to give a lie detector test to your aunt and uncle."

"I thought those didn't work."

"Just asking would be interesting, to see how they reacted. Or you could enlist their help. Instead of being suspicious of them, get *them* to hound the detective."

"I wasn't suspicious of them until recently. And they never did anything before to get him to consider different angles."

"You know that for sure?"

"No. I guess not. What else?" I put my half sandwich back in my lunch bag and set it in the fridge.

We picked up our water bottles and went outside. Again, as if by agreement, we walked through the garden to the wooded area at the back of the property where I'd seen my first ghosts. We sat on the bench.

"Thank you for telling me," she said.

"Thank you for telling me your story."

"I won't tell Joe or anyone," she said.

"I know."

"Although you don't need to keep it a secret."

"Usually, people treat me differently when they find

out. So it's better to not let it get in the way."

"All people, or some people?"

"Okay, you're right. But most people."

"Maybe that's in your head."

"What do you mean?"

"Maybe you feel differently once you tell people, and you think it's their behavior that's changed."

"I'm not sure about that."

"It's something to consider," she said.

"Don't try to push me."

"I'm not. Not at all."

"Okay."

"Are you going to do it?"

"What?"

"Ask to see the files?"

"You just gave me the idea five minutes ago. I have to think about it."

"You would bring a totally different viewpoint than a detective. Especially as a woman." She held up her hand and began ticking off the list on her fingers. "You're a woman. You're not a cop. You're more intuitive than ninety percent of the population . . ."

I laughed. "That's only three."

"You see ghosts!"

"I doubt there's anything related to ghosts in the file."

"No but, because of that, you see the world from an unusual vantage point."

We finished our water and stood. We walked back along the path, past the rose bushes, and down the stairs to the offices. When we got inside, Kate took my water bottle and put both of them on my desk. She turned back and gave me a hug.

"You are an amazing person," she said. "I feel lucky to be your friend."

"Same here."

She picked up her bottle and walked out the door, headed toward her office. Her footsteps were loud and sharp and determined, all the way across that vast, scary cave, and then it was silent.

I sat at my desk and woke my computer. I hadn't finished Joe's sermon notes, but my head was in such a different place, they seemed totally irrelevant at that moment. I opened the browser window and searched private investigators, but after about five minutes of that, it made my head hurt and I closed the window.

I wasn't sure what I wanted. Looking for a private detective made me realize I'd given up altogether on the idea of professional investigators. How would a detective hired by me be any different than one paid by the city? I no longer had any confidence a detective could figure out anything. And even beyond wanting to know who killed them, and why, what I really wanted, more than anything in the whole world, was contact with their spirits.

I thought again about the diaries. Another reason I needed to go back for a second visit this summer.

I began typing Joe's notes. At least I no longer felt like the worst person on earth. I'd made a mistake. A terrible mistake, but not the worst one in the world.

Seven

WEDNESDAY EVENING WAS the church's monthly business meeting, and I was there to take notes. They needed to know who said what and record the number of *yeses* and *noes* for each initiative that was put to a vote. In all the time I'd worked there, no one went back and read my notes, but that didn't stop Pastor Joe from reminding me every month how important it was. Maybe just knowing their words were being recorded and their votes captured made people behave differently. Who knows.

The sky was still pale blue when I arrived at the church at seven-fifteen.

I love summer, love feeling as if the sun is out forever and that the days truly have more hours, stretching into the evening. I love the warm air and that I don't have to race through icy, drenching rain or feel metallic cold filling my bones, no matter how thick my coat and how tightly wound my scarf. That sounds ridiculous, living in California where it's rarely below fifty degrees during the day, and not much lower than forty-five most nights. But I get cold. I like warm weather, even hot weather. Everyone complains when it's in the nineties but I'm like a cat, purring in a pool of sunlight.

The parking strip was full — Joe's car, Kate's car, and a few of the early birds who are so excited for the business meeting they arrive at seven so they can start debating topics among themselves. They also gossip, although they're careful not to call it that — passing on prayer requests, expressing concern — are the favorite euphemisms.

I left my Beetle in the back parking lot. The business meeting isn't for the entire congregation, just elected officers of one committee or another, the church treasurer, and the deacons. The deacons are more or less unpaid minister proxies. I can't really see that they ever do any actual ministering, beyond visiting people in the hospital and at retirement homes, and everyone does that. Or most of them.

I went into the fellowship hall and took my seat in the front row at the far left. It's awkward sitting on a metal folding chair and taking notes, but there are worse jobs. Much worse.

While I waited for things to get going, I took out my phone and surfed the web a bit. JD texted me that the bar was overflowing because of the nice weather — clear and sunny at the coast, rather than the usual summer fog. The outside patio was standing room only. I texted back that I'd rather be in a packed bar than sitting on a metal chair in a large room, seated next to a woman who was wearing too much perfume. He texted me that there was plenty of perfume at the bar and no available chairs, so maybe I was better off. I texted back a smiley face.

At seven-twenty-five, they still didn't look close to getting started. Joe stepped away from a cluster of people, moving abruptly, as if he were snapping a stalk of celery off from the bunch. He walked over to where I was sitting. He grabbed a chair from the second row, dragged it around, and angled it toward mine. He sat down.

"How are you doing?" he said.

"Good."

He lowered his voice. "Cindee said she came by the other day."

"Yes."

"Everything okay?"

I didn't like that at all. Obviously I had no idea what Cindee had told him, and I wasn't sure if he was asking if I was worried about my job, angry at Cindee, thinking of quitting, harboring bad thoughts about him, or something else entirely. She'd been pretty clear she didn't want him to know anything about what the ghost had accused him of. I couldn't imagine her telling him about the ghost at all.

"Well?" he said.

"What did she say?"

"That you were upset."

I glanced at the woman next to me. She was talking on her phone, but still, that didn't mean part of her brain wouldn't pick up on our conversation, so I wasn't sure why he was asking me this question now, in this place, with the meeting due to start.

"I'm fine."

He stood. "You're sure?"

I nodded.

"She was crying."

"Really? Well what, exactly, did she say?"

He glanced at the woman next to me.

"I can stay a few minutes after the meeting," I said.

He smiled, but still looked like he didn't want to wait that long. I guess he didn't like his wife crying, but that sure wasn't my fault. In fact, I could have argued it was his.

The president of the council announced they were ready to start. Only six minutes late. The agenda was long — fifteen items. They hadn't had the June meeting because so many people were gone on vacation. I tried to get comfortable in my hard, cold chair because we were going to be there for at least two hours, but there's no way to get comfortable in a folding metal chair.

They plodded through the list of topics. The first two — purchasing four new rosebushes for the garden and getting a new toilet for the education wing — were no-brainers, one more than the other.

Then they started a discussion of the janitorial service raising its rates. It took forever, with debates about the quality of the janitorial work, whether the company was holding the church hostage, whether or not they'd been loyal — whatever that meant — whether a "service" can even be loyal, whether it would cost more in the long run to try to hire another company, what if they couldn't find another service . . . and on it went. Silicon Valley was booming, buildings were going up everywhere, and all of them needed cleaning services. Next, they veered off into a discussion of whether the company was just raising rates because they knew how much cash was flowing around high tech companies, and really they should give the church a *reduced* rate, because it wasn't a for-profit organization.

The whole thing took thirty-five minutes. I looked at the list of twelve more topics and yawned, wishing I'd stopped to fill my travel mug with an iced latte.

There were several topics related to the childcare center. They have their own board and their own business meetings, but sometimes things like space requirements, or insurance, are discussed at the business meetings because the church has to vote on them too. Luckily they moved through those topics quickly. I think the president looked at the clock, did the math, and hurried people along when the comments got repetitious.

The second to last topic was about the high school youth group. Although Kate was the minister in charge of activities for teenagers, a middle-aged couple helped out as volunteers. They planned a lot of the activities, chaperoned the events at church, and enlisted other chaperones for camping and ski trips and community service outings. This couple — Phil and Tina — was proposing that the Friday night social events run all night.

Kate was in agreement. Their thought was that kids left the youth group at ten o'clock, and the ones who could drive didn't always go home. They went to parties, and most of those parties featured drinking and pot smoking and all kinds of other "ungodly" activities, according to Phil.

"We'd like to continue the pizza and movies that we have now, and then invite the teens to bring sleeping bags and spend the night," Phil said. "We'd provide a light breakfast and send them on their way by eight on Saturday mornings.

Tina, a very tall, thin woman with hair to her waist, stepped in front of her husband. "We'd have board games. They could sleep or not. They could talk, we'd be here, of course, and we'd take shifts so there would always be . . ."

Joe stood. He raised his hand as if he was saluting her, or telling her to talk to the hand. "They belong at home with their families."

". . . two adults awake." Tina kept her voice calm, moving past his interruption as if he'd immediately recognize his mistake.

"Let them finish," Kate said.

Joe looked at her. He kept his expression neutral, but he held her gaze as if he was waiting for her to agree with him, or admit it was a bad idea before it was even discussed.

People began calling out questions. They asked about the plan for keeping the kids inside, about kids sneaking in their own party supplies, about boys and girls sleeping next to each other, about where they would change clothes so the sexes were kept separate. It swirled around, gathering energy, a big parental hurricane of worry.

Phil and Tina countered each question, but as it continued, they answered less and less, looking sort of defeated and disgusted. Several times, Tina glanced at Joe. Her face got harder each time. I could see that she blamed him for launching the discussion in a negative direction before they'd even explained the details.

The more people talked, the more they fed on each other. After fifteen minutes or so, you'd have thought Phil and Tina had proposed hosting their own blowout drinking bash at the church to try to have the best party in the neighborhood, to lure kids away from other parties. It was almost funny.

When they finally quieted down for a few minutes, Tina spoke softly, but clearly. "I think you're looking at this the wrong way. Not all the kids have to stay all night, but you have to recognize the reality of what's happening after the youth group meetings. They aren't going home. They're almost adults. We can't force them to behave by assuming they're going to do what they should. We have to provide opportunities for them to find better ways to have fun. They want to be with their friends. Even if they do go home, they're texting all night and drifting around on social media. And that has its own problems. This way, they have spiritual guidance and they learn by doing, not by getting lectured."

"If they aren't going home, that's the parents' problem," said the woman seated next to me.

"I disagree," Phil said. "We're a community, we need to work together to keep our teens on the right path."

Joe put his hand on Tina's forearm. "Your intentions are good, but I would not allow my daughters to attend something like that. I don't want them thinking it's okay to sleep in the same room with males, to run around in their nightclothes. It's just not right."

I thought he was an idiot. He sounded just like all the other nervous parents who were worrying themselves blind. Worrying about something that would probably be a good thing, and not worrying about what they didn't know. Thinking they had a handle on what their kids were doing. Teenagers now know more about the world and life than their parents did when they were twenty-five or thirty years old.

Kate moved out to the side aisle and turned to face everyone. "I think we're off track. There are some legitimate concerns, but this idea has a lot of potential. Let's not rush to a decision when this is the first everyone has heard about it."

Finally, they set up a committee to meet with Phil and Tina, rather than voting on it — a partial victory. But watching Joe derail a good idea, and be so overprotective of his daughters and not comprehend all the good points in the suggestion, put me in a fighting mood, which was not going to be good for our discussion of why I was "upset" after I'd talked to Cindee. I wondered if he knew she'd been more upset than I was. Three weeks ago I was ready to call her my BFF, and now . . . I guess I saw that her loyalty was with her husband, which it should be, but does marriage require blind, deaf, and mute loyalty?

The meeting didn't end until ten-fifteen. I regretted my impulsive offer to stay late. Especially since, as I should have known, six or seven people had to grab Joe's sleeve, insisting on a personal conversation and summary of the meeting. I'd seen it every time. It would be another fifteen or twenty minutes before he escaped the fellowship hall for our little chat.

I went downstairs and sat in one of the armchairs in the main office, staring at my empty desk. Although part of me didn't want to wait, I was very curious what Cindee had said. I was also a little nervous about telling him to his face that I questioned his integrity, or whatever I was questioning. I wasn't even sure. And now that I'd seen my own behavior in a more truthful light, I wondered whether I was a person to be questioning anyone's integrity.

He hurt his flock, the ghost had said.

He betrayed them, every single one of them.

I lost my daughter because of him.

Finally, the door opened and Joe stepped into the office. He locked the door. Not a good sign.

"Give me a second." He went into his office and I heard him rummaging around.

I felt like a serf, waiting to be summoned by the king. I wondered if he realized that the more things went on like this, the less I liked my job. JD told me it was a bad idea to get caught in the middle of their marriage. Not that I needed that advice, it was obvious. But here I was, drifting into the nucleus of their marriage.

"Madison?"

I stood obediently and went into his office.

"Have a seat."

"Is this a *boss-employee* conversation, or a *you're-my-wife's-friend* conversation?"

He smiled. "Why do you have to draw such sharp lines around everything?"

"Don't you do the same?"

"Okay. Touché. I'd feel more comfortable if you sat down."

I moved to the couch and sat on the edge.

"So what happened with you and Cindee?" he said.

"Shouldn't you be asking her?"

"I want your side."

"My *side?*"

"We can't have this kind of conflict."

"You know, have you ever thought about how weird this job is?"

"How's that?"

"You're my boss because you hired me and give me work. Kate is my boss because she gives me work, the church board is my boss because they decide my salary and vacations. Cindee is, what? Is she my boss too? Why is it a problem if there's conflict? I'm sure we'll work it out, and if we don't we'll be professional and polite."

He leaned back in his chair. Outside, I heard a siren, a pause, and then it spun up again, another siren joining in. The lights flickered. He glanced toward the main office then back at me. "You're right, it's not a traditional workplace. It's a ministry. And my job has the same challenges as yours — the lines aren't always clear."

"Well am I in trouble for having a disagreement with your wife?"

"I don't like seeing her upset."

"I'm sure. But you're blaming me?"

"There's no blame about it. I wanted to see if there was something I could help sort out."

"So you don't know why she's upset?"

"Not really."

"Shouldn't you be asking her? She's your wife."

"She said she didn't want to betray your confidence."

I folded my hands in my lap. I looked up at the ceiling, waiting for the light to flicker again, hoping I wasn't damaging my eyes, staring into the fluorescent bulbs. But I didn't want to look at his face. I was surprised and sort of honored that Cindee didn't tell him much of anything. Maybe she was protecting his feelings more than mine, not wanting to confront him with anything he may have done wrong. But still, she could have said I was talking about another ghost. Although I guess she didn't want to get me fired. So in the end, I was honored. Even if her motives were mixed.

"You don't have to tell me, of course."

"You're absolutely right about that," I said.

"Look, a church is like a family . . ."

I closed my eyes. I had no memories of my father lecturing me, telling me in that authoritative voice that he knew more than I did, and if I wanted to survive in the world, I'd better listen and follow his guidance. To be fair to Joe, I wasn't sure if he knew he was coming across as a father wannabe. And maybe I was reading into it. Maybe every role in Joe's life was one of telling other people how to live — his daughters, his parishioners. I felt a wave of grief for not remembering my father, not remembering enough to even know if conversations like that had ever happened. Maybe when he died, I wasn't yet at the stage in life that invited lecturing.

"Are you listening?"

I nodded.

"I know it's your job, and it's mine too. But we can't act as if it's just a job with professional interactions. Whether you like it or not, we're a family."

"But you said from the get-go that you hired me to be outside of the *family*."

"Yes. But that doesn't mean you haven't formed relationships over the years. And I don't like it when there's conflict that can be talked about and resolved."

"Like you wanted everyone to work through the conflict over the all-night youth group get-togethers?"

"They formed a committee."

"Yeah, but you would have preferred they drop the idea."

"The conflict is going to be worked through."

"And will you win?"

"It's not a contest. The point is, Cindee's extremely upset. And if something is bothering you, if you had a bad experience when you went home, I hope you know you can talk to me. Or if it's a boyfriend problem . . ."

"It's nothing like that."

"I felt we were close, and the dynamic seems to have changed. You seem angry. Whether it's with me, or life, I don't know. But I hope you're not taking your anger with me out on Cindee."

"I would never do that. Why would you say that?"

"Just trying to understand."

"No, you're trying to guess. Cindee won't tell you and I won't tell you and you're trying to guess. Well I feel stuck between the two of you."

"Why is that?"

I scooted forward so I was almost sliding off the couch. "I don't see the purpose of this conversation."

"So you're not going to tell me what happened?"

"Not if Cindee didn't."

"Okay." He pushed his chair back. "Thank you for talking to me. Thank you for staying so late. Be sure to put it on your time card."

Everything inside of me wanted to tell him the whole story. Well, most of the story, not the going through his papers part of the story. I was tired of watching what I said. I'd spent my whole life hiding the story of my parents. I wondered if I should blurt it out right then. Why not? But that would make him interfere more, then he'd go all out trying to be the father.

Both of us stood at the same time. Before we could move further, the office door slammed shut. For half a second, I thought that the sudden movement of both of our bodies had caused some kind of vacuum.

The lights flickered, darkening for several seconds.

"Huh," Joe said. "I wonder what that was about." He stepped to the side of his desk.

The room was cold and getting colder. I heard two more sirens. I watched him, wondering if he felt the cold, wondering if the ghost was actually going to appear when he was there. I was filled with a strange excitement. If he saw the ghost, it would change everything. Then I was afraid. What if the ghost appeared and I felt her, or it, and saw her and heard her, and Joe felt nothing?

A third siren sounded. Maybe that's all I'd heard the other night. Maybe my own mind magnified it into something terrifying and unbearably loud.

The lights went out and the room was completely dark.

"Don't move," Joe said. "I'll find my phone and turn on the flashlight."

He didn't need to say that. I couldn't move, my feet were frozen to the floor again. I was so cold, I was shaking. The room was silent — no sound of him moving. I couldn't even hear him breathing.

"Joe?"

He didn't respond.

Near the door, the yellowish figure appeared. The red

gash was as ugly as ever, but again, no longer bleeding as it had that first time. The silence grew heavier as the thing hung there. I wanted to speak but was afraid that Joe was experiencing nothing but a power failure and he'd think I was mad.

Then I heard a strange sound from the opposite side of the desk. I held my breath. A very soft whimpering. I took a shallow breath and held it again. Once more, a quiet whimper.

The figure moved toward me and the whimper turned to a groan.

Suddenly, Joe shouted, a sound I can't describe — something between the groan that came just before it and a wordless cry of pain, a question, although there weren't any words I could make out.

The figure came closer until I felt the yellow stuff was touching my arm. I was so cold my teeth rattled against each other, my eyeballs jiggled in their sockets, and my spine vibrated down the length of my back. The spirit moved past me.

"Don't!" Joe shouted.

I squeezed my arms around myself trying to keep warm, but it did no good.

For several minutes, maybe longer, maybe an hour, maybe only seconds, the thing hovered in the room, not speaking, spreading its icy cold like a thick, damp blanket. Every few minutes Joe made the sound of a wounded animal. Terrible noises partway between pain and terror.

There was a thud on the other side of the desk. The

creature began to fade, only the red wound remaining, until that also disappeared. The room warmed, but not by much. The lights remained out. I walked slowly, sliding my feet on the carpet to avoid bumping anything, although I knew there was nothing between where I'd been standing and the door. I put my hands in front of me. After a few more steps, my fingertips touched the door. I felt my way over to the doorframe and then along the wall for the light switch. It was still in the up position.

A moment later, the lights came on. I was afraid to turn, not sure what I'd see. It flashed across my mind that he'd surely fainted, but possibly had a heart attack. I turned.

The desk blocked my view of him. Slowly I walked closer and looked behind the desk. Joe was curled in a fetal position next to his chair. A thin cut ran down the side of his neck. Blood was bubbling up along the cut and running toward his throat. His eyes were closed.

I looked around to see what had cut him, but nothing was obvious. He'd fallen without hitting the desk and because of the way he was curled up, it almost seemed as if he'd taken that position deliberately. But I'd heard him fall.

"Joe?"

He didn't answer. I moved closer and knelt down. I was afraid to touch him, embarrassed, really. Afraid I was violating his space, his dignity. When he woke, if he woke, he'd feel humiliated. I touched his foot. He didn't respond. I shook his foot. It felt loose, as if his joints had broken apart. I touched his shoulder and shook harder. "Joe. Are you awake?"

He didn't respond.

I sat back on my heels. I knew I should call 9-1-1, but I had no idea how I would explain this. The truth, of course, but they wouldn't believe me. Never in a hundred years. I wondered if they'd accuse me of hurting him. It wasn't as if he was bleeding so badly he might die. And it was odd that he seemed unconscious yet he didn't appear to have hit his head.

I leaned forward and put my face close to his. There was a light, cool puff of his breath on my skin. I put my finger on his neck. The throb of his pulse was rhythmic and strong. I felt less urgency, but I had to make a decision soon. I really did not want to make an emergency call.

Sitting on my heels again, I tried to remember the last thing that had happened before I heard the thud. I tried to remember if there'd been any other sounds aside from his moaning. I didn't think so.

His eyes fluttered and I let out my breath. If he opened them in the next minute or two, if he spoke, I wouldn't call. I started worrying about what he'd remember. I imagined him waking, sitting up, asking what happened. I'd ask what he remembered. He'd say — *nothing. The lights went out.* Maybe he'd mention that it got really cold, he'd heard a siren. Maybe he wouldn't mention any of that and all he'd remember was thanking me for staying late and talking to him.

His eyes fluttered and opened. He stared at the ceiling as if he wasn't sure where he was. I realized I'd been holding my breath again.

He groaned and unclasped his hands from around his knees. He lifted himself on his elbow and looked at me. The spread of his lips and his unblinking eyes had a look of terror. He sat up and cleared his throat. Still not speaking, he pushed himself to his feet.

I stood.

He touched his neck and pulled his fingers away, staring at the blood as if he wasn't sure what it was.

I grabbed the tissue box off his desk and handed it to him.

He wiped at his neck and dropped the bloody tissues in the trash can. Blood continued to seep out of the cut. "Well," he said.

I watched him watching me, then his eyes shifted to the side, unable to hold my gaze.

"Well." He grabbed another tissue and held it to the wound.

"Is that all you're going to say?"

"I need to think about this."

"About what?"

"I need to reflect on the meaning of what happened."

"And what do you think happened?"

"I said I need to give it some thought."

"You won't even say it?" I wanted to smack him. Clearly he'd experienced something, and it wasn't something he'd expected. It wasn't something that fit with all the books lining the shelves on two walls, floor to ceiling, explaining how the world worked and all the details about god and what he or she wants, although in Joe's mind, it was definitely a he. All those books and rules and assertions, filled with supreme confidence that the people writing them are one hundred percent correct, even though they don't have a clue. They've never experienced death, never heard god speak in an audible voice.

He was so stubborn. I couldn't believe he would rather stick with those books than sit down and talk to me about what had happened.

I was dying to know if the ghost had spoken to him, if he'd been accused of anything, if he'd known immediately who it was. I had so many questions, I could hardly straighten them out in my mind. Maybe having time to think about it would be good, but I wanted to talk while it was fresh. He was so unfair, refusing to admit that I was telling the truth. All this time I'd been telling the truth. He couldn't admit he'd been harsh or close-minded, or absolutely wrong about the rather fluid line between the living and the dead.

He walked around his desk, grabbed a few more tissues, and went to the door. He opened it and stood back. "I'm going to wash up and head home."

"Really?"

"Yes."

"You aren't going to talk to me?"

"Not right now."

"Maybe never?"

"I didn't say that."

I stood there.

"It's late. You should get home."

"Fine." I grabbed my bag off the couch, walked out of his office, and opened the outer door. I didn't turn to say good-bye or suggest that he might want to wait before he jumped behind the wheel of a car. I ran up the steps, along the path, and out toward the back parking lot. It was completely empty. Breathing the night air felt good.

More than anything in the world, I wished JD was there. For one half of a maddening second, I thought about driving to Half Moon Bay. But it was after eleven and I had work the next day. Although right then, I didn't want to go to work. I didn't want to see Joe or the basement or that church or that restless spirit ever again.

Eight

I SLEPT UNTIL eight the next morning. When I got up, I brushed my teeth, put on leggings and a sports bra, and rolled out my yoga mat. I opened the sliding glass door. As I started my poses, the cool morning air soaked into my lungs and spread through my blood, pushing the toxic feelings from the night before out through my skin, forming a thin coat of perspiration. I breathed so deeply, I thought my head and chest might explode. When I exhaled, all the fear and anger drained out and I felt clean and fresh.

I stood in the warrior pose, holding it twice as long as usual, first with my right leg forward, knee bent, and then my left, my arms stretched parallel to the floor. I felt like the pose was preparing me to battle Joe and his blind stupidity. There was a very good chance he would refuse to acknowledge what had happened in his office.

I didn't care that I was late for work. I felt a little bad that Kate probably wondered where I was and why I hadn't called in, but I definitely did not want to be sitting at my desk like a maid in waiting when Joe arrived. He could wait for me this time.

On Thursdays he usually prepared the bulk of his sermon for the coming Sunday, spending the morning in his office. In the afternoon, he went for a long walk, returning to fill the holes in his message with all the thoughts that had come to him as he wandered through the park. He attributed those thoughts to god, which I guess explained his pigheaded view of the world.

After yoga, I took a shower and chatted with the birds. I fed the birds and fish and watched the fish swim while I ate a cup of yogurt and a small bowl of red grapes. I was still hungry, so I made two pieces of sourdough toast, buttered them, and took them out on the back deck with my coffee and cigarettes.

It was already seventy degrees. I sat down and closed my eyes for a minute, letting the sun warm my face while the coffee warmed the inside of me. The iciness of Joe's office, both when the spirit was there, and after, when Joe exhaled his own variety of icy breath, began to feel like a long-ago memory.

I opened my eyes and ate my toast. I finished my coffee and lit a cigarette. Halfway through, I realized I wasn't enjoying it as much as I should, my mind chewing over Joe and the ghost and the list I'd made a few days earlier. I snuffed out the cigarette. I was quite proud of myself for stopping instead of mindlessly sucking in smoke. If I wasn't smoking to relax and settle my mind, it wasn't serving its purpose. I picked up my mug and went inside.

Since it was going to be another hot day, I did my hair in a french braid, which took a fair amount of time, juggling all those strands behind my head, weaving each section without getting all tangled in fingers and hair.

When I arrived at the church, Kate's and Joe's cars were parked out front.

I climbed the steps to the garden. As I walked along the path, my heels dragged on the concrete, slowing with each step. I paused at the top of the stairs leading down to the offices. I closed my eyes and tried to picture what was going on in there right that minute. Probably nothing remarkable — Kate working in her office, Joe in his. The coffee lingering in the pot, making the office smell rich, at first, and then stale. I wondered what they'd do when I walked in. Would Joe come out and greet me? Would he even notice I'd arrived? I was absolutely certain he hadn't said a word to Kate about the night before. Would I?

I walked down the stairs, opened the door, and stepped inside. Joe's door was open. A surprise, because he usually closes it when he's working on his sermon, when he's doing any kind of studying. In fact, it's closed most of the time when he's in there, unless he's expecting an appointment any minute.

I stepped into his doorway. "Hi."

He looked up. "Good morning."

At least he had the decency to not chastise me for being two hours late.

He moved his laptop, angling it away from the door. He put his fingers on the keyboard.

I waited another moment, but he started tapping computer keys. I turned and went to my desk. I'd been right about everything. He wasn't going to mention the previous night, or if he was, he didn't feel any urgency. And the office smelled of stale coffee.

As I put my bag in the bottom drawer, I realized I'd forgotten to bring a lunch. I was so used to doing yoga at night instead of before work, that my morning ritual was messed up. Maybe I'd take Kate out to lunch. Usually she asked and she paid, no matter how many times I offered. In fact, maybe I'd tell her all about what had happened with Joe, depending on what he did in the next two hours.

At quarter to twelve, Kate came into the main office. She didn't comment on how late I'd been, maybe she'd been toiling away so hard all morning, she hadn't even noticed. "I'm running some errands. See you in an hour or so." She smiled and walked out, letting a waft of warm summer air inside as the door drifted closed behind her.

I continued working. I'd eaten breakfast so late, I wasn't hungry yet. I decided I'd stay glued to my chair until Joe came out. Eventually his body would demand either the restroom or food. It annoyed me that once again, I was waiting for him. The thought almost made me want to go out anyway, but the desire to see what he would do was much stronger than my irritation.

The minutes ticked past. Every three or four minutes, I glanced at the clock on the wall to my left. The second hand dragged its way up to the top, falling down the other side at the same pace it rose, giving the impression it was climbing slowly and falling fast, despite the steady pace.

At twelve-twelve and seventeen seconds, I heard Joe close his laptop with a click that sounded like it was right next to me, the rooms were so deathly quiet. I turned to my computer and tried to look busy. From the corner of my eye, I saw him appear in the doorway.

"Can I get you anything from the deli?"

I looked up. He wore a shirt with a collar. I couldn't see the mark on his neck, but felt I could see the shadow of the bloodstain. I knew I was imagining it, the image from the night before planted over his actual presence in the doorway. I wanted to know if he'd scrubbed it off, if he'd rubbed his skin raw with industrial paper towels, trying to clean off the blood before he went home to Cindee — and maybe that's what I was seeing. I wondered if she'd noticed the scratch, how he'd explained it. Even more, I wondered what caused it. Had the spirit done it? Was it possible the ghost's appearance had distorted my sense of time, or rendered me unconscious on my feet, so I didn't know something more had happened? Was that even possible? Of course, anything is possible with beings who aren't bound by the laws of physics and time and rational thought.

I wanted to smack Joe. I wanted to scream — *Are you going to pretend nothing happened?* I did not want to be the one to break whatever weird code he was following, did not want to be the one who needed to talk about it, did not want to be the one who showed my hand first. Had it really come to that? Playing some petty game to get my boss to admit he was wrong?

"I'm not hungry," I said. The power of saying no was satisfying. I'd probably regret it in an hour when I'd be suddenly hungry and would have to go out in the heat of early afternoon and get inside my baked car.

"You sure?"

"Yup."

He went back into his office. I heard the desk drawer open and his keys rattle as he picked them up and shoved them in his pocket. Then it was silent.

I looked at the clock.

Three minutes, seeming like thirty, passed before he came to his office doorway again. "I suppose this is as good a time as any to mention that unsettling situation last night."

I pressed my lips together to keep from smiling.

He went to the armchair and sat down. He glanced at his watch, even though there was a clock staring him in the face. He half-crossed his legs, putting his left ankle on his right knee cap. Then he uncrossed them and did the same with his right ankle. When he was finally settled, he looked at me. "I'm sure you have an explanation for what happened."

I opened my mouth. No words came out, not even a sound.

"An explanation that's contrary to the revealed word of God," he said.

"What's your explanation?" I was stunned at my wisdom in not going in for the attack. I smiled. I picked up a paperclip on my desk and pulled the exposed tip away from the curve so it looked a bit like a fishhook.

"I honestly don't have one."

"Are you sure?"

"Nothing like that has ever happened to me before."

"I know."

"It was . . . disturbing."

"How?" I thought he'd look at me with disdain for asking the obvious, but he didn't.

"This is hard for me to put into words."

"Did you say anything to Cindee?"

"No."

"Why not?" I could hear JD's voice whispering inside my head — *Don't get in the middle of their marriage*. But this had all started because of Cindee, sort of.

"I heard some things, as if someone was speaking to me . . ."

"The ghost."

"I thought it was you, the tricks being played on my senses by the sudden darkness."

"Oh, come on."

"I said this is hard to talk about, can you at least let me finish?"

So much for my fleeting wisdom.

"The shrieking, the ugly accusations, the feelings of . . ."

I waited, gritting my teeth, forcing the words to stay

inside of me. Apparently, he did have a different experience of the ghost than I'd had. It was similar, although not exactly the same, as what happened when I'd seen the murdered girl's ghost a few weeks earlier. I'd seen her, but Roseanne hadn't, and she'd been looking right at her. Different experiences of the same spirit, but Roseanne's experience was no experience at all. Thinking about it made my head ache. Maybe with the mysterious and unknowable things in life you just can't explain every little angle.

Joe went on, "The feelings of . . ."

I straightened the paperclip into a wavering strand.

"I really don't want to get into it too much." He bent forward, propped his elbows on his knees, and put his face in his hands.

After a moment, he sat up again. I thought he'd stand and leave, unable, still, to admit he was wrong, that his rules about how things worked were incomplete, if not wildly off base.

"I guess there's someone I counseled who is haunting the church, if you will. Haunting me."

I held my breath. I told myself to keep holding it, to not blurt out any questions, to wait and let him talk. If I started going on too fast, I'd never understand what he was thinking. Maybe he had to talk himself around to recognizing the existence of ghosts. Of course it seems unbelievable when someone else tells you about a supernatural experience. Until it happens to you, there's no way to understand. If I was the first person on earth to see an alligator, and no one else had seen one, they wouldn't believe that, either. We all believe similar things because our experiences of the world are more or less similar — fire burns, lack of food makes your stomach ache. Once you have an experience outside the norm, you're isolated from everyone else. When your parents are murdered, no one else can comprehend how that consumes your life. They want you to let go and move on. Everyone but Kate — her experience with her brother gave her an existence similar to mine.

"I honestly don't know what to say. And I'm not sure I should be talking to you about this."

"Why not?"

"Because you're a child. Because . . ."

"I'm a child?"

"That's not to belittle you, you're just naive."

"I'm anything but naive, Joe. You hardly know me. You know one facet — the person managing the church office. You know next to nothing about my life."

"Okay, maybe that wasn't fair. I'm sure you gained some maturity beyond your age, losing your parents when you were so young. Calling you a child was disrespectful, I'm sorry."

I held onto the paperclip and waited, longing for a drink of water, but I didn't want to break the bubble of conversation that had formed around us.

"But you're also my employee. And . . ."

I swallowed, still waiting. Not interrupting was getting more difficult, especially since he was providing all kinds of open spaces for me to put words in his mouth. Possibly, to twist what he wanted to say into something else entirely. I wondered if I did that with other people, with JD.

He sat up and folded his arms across his chest. "Obviously there was some kind of power disruption last night. My senses were distorted and I had a hallucination of sorts. I think there was some buried . . . regret . . . of my own, I don't know."

I couldn't believe what I was hearing. Was he really going to turn this into a group hallucination? I couldn't shut up anymore. "You think two people can have the same hallucination? That's a bit far-fetched."

"Yes, it's possible."

"A ghost is also possible. And how do you know we experienced the same thing if you won't tell me what you saw, and heard?"

"Did you hear anything?"

"Twice before when I saw it, she spoke to me."

He glared at me. He obviously didn't want to hear about any time before. "Did you hear a voice of some kind last night?"

"No."

He looked relieved. "Then it seems I had an auditory hallucination. There was a visual disturbance with the lights suddenly going out and then, I think . . . because I was tired, and . . ."

"There was no visual disturbance." I sat up straighter in my chair and dropped the paperclip. It made a tiny ping on the desk. "There was a ghost in your office and you don't want to admit it."

"I'll have to do some research. But I think the lights suddenly going out, and the halo effect — that yellow glimmer . . ."

"No. That's not how it is. What made you pass out? What made that gash on your neck?"

He put his hand to his neck. "I can't explain that."

"Exactly."

He stood. "You're sure you don't want anything from the deli?"

"Is the conversation over?"

"If I have time when I get back with my sandwich, we could talk for a few more minutes. I'd like to clear the air and put this aside."

"You're not doing a very good job of clearing the air," I said.

He moved toward the door.

"Okay. I'll have a turkey sandwich. With everything. On dark rye."

"My treat," he said. He opened the door and went out.

The office was so quiet it felt as if the tick of the clock had crept inside my ear canal. I had a headache. I turned and picked up my water bottle, took a few sips, and stood. I went into the basement and around the corner to the conference room where the floor is carpeted. I laid down on my back and closed my eyes.

Suddenly, I didn't care if he believed me. I didn't care

if he'd seen the ghost, or had been too ashamed to reveal that to his wife. I didn't care if he thought I was lying and I didn't care if he wanted to revise the experience into something that fit his pre-existing view of the world. I didn't even care if he came back and ate his sandwich in his office and we never talked about it again. All I cared about was encountering the ghost as many more times as it took to find out whether she wanted any help from me, and if I could do something to help her find a restful place. Joe could wind his little brain into knots of doctrinally correct opinions and categorize me as a liar. There were too many other things I cared about.

I was not on some crusade to get people to believe in ghosts. They're out there, and I know it. JD knows it. Over forty percent of the people in America know it. I've read that eleven percent of Americans who go to church have encountered a ghost! That was more than enough for me. Even without the forty percent, and the eleven percent, it was enough for me. Still, there are probably a billion people on the planet who know that not everyone slides easily into the next world.

When Joe returned, I was seated at my desk, working diligently at my computer, although my brain was still somewhere else, perhaps whispering my thoughts to the ghost, asking her to visit again. I'd finished my bottle of water and was happy to see he'd brought a fresh bottle with my sandwich.

He put the water and sandwich on my desk, went to the armchair, and sat down. He put his sandwich on the small table and unwrapped it.

"Look," he took a bite and chewed slowly.

I guess saying *look*, then shoving food in his mouth, was his way of saying he was going to speak first — controlling the conversational flow — so he put a sound out there, and then took time to eat. Sort of like a dog marking his territory.

"Something unusual obviously happened, and it certainly gave me some things to contemplate, to take to God in prayer, and to wait for some insight."

"Whatever." I took a bite of my sandwich. Chewing, and the taste of the bread and turkey and salty mayonnaise, the bite of the onions and the sweetness of the tomato, calmed me. It occurred to me that encountering the ghost the night before had left me quite hungry. I took another bite.

"Don't be childish," he said.

"That's the second time you've called me a child."

"Sorry."

"You're forgiven." I smiled, hoping there weren't pieces of dark rye bread stuck between my teeth.

He ignored my sarcasm, or didn't notice it, I wasn't sure which. "I'm going to discuss it with Cindee. And pray about it."

"That's nice."

"Clearly there's something you want to say, so why don't you?"

"I was told not to talk about ghosts."

"I'll make an exception."

Did he have any idea how condescending he sounded? Maybe he thought he had an employer prerogative. In other jobs, I'd had condescending bosses — and not just males. I'd thought a minister would be different. Maybe I'd thought Joe was different. Or maybe I don't like being talked down to. I don't think anyone does, but I was also starting to wonder if I had a problem with any kind of authority. When I considered my attitude toward Detective Smith, and now Joe — *Pastor Joe* — and possibly Gloria and Paul, it seemed that I did. Was my life just filled with condescending people who wanted to be surrogate parents? Or was there something inside of me, fighting against anyone that even hinted at parental authority? Maybe I was behaving like a defiant teenager and so they all treated me like I was one. Maybe my parents' horrible deaths right in the middle of being a teenager had locked me there forever. Or maybe, I'm just strong willed and self-reliant and I was over-thinking it. The whole thing made my head ache even more. I took several sips of water and looked down at the remaining quarter of my sandwich that I now had no appetite for.

"You're going to be stubborn?" he said.

"I don't think I'm the only stubborn person in this office."

"Fair enough." He grimaced and glanced at the clock.

"Do you have an appointment?"

"No."

"You looked at the clock."

"Habit."

"Before you looked at your watch, so I don't think it's that big of a habit."

"Are you tracking every movement?"

"No, just making an observation." I smiled.

He didn't smile back. "I do need to get back to work on my sermon. Are you going to tell me your thoughts about last night?"

"Now that I have permission, sure."

He ignored the sarcasm again.

"I've seen that ghost three times now. The first time, she told me you were hurting your flock. The second time, she said you'd betrayed her. That she'd lost her daughter because of you. Lost her daughter forever."

Everything about his face said he wanted to interrupt me but he was hanging on tightly to his pastoral hat and doing his job as a professional listener, waiting for me to finish, even though he wasn't really listening. He was holding his breath, eager to contradict me, and the ghost.

"The second time, her presence emitted this horrible screeching sound that I can't even describe. It was so painful I thought I'd lost my hearing. Then, last night, I heard what sounded like sirens before she appeared. They might have *been* sirens, I'm not sure. After that, she didn't make a sound. And I'm left wondering if she spoke to you and somehow prevented me from hearing. Because she'd managed to find the person she really wanted to communicate with."

Joe got up and went to the coffee pot. He filled a mug, took a small swallow, curled his lip, and put the mug back on the coffee stand. Keeping his back partially turned toward me, he said, "That's quite a story."

"Why did you force me to tell you if that's how you're going to respond?"

"I didn't force you to tell me."

"You sort of did."

"No, I felt you had something to say and I encouraged you to tell me, if you wanted."

What I really wanted, right then, was to laugh. But I resisted. "That's what happened. There's a ghost here and she wants something from you. You can pretend she doesn't exist. You can explain it as a trick of light, a confused sense of hearing, hallucination, unresolved *regret*, the work of the devil — whatever you want. But I expect she won't leave you alone until she gets it."

"Is that right."

"That's my experience."

"I won't disagree that something strange happened, but I know from the word of God that we shouldn't be conjuring up spirits."

"Oh, so the word of god admits they exist? That's pretty funny. After all this time, I had no idea. So the issue isn't the existence of ghosts, it's that you think I'm some sort of conduit, inviting them here and tarnishing the church."

"It crossed my mind."

"Well it crossed your mind wrong. I don't conjure anything." I paused. I sure wished that were the case. If I could call on ghosts at will, I wouldn't be wrestling with despair over my parents, still aching with the empty feeling I'd experienced inside my former home. He made it sound so easy, as if I had some agenda of my own. And I suppose with my parents, I do, but with the others, and with this one now, there was no agenda. "Anyway, that's what happened."

A shadow passed outside the window and a moment later, Kate walked into the office.

Joe stared at her as if he'd seen a ghost.

I laughed.

"Wow," Kate said. "Should I go run a few more errands? I feel like I walked in on something I don't want to know about."

"Don't be ridiculous." Joe walked to the table, wadded up his sandwich wrapper, and held it in his fist, glancing toward me as he realized the only trashcan in the main office was under my desk. He picked up his water bottle and walked toward his office.

Kate moved out of the way.

He stepped into the doorway of his office. With his back facing us, he said, "Just talking. Good timing, because I need to get back to work. I've run into a bit of a wall on this week's message."

I smiled. I bet he had. It's probably not good when you're a minister and your most recent and vivid encounter with something unseen is an angry, grieving, possibly vengeful ghost, rather than god."

Kate looked at me. She scrunched up her face as if she was trying to form a question mark with her skin.

I shrugged.

She walked toward the door to the basement, sniffed in the direction of the coffee stand, and flipped the switch to turn it off. She turned and said softly, "I still think I walked in on something. But I have a pretty good idea what it was, and I'm glad I missed it." She smiled and disappeared through the doorway.

I folded my sandwich in the wrapper. I grabbed my bag and water and the sandwich and went outside. I walked up the stairs slowly, enjoying the heat on my skin, glad to be out of the claustrophobic presence of Joe's ideas. I went up to the kitchen, put my sandwich in the fridge, and went back outside. I stood in the garden debating whether I wanted to go sit on the bench in the grove of trees and enjoy the birds and squirrels, or if I wanted to have a cigarette. I couldn't smoke in the grove, and I couldn't smoke anywhere near the childcare center, obviously, even though they were all inside having their afternoon quiet time.

I walked out to the parking lot behind the church. I stood near the room where the gardening tools and supplies are stored. It was the spot where I used to stand with Fred, the church gardener who was murdered. We'd smoke and talk about life. Thinking about him created a tiny pinch inside my chest and my eyes watered.

I dug in my bag for my cigarettes. Only three left, and I knew I didn't have any more at home. That was a good thing. I could see how the day might be headed toward exceeding my three smoke limit. If I could manage to limit one to a half smoke, I'd stay on track.

The first intake of smoke burned slightly. My throat was a little raw and I wasn't sure why. Maybe from the ghost, freezing my insides, and then having them thaw quickly, leaving them sore and pulpy. With each exhalation, I watched the smoke hang in the still air. I hoped it would dissipate as soon as I was done.

Footsteps echoed in the corridor along the education building. I turned. Kate was headed in my direction, walking quickly. I looked at my half-finished cigarette. This could be my other half for the day. I hated to let it go. I was enjoying the quiet and warm air, but I wouldn't enjoy it with Kate standing there, trying so hard not to pinch her nose. I dropped it on the ground, smashed out the embers, picked it up and dropped it into the plastic bag I always have handy.

"Want to go sit in the shade?" Kate said.

I nodded. As we passed the trashcan at the end of the corridor, I dropped the plastic bag inside. We went to the grove of trees and sat on the concrete bench.

"What happened?" Kate said.

"Joe saw the ghost. He won't admit it, but he saw the ghost."

She stared at me, her mouth partially open.

We sat there like that for almost five minutes. Every so often, her lips would move, but she didn't speak.

"First he wrote it off as a trick of light, then he accused me of conjuring it up. I think the ghost spoke to him. I couldn't hear, but he seems disturbed, like he's feeling upset about something. Maybe a secret he's keeping."

"So you think he *has* done something to hurt the people who belong here?"

"I already thought that," I said.

"Wow. I don't know what to say. I really don't know what to say."

"He's twisting it around. It sounded like maybe the Bible does say something about the existence of ghosts. News to me. So now it's not that he doesn't believe, it's that I'm the one inviting them to reveal themselves."

"Oh."

"I'm not sure what to do. He asked me to tell him what I'd experienced when she appeared, but then he got upset when I did that."

"When did this happen?"

"Last night."

"Is that why you were so late?"

"Yes."

"Tell me what happened."

I explained the whole thing, including the blood on his throat and my fear when he was lying on the floor, not responding.

"What are you going to do?"

I realized right then I didn't want to tell her. I already knew, although I hadn't thought it through, but it must have been floating through the bottom of my mind and her question made it rise to the surface. I was going to come back to the church that night and see if I could entice the spirit into being more precise.

"Why won't you tell me?"

"Tell you what?"

"I can see your mind working on a plan."

I smiled. "You can't see my mind doing anything."

"Yes, I can."

"I don't know exactly."

"Fine. You don't have to tell me everything. Maybe it's better if I don't know." She stood. "But thanks for letting me in on what happened. When I came into the office I could feel something so heavy it was like another presence there."

"Maybe you felt the ghost. Maybe she's there in the daylight, waiting."

"Mostly, I felt this incredible tension between you two. As if one of you would have physically attacked the other if I hadn't walked in right at that minute."

"I doubt that."

"You looked like you could kill."

"I'm kind of frustrated."

"That's an understatement," she said.

"He didn't tell Cindee, just so you know."

"I'm sure not. He wouldn't have told anyone if you weren't right there."

"I guess twisting it around like he is, he's trying not to tell me either."

She laughed. "Trick of the light. That's funny."

"I know."

We grinned at each other. I stood up and we walked

back to the stairs leading to the office. As we started down, I glanced at the parking strip. Joe's car was gone. Even though it was his habit to go for his sermon-contemplation walk, I thought he must have bolted awfully fast when Kate went outside. We hadn't been talking for more than ten or fifteen minutes. I had the feeling he wanted to sneak out without having to face either one of us. Especially me.

Then, I had a fleeting thought that he'd sent Kate out there to keep me away while he packed up and left, but I quickly decided I was being too cynical. She'd become a true friend and she'd never do that. She was too blunt.

KATE LEFT ABOUT four o'clock to go grocery shopping for her dinner guests.

At four-twenty, just as I was putting my bag over my shoulder, the phone rang. I decided I'd better answer, since my scheduled quitting time was five.

"Central Avenue Church, this is Madison," I said.

"Hi. It's Cindee."

I sat down. "Hi."

"Are you going to be there a bit longer? I wanted to come by and have a chat."

"I'm really tired. I didn't sleep much last night. Kate and Joe are gone, so I was just heading home."

"Oh."

The line was silent for several seconds.

"Don't you want to talk things out?" she said.

"Yes, but does it have to be today?"

"I'm having trouble sleeping myself. I don't like not having things resolved."

I smiled. She must have a tough time going through life if she didn't like things unresolved. No one likes things unresolved, but that's sort of how life is. She should have asked *me* about unresolved situations. I bet I'd beat her, if someone were keeping score. "I really am super tired. I was going to go home and take a nap. How about if you meet me here tonight."

"Tonight? Why would we do that? Wouldn't a restaurant, or the Coffee Cafe be a better place?"

"I need to come back here tonight. I already planned it. If you want to get together, that's the only choice. For today."

She was quiet for a minute or so. I knew she knew why I was coming at night. I could feel her looking worried, wondering what Joe would say. She was worried about letting me have the upper hand, and maybe just a little scared that if there really was a ghost, and it showed up, she'd freak out.

"Why are you doing this?" she said quietly.

"Because I have to."

"Do you?"

I waited.

"Where would I meet you?"

"In the parking strip, on the church steps, in the garden, in the office. It doesn't matter."

"What if someone sees me?"

"No one is ever here that late at night. At least no one living."

She sighed, sounding a little annoyed. "What time are you thinking?"

"One o'clock."

She yawned. "Uhm, okay . . ."

"Okay, you'll meet me?"

"I don't know."

"Are you worried Joe will wake up?"

"No. He sleeps like the dead." She gasped softly. "I mean, he won't notice, but . . ."

She was quiet for a few more seconds. I wanted to yawn myself. I was tired, that was true. And if I was getting up at twelve-thirty to drive to the church, I needed a decent nap, not a long phone conversation, or non-conversation while she tried to figure out how much courage she had.

"I should get going," I said.

"Okay. I'll meet you at one."

"It'll be fine. Don't worry."

"We'll see. Bye." She hung up.

I went outside and locked the door.

A dove was cooing in the huge pine tree on the side of the ivy-covered hill that slopes down toward the walkway outside the offices. I paused and listened to her. The sound was so deep and contented, so rhythmic, I felt like she was reassuring me everything was working out. Whether that meant I'd get anything resolved, was still up for discussion.

Nine

AT TWELVE-FORTY A.M. the street in front of the church was deserted. Streetlights cast pale circles of light on the pavement but did nothing to alleviate the thick darkness of a street lined by mature trees, shielding houses with their exterior lights turned off. Before I turned off the engine, I pulled my phone out of my bag and clicked on the flashlight app.

Inside the office, I woke my computer to provide some light. Other than that, I wanted to keep the dark, quiet atmosphere. I wanted the spirit to know I was inviting her. Maybe Joe was right after all, I was conjuring a spirit — this time. I really hoped that my open, welcoming attitude would prevent her from emitting those unearthly shrieks.

Cindee arrived at ten minutes to one.

I was standing near the counter that runs behind my desk and along the wall opposite to the exterior door. My bag was on the counter and I was scrolling through photos I'd taken the last time JD and I went to the beach.

As Cindee locked the door behind her, I closed the photo app. At that moment, the computer went back to sleep and the office was completely dark except for the small, rectangular glow of my phone. It was enough to see her reach for the light switch.

"Don't turn it on," I said.

"It's creepy in here."

"Are you afraid of the dark?"

"No, but . . . I can barely see you."

"I want it dark."

She sighed and took a few steps into the office. "I can't see where I'm going."

I stepped over to my desk and moved the mouse. The computer light made the furniture visible.

She came toward me and wrapped her arms around me. "I don't know what happened the other day. I thought we were friends."

"You'd rather defend your husband to the death than know the truth. That's what happened."

She let go of me and walked slowly to the armchairs. She sat down. I couldn't see her face clearly despite the computer screen glaring at my left.

"That's an exaggeration, don't you think?"

"No."

"Of course I want to defend my husband. I'm not going to believe unsubstantiated gossip about the man I love. The father of my children."

"If a living person said those things, I could see why

you'd react that way. But I don't think someone comes back from the dead to gossip, do you?"

"I'm not sure anyone comes back from the dead, period."

"Well apparently the Bible says they do, you're just not supposed to talk to them."

"Where did you hear that?"

"Your husband."

"Oh."

Since she didn't say anything more, I figured I was right. Maybe it was some obscure passage she'd forgotten about. Maybe they took one story and turned it into all kinds of rules, which is what they tended to do, from what I'd noticed. "Did you talk to Joe tonight?"

"About what?"

"He didn't say anything about today?"

"He told me he was having trouble with his sermon."

"That's all?"

"Why? Did something happen?"

"A lot of things happened."

"What are you talking about?" she said.

"He didn't mention our conversation? He didn't tell you he wanted to pray over something?"

She stood. "What's going on?"

I put my hands in my pockets and tried to think about what to do. For some reason, telling her what had happened the night before, and relating our conversation, felt like a betrayal of Joe. But the experience belonged to me as much as it did to him. My encounter with the ghost and my frustrating discussion about whether or not the experience was even real — those things were part of my life as much as his. Besides, he'd said he was going to tell her. It wasn't my fault he was dragging his feet.

"Your husband saw the ghost last night."

"No he didn't."

"Well, actually, that's what he's debating. He's hoping to turn it into a hallucination, but in the end, I think he can't quite convince himself of that."

"I don't believe you."

"Really? That's how you want to fix our relationship?"

"I mean . . ."

"He dragged me into his office after the business meeting to try to play peacemaker between you and me. While we were talking, the ghost appeared. He passed out."

"He would have told me. That's all I'm saying."

"Well apparently he hasn't quite worked up the courage to do that yet. He said he was going to pray over his experience and talk to you."

She flopped back down in the chair and straightened her legs so she was almost lying flat. I still couldn't see her face, but I could feel the hurt. Her continued silence made the feeling grow stronger until I wanted to rush over and give her a hug. Several minutes passed. Finally, I said, "Aren't you going to say anything?"

"I think I should hear the details from him."

"Okay." Her loyalty was impressive. I tried to think how I'd be if something similar happened with JD. The problem was, I couldn't imagine anything even sort of the same. I think I'd stick by him, but would I do that if he were being stupid? Maybe that was the part of marriage I didn't get. Or maybe it's not all marriages, just Cindee and Joe's, or just some marriages, or marriages with children, or ministers' marriages.

There were too many variables.

"Did it . . . did it say anything to him?"

"Not that I heard."

"What do you mean?"

"I didn't hear her speak, she didn't say the things I told you about. But maybe she assumed she didn't have to. She'd already told me. But I think Joe heard something. He's a bit vague on that point."

"Oh."

"Well where is it?"

"Where's what?"

"The . . . Thing."

"I don't know."

"So we'll just sit here all night waiting for it?" She yawned.

If the ghost decided to appear, Cindee wouldn't be yawning then. I smiled, but I don't think she could see my face any more than I could see hers.

"Why are you smiling?"

"How can you tell?"

She nodded her head toward the computer that was much closer to where I was standing.

"I smiled because you're acting all sleepy. Trust me, if

she reveals herself, you'll be feeling anything but tired. Or bored."

"I'm not bored."

"So are there ghosts in the Bible or not?"

She straightened in the chair, warming to the topic. I could feel her whole body waking up, filling with energy at the chance to tell me about the Bible. "There's a story about one of the Old Testament Kings. He asked a witch to contact the ghost of the prophet Samuel."

"There are witches *and* ghosts in the Bible?"

"Yes."

"All this time, everyone's acted like I'm crazy, or a liar, and no one thought to mention you all believe in ghosts?"

"Well we don't, not exactly. I mean we didn't. I guess I'm not sure what I think."

"But you believe every word in the Bible and it says there was a ghost to consult."

"I said I'd forgotten about that story."

"What made you remember?"

She sighed. The room got suddenly cold, as if the air conditioner had come on, but the church doesn't have an air conditioner in the basement. It stays cool enough, even most summer days, all by itself.

I shivered, but Cindee didn't seem to notice the cool air or my shivering.

"I looked it up," she said.

"When?"

"After you and I argued the other day."

"Did you mention it to Joe?"

She shook her head.

"Why not?"

"I don't know. I guess I didn't want to seem like I was arguing with him."

"You aren't allowed to argue with him?"

"It's not like that. I was going to tell him, at the right time."

"Oh."

"He has a lot on his shoulders. You don't understand."

"Actually, I do."

"Okay. Maybe."

The room got colder. Cindee shivered, but she didn't seem to attribute it to anything except a slight chill because it was dark and late at night.

Slowly, the spirit began to materialize in front of Joe's office door. I glanced at Cindee. Her arms were crossed over her ribs and she had her hands wrapped around her upper arms. I wanted to ask her how she felt, tell her to turn and look at the door to Joe's office, but at the same time, I didn't want to speak. I wanted to wait and see if the spirit spoke first.

The computer went to sleep, darkening the room. The yellow figure grew brighter. The red gash seemed larger than I remembered, circling the neck.

"Her," the ghost whispered. "You brought her here."

Cindee was shivering violently. The buckles on her boots rattled against each other. She didn't indicate that she'd heard anything.

I moved away from the counter and took a few steps toward the center of the room. The spirit remained where she was, almost as if she wanted to block the way into Joe's office. Or maybe it was the opposite, maybe she wanted to get inside, lead us into that room. It was very likely whatever had happened to her, whatever he'd done to betray her daughter, or her, or the entire congregation, had happened in that room.

Cindee started crying.

"It's okay." I spoke softly and I wasn't sure she heard me. I took a few steps closer.

Cindee bolted out of her chair and stumbled toward me. She shivered next to me, her shoulder bumping mine. Her hair covered the sides of her face.

"Who are you?" I said.

"Diane," the ghost cried. "Diane McAllister."

"I know!" Cindy said. "I know. I'm sorry. I know."

The spirit rushed across the small space between Joe's door and the spot where we stood. The thing seemed to envelop her, although I could still make out Cindee's form.

"Why are you doing this?" Cindee's voice was almost a scream.

I thought about putting my arm around Cindee, but I wasn't sure the spirit would allow me to touch her.

"You destroyed my life. You and him."

"I didn't . . ."

The spirit let out an unearthly scream. "You did. You know what you did."

"I'm sorry. I thought I was helping."

The ghost howled. It echoed through the room, making it seem as if the walls had fallen away and we were in an open field that went on forever, a desolate place with nothing but acres of weeds and dirt, covered by an unrelenting black sky.

Cindee collapsed to her knees. Although her kneecaps made a crunching sound from the impact with the floor, she didn't acknowledge the pain. It felt as if she was shrinking, not because she was on her knees, now sitting on her heels, but her body seemed to be withering under the rage coming from the spirit.

Cindee started crying harder. "I'm sorry. I'm sorry. I wanted to help."

"You should suffer, like I did."

"Please don't. Don't take my children. Please. I'm begging you. I'm so terribly sorry." Cindee was flat on the floor, sobbing.

The ghost howled.

Cindee screamed, a sharp cry this time, as if she'd been stabbed.

The yellow image began to fade, and then she was gone.

I knelt beside Cindee and put my hand on the back of her head. She continued crying, curling into a fetal position, exactly as her husband had done.

Her long, wavy hair was tangled as if it had been caught in the branches of a tree. Her scalp was wet with perspiration, or maybe blood. I yanked my hand away. I stood and went to the light switch. I didn't want to turn it on. I didn't think I could bear the bright, unforgiving light. I stumbled to my desk and woke the computer. Even though the screen glared, it was more soothing than flooding the ceiling with tubes of light.

I returned to Cindee's side and sat next to her. "Are you okay?" I touched her shoulder and she moaned.

After quite a few minutes, she slowly straightened her body. She pushed herself up to a sitting position. There was a long, deep wound that ran from her temple, across her left cheek, and ended at her jaw. For such a deep cut, it was strangely lacking in blood. Some drops bubbled out, but it had the appearance of an injury that had been there for months. The skin around the gash was puckered, as if her flesh had been sliced with something burning.

She put her hand to her face and recoiled. "Is it awful?"

"It's pretty deep, but it's not really bleeding." I stood. "I can drive you to the emergency room."

"No!"

"It might need stitches. It's really deep."

"No, I think it will be okay."

"It's not."

I helped her to her feet and walked her over to the armchair. She sat down carefully as if she was afraid she might snap a bone if she moved to quickly. I sat in the other chair.

She put her face in her hands and began crying. "Can

it come back? Can it . . . can she hurt my children?"

"I don't know. Why would she do that?"

"You heard. She wants me to suffer."

"Who is she?"

"I don't want to tell you. I'm so . . . I'm so ashamed."

The minute she said that word, I knew what word Joe had been trying to say. But apparently his shame was so deep he couldn't even form the shape of the word.

"It's okay." I reached across and put my hand on her forearm.

Her muscles unclenched and her body settled into the chair.

"I really think you should see a doctor."

"I would never be able to explain this. And if this is all I have to suffer with — a horrible scar — I'll get off easy. I will." She put her hands over her face. "Do you think she'll come back?"

"I have no idea."

"I suppose I owe you an explanation."

"You don't owe me anything."

She took a deep breath. "Can I have some water?"

I jumped up and grabbed a mug off the coffee stand. I ran through the basement, not even thinking of its horrors, and shoved my way into the bathroom. I filled the mug with water and walked as quickly as the full mug would allow back across the basement, now aware of my footsteps, echoing through the empty space. And it was definitely empty — not even the suggestion of Diane's spirit lingering in an even darker corner.

I stood in front of Cindee and handed her the mug. She held it with both hands and took a long drink, swallowing almost half the water in a single gulp. She put the mug on the table.

The computer had gone dark. I walked over and woke it up.

When I was seated next to Cindee again, she began talking. Her voice strained, as if the skin inside her esophagus was as damaged as the skin of her face.

"Diane went to Joe for counseling. She was terribly worried about her daughter."

I wished I'd gotten my own cup of water, but I wasn't going to walk back to the restroom now. I swallowed and waited for her to continue.

"Her nineteen-year-old daughter was in a relationship with a man who attended this church. He was thirty-five and Diane was desperate to break them up. Joe told her to pray, to make sure she listened to her daughter, to not lash out, things like that. Then, she didn't come to see him for a long time. The next thing he knew, the man had left the church.

"Diane came back to talk to Joe again a few months later. It turned out that she'd told the man her daughter had had three abortions and would never be able to be a mother. Then, Diane came on to the guy. She kissed him, tried to seduce him. She told him she was able to have children and he should go with her."

For a few seconds, I couldn't see what any of this had to do with Cindee. And then, as she took another long sip of water, I understood. How did she know all of this?

She let out her breath slowly. "She was crushed with guilt. And so ashamed. She started meeting with Joe several times a week. She was inconsolable.

"Joe felt so helpless, so burdened by it all, he told me about it. A few months passed and there was another woman at church who was frantic about a man her daughter was seeing. It was a completely different situation. This daughter was in her forties, divorced twice, different story with the guy. But for some reason, I don't even know why, I thought she'd get her priorities straight about not interfering if I told her Diane's story. I knew with every word I spoke I shouldn't be doing it, but I did.

"That woman went and told Diane's daughter everything! I was furious, but it was too late. And I shouldn't have been furious at her. I mean, I was. But I was furious at myself. The daughter confronted Diane, and then moved to New Zealand. She cut off all contact with her mother. About six months later, Diane hung herself."

Cindee bent forward, her upper body collapsing on her lap. She sobbed with deep, guttural sounds, gasping for air. She cried for a long time. Eventually, she ran out of tears and breath and slowly sat up. The room was dark, but I left it that way.

"Does Joe know why Diane killed herself?"

"The daughter didn't even come to her mother's funeral. I guess I don't know how she would, no one knew how to reach her, and obviously she didn't hear about it through an obituary. Or maybe she did. I don't know."

I waited for her to answer my question, but she didn't.

"I can't believe I betrayed her confidence, Joe's confidence. I'm so ashamed. I don't even know why I did it. Maybe I just needed to get it off my chest. Maybe I couldn't believe women would meddle in their daughters' lives like that. Maybe I was even afraid I could be that woman — so sick with worry about my daughters I'd do something equally awful. I don't know."

I yawned. I hoped it was soft, that she didn't hear me feeling tired when she was in so much pain. It was too dark to see the clock on the opposite side of my desk, but I guessed it had to be two in the morning, maybe later. I was tired. Part of me was horrified by what she'd done, but another part of my mind whispered to me that I wasn't above reproach. Of course, I hadn't told anyone about the secrets I'd pried into. Are there varying levels of betrayal? Despite how wrong Cindee was, she was still ignoring Joe's part in it. He was the person Diane had trusted. He was the one assigned with keeping her secret. He was the one who broke his professional code of ethics.

Cindee seemed to completely excuse what he'd done. All that stuff the other day about what a good man he was. Why was she chastising herself when he was the one who was more wrong? I don't think there can be a "more wrong" aspect to something like this, just like there aren't varying levels of betrayal. They were both wrong. We were all wrong. But she was giving him a pass and it wasn't right.

I wondered what the ghost felt. Did she feel satisfied that she'd scarred Cindee? She'd been more vicious to Cindee than Joe. Why was that? I suppose Cindee was the one who overtly caused the most damage. Would she be back? Would she drive them out of the church completely? Drive Joe out of the ministry? I couldn't believe a gouge across the face, no matter how disfiguring, would compensate for losing your daughter. For feeling so lost that you ended your life.

Cindee was crying softly. She'd leaned forward again, gripping her thighs as if she needed to hold her body together.

I reached across the table and put my hand on her shoulder, but as far as I could tell, she didn't notice my presence — not my hand, or even that I was sitting next to her. She almost seemed unaware that she was in the church office. "Cindee." I patted her shoulder. "It's late. You need to . . ." What did she need to do? Some sort of cliche? Was that what I planned to feed her? I spoke louder. "Does Joe understand why Diane killed herself?"

Without warning, she let go of her legs and sat up straight. She stared into the darkness, turning her head slightly away from me, maybe ashamed to let me see her tear-swollen eyes and lips, her running nose. There's an instinct to hide your face, to not allow another person to see the weakness of a face torn up by grief, even though the darkness hid all of that.

"I don't know," she said.

"What do you mean, you don't know?"

"Just what it sounds like. *I don't know.*"

"So you never told him what you did?"

She shook her head once. "Unless that . . ." She waved her hand in front of her. "That, ghost, spirit, thing . . . Diane's ghost. Unless she revealed it to him the other night." She started crying again. "I should have told him. I knew I should have told him."

I realized I was right in the spot where JD advised me not to go. Smack in the middle of Cindee's marriage — privy to all the details of what she'd done to betray her husband. He trusted her, and she blabbed. But then, maybe Joe knew more than Cindee realized. When he'd hired me, he'd been so insistent that the office manager not be a member of the church, so there would be no avenue for gossip — as if that were the only criteria.

I yawned again. I wanted to escape. I wanted to get out of that office, away from her regret and away from the enormous thing that had grown up between them. I didn't want to know what she was going to do. I just wanted out.

I stood.

"Where are you going?"

"It's really late."

"Coming here in the middle of the night was your idea."

"It was, but now I'm tired. In three or four hours, I have to be back here and manage to stay awake all day."

She gripped the arms of her chair. I went to the door and flicked on the lights. She blinked and turned her head away from me, shrinking into the chair as if she wanted to disappear. "I don't know what to do."

"Maybe if you can get a few hours of sleep, it will become clear."

She whimpered. "I can't go home and get back into bed beside him. He'll know."

"What do you mean?"

"He'll know I was crying. And this." She touched her face. "What about this? I deserve it. I do. But how will I explain it?"

"I don't know."

"Can you turn out the lights?"

"We can't stay here until the sun comes up."

"Why not?"

"I'm tired. You're tired."

"But this!" She plastered her hand flat across her face, as if she thought she could cover it. After a moment, she pulled her hand away. There was a line of blood across her palm. Not a lot, just a thin streak. "What will I say? Help me think of something."

"How about the truth?"

"To my husband? To my daughters? They'll have me committed."

"Well I'm not going to help you lie. And it would be impossible to explain your face without making up something equally fantastical."

She covered her face again. "Will it be like this forever?"

"I don't know."

"I'm being punished?"

I didn't know how to answer that. Punishment seemed like too simplistic. To me, it seemed more like a lashing out, wanting someone else to feel your pain.

"Where is God?" Cindee cried, her voice piercing despite her mouth still being covered by her hands, pressed close to each other.

I couldn't answer that question.

Slowly she removed her hands from her face. She looked at me with her swollen eyes and blood-red nose. The ugly gash seemed to throb under the lights. She was a beautiful woman. I wondered what would happen to her now.

"I can't tell the truth. Joe could lose his job if we start going around talking about ghosts."

"You don't have to blab it all over. But I don't see how you can be married and not tell your spouse the truth."

"In marriage, you have to accept your mate as he is. Or you'll never survive."

"And that means lying?" From the outside, marriage looked very confusing to me at times. I understood the idea of accepting someone — that's sort of how all relationships should be. So what, exactly, did she mean?

"No, that's not what I'm saying. I don't know what I'm saying. I just don't know what he'll think about what I've done. I don't know what he'll think of the ghost. If he saw it, and he doubts that experience . . ."

It was too much for me. I wanted to escape more than ever, but she wasn't budging from that chair. I walked to my desk and picked up my bag.

"Don't go."

I felt heartless. I was the one who insisted she meet me . . . although it wasn't as if I forced her. She could have waited a day, met me in a nice, safe coffee shop like she'd suggested.

"I don't know what else to do."

"I need your help."

"This is between you and Joe."

"I can't tell him."

I perched on the edge of my desk, so she didn't think I was settling in long term again. "You have to."

"What if he leaves me?"

"It's half his fault."

"But the reason she killed herself was because of me. Do you know how that feels?"

"I thought you believed in forgiveness? Doesn't god forgive you?"

Her eyes filled with tears. She traced her finger along the gash. She put her hand back in her lap, then stood.

"It will be okay," I said.

"I really don't know."

I hugged her, careful not to brush my shoulder along the open wound.

We walked out together and didn't speak another word, up the stairs, and down the second set to where our cars were parked. She hugged me again, got into her car, and drove away.

WHEN I GOT home, I was too wired to sleep. The birds seemed equally wired, partially because I'd forgotten to cover the cage before I went to the church. I put the cloth over them, but they still chirped and hopped around, batting their beaks at their toys, rattling the cage with all their busyness.

I opened my iPad and sent JD a long email telling him what had happened. I told him I'd call during my lunch break.

The bed was warm and soothing and I didn't realize how much I ached, how tense my muscles were from the encounter with the ghost. I closed my eyes and the last thing I saw before I fell asleep was an image of her yellow form with that blood-red gash caused by the noose. The colors bled across the backs of my eyelids.

Ten

THE NEXT MORNING I got up early. With only four hours of sleep, I yawned my way through a little bit of yoga, and got ready for work. No matter how tired I was, I had to be there to get a sense of Joe's mood, to look at his face for a signal that he recognized it wasn't all on Cindee.

On the way to the office, I stopped for a large latte, even though I'd had a cup and a half of coffee at home. It was only eight-twenty when I arrived, but both Joe's and Kate's cars were parked out front. I got out of my car and put my hand on the hood of Joe's Miata. It was cool. Maybe he'd been waiting for me.

First, I went to the kitchen and put my lunch in the fridge. I went downstairs to the office. Joe's door was closed. I put my bag under my desk and went to the doorway into the basement. Kate's door was also closed. Kate never, or hardly ever, closes her door. I think it was lonely enough for her rattling around back there, needing to cross that hollow space every time she wanted face-to-face human interaction.

I sat down and stared at my computer. I couldn't even remember what I was supposed to be working on. I couldn't remember what I'd done the day before, if anything. I took a sip of my latte. There weren't any messages showing on the church phone. I bent down and pulled my phone out of my bag and checked for messages from JD. Nothing. Which made sense. He was probably still sleeping. I was jealous of him — lost in a dream world while I sat there, strangely alert and jittery from caffeine and wanting to know what was going to happen, but also supremely tired. I yawned.

After a few minutes spent mindlessly sipping my latte and staring at the dark screen, thinking of the warm glow of light the computer had provided the night before, I moved my mouse to wake it. For a fraction of a second, as the screen flashed to life, I thought I saw the hazy image of the ghost.

I checked my work email. I was disappointed there was no message from Cindee. Of course, she was probably sleeping more soundly than JD. I yawned. Would Cindee wake and, for that small instant before her eyes focused and she began to re-enter the conscious world, wonder if the whole night had been a dream? Then, she'd touch her face and know her life was changed forever. I shivered.

My cell phone rang. I looked at the screen. Detective Smith.

I really did not want to talk to him at the office, but with all the closed doors, it was probably safe. Still. I hesitated. What if it was bad news? But what if it was good news? I answered. "Hi."

"Good morning, Madison."

What did that formal greeting mean? I picked up my cup and took a sip. I took a second sip before he spoke again.

"I have an update on your parents' case."

My heart started to thud as if someone was inside, pounding on the walls with her fists. My hands turned icy and the aftertaste of the latte was sour. I wasn't sure if I was feeling unbearable excitement or dread.

"I know you're not going to like what I have to say, but it's been decided that your parents' case will no longer be actively investigated."

I screamed. I threw the cardboard cup across the room. It hit the armchair. The lid popped off and coffee drenched the seat of the chair as if my insides were spewing out.

Joe's door opened. He stared at me. From far away, in another part of my brain, I heard Kate's office door bang open.

"You can't do that!"

"There aren't any leads. It's been considered a cold case for . . ."

"You can't just quit! What kind of detective are you?" I was shouting.

Joe stared at me, his mouth partially opened. Kate

was now in the doorway, also staring. Her face had a knowing look, while Joe's was confused and slightly scared. I swiveled my chair so I couldn't see either one of them.

"I'm sorry. I said you wouldn't like it."

"Don't be so condescending. Why would you even say that?" I stood up. My left fist was curled into a tight knot. With my other hand, I gripped the phone so hard I thought I might crack the glass. "You can't do this. You have no right to make that decision."

"When there haven't been new leads for a significant amount of time, we move investigations to inactive status. We can't give resources to cold cases. It's a small town, we're understaffed, it's . . ."

"You weren't giving resources before. How is this different?"

"That's not completely true."

"Yes it is."

"The files will be put into storage. I'm afraid I won't be able to take your calls."

"You're a terrible human being!" I screamed. "Even if you aren't doing your job as a cop, and I question how good a cop you are, as a member of the human race you should be fighting for this. What kind of self-respect can you have if your job is to solve crimes and you just give up? Someone out there did this and they got away with it! And you couldn't care less."

"Not true."

"You're just walking away. Washing your hands, as

they say. Well their blood is on your hands. Their blood is all over you and I hope you never have a good night's sleep again."

"Madison. Please. You need to take a breath and think about whether you want to live your life obsessed with something you'll never have the answer to."

"Someone has to be obsessed, since you're not. And I will have the answer. I will."

"Good-bye, Madison. I wish you well."

He ended the call. I wanted to throw my phone as I'd hurled the cup of foamy coffee, but before I could take another breath, Kate was standing next to me. I hadn't even noticed she'd crossed the room. Maybe she'd been standing there for a minute or two.

She looped her arm around my waist and took the phone out of my hand. "Come sit down."

I shook my head. My face was slick with tears, my eyes so blurred I couldn't see the chairs.

Kate tugged gently. I released my frozen stance and let her lead me to the chair that wasn't soaked with coffee. I sat down.

She looked at Joe. "Come here."

She hurried to my desk and wheeled my chair over. Joe sat down and Kate ran back to her office. She returned with a bottle of water. She broke the seal on the cap and handed the bottle to me.

"What happened?" Joe said.

"Give her a minute," Kate said.

"Why are you talking to a detective?" Joe said. He ran

his fingers over his beard as if he were petting a small animal. He glanced at the door then back to my face. He looked at Kate.

"Give her a *minute*."

I sipped some water, but it didn't want to go down. It swished around in my mouth, threatening to spill out between my lips. I tried again to swallow but it stayed where it was. I tipped my head back and finally it seeped down my throat. I put my head up and coughed. I screwed the cap back on the bottle.

This couldn't be happening. I closed my eyes. I thought about Kate's advice to look through the files myself. Was that not going to be allowed? Were they putting those boxes of photographs and interview notes somewhere in the basement of their building, and Detective Smith would refuse to even speak to me, much less give me access? He'd said he wouldn't take my calls. Surely he didn't have a right to dismiss a member of the public like that. There had to be rules, professional guidelines . . . something.

I started crying. I couldn't believe he could just walk away. Part of me was so angry at myself. I should have thought about all this when I was younger. But when I was a teenager and just into my twenties, it never really occurred to me that I could have an influence with the police. Although it was looking like I didn't have any influence after all. He must have a boss. I'd find out who his boss was and demand they pay attention to me. My parents deserved justice, they deserved an investigation, not just some slacker who was too lazy to keep digging. People don't get shot in their bed for no reason. There had to be a reason. Did they want a murderer out there wandering around, killing again? Maybe he already had. Or she. It didn't have to be a he.

Kate put her hand on my shoulder. "You can fix this. You're not giving up."

"Will someone tell me what's going on?" Joe said. He stood and pushed the chair back to my desk. He leaned against the counter and folded his arms.

In that instant, a cold, calculating part of me took over. "Why don't you tell us what's going on first."

"What?"

"Don't pretend you don't know what I'm talking about," I said.

"Now isn't the time."

"Why not?"

"You're obviously very upset."

"I'm getting it handled." I unscrewed the bottle cap and took a long drink of water. The empty coffee cup was still on the floor. I regretted what I'd done. I really needed a sip of warm, strong coffee. "Sorry about the chair. I'll get it cleaned."

"No worries," Kate said. "You have a right to be upset."

Joe glared at her. I guess he didn't like her having the inside scoop when he didn't.

"You tell us what's going on and I'll tell you what happened," I said.

He looked down at his feet. He was quiet for a few minutes. Then he looked up. "I can't talk about it right now."

"Neither can I."

"Fair enough." He walked across the room and went into his office. He closed the door.

Kate looked at me. "Why won't you tell him? You're so stubborn. He heard everything you said. He can probably guess, if he thinks about it for a few minutes. He knows your parents died."

"Then let him guess."

"Don't be like this."

"I can't help it."

"Yes you can." She took her hand off my shoulder. "You're as stubborn as he is."

I laughed.

"I assume they've decided to stop working on your parents' case?"

"Yes. It's considered inactive. I'm not supposed to call him."

"You still have a right to look through the files. If you think about it, what does that even mean? I'm sure it feels terrible, like they're giving up, but like you said, they weren't doing much anyway."

"They weren't doing *anything*."

"So really, it's psychological. Do you see what I mean?"

"I guess."

"In their minds it's filed away so they don't have to

face it, or feel bad about it. But nothing has changed for you."

I stood up and hugged her. "You're very wise." I stepped back.

She was smiling. "Not always, but thank you."

Then I turned and went to Joe's door. I knocked.

"Come in."

I walked directly to the couch and sat down. "Do you have a minute?"

He smiled and nodded, although he looked a little sad. "Of course."

"My parents were murdered."

He looked even more sad. Shocked and sad and tired. He didn't say anything, which made me really happy.

I glanced over and saw Kate standing in the doorway. I looked back at Joe. "I came home from school one day and the house was really quiet. Empty. I couldn't find my mother. I finally went to my parents' bedroom. The door was closed, which it usually wasn't during the day."

"Oh, Madison," Joe said.

His eyes looked slightly damp, which stopped me for a minute.

My throat tightened. I sat up straighter and tried to take a deep breath. "They were lying in their bed. There was one bullet hole in the center of their foreheads. They looked peaceful. At least I like to think they looked peaceful, that I felt it at the time. To be honest, I really don't remember. But no memory tells me they didn't look peaceful, so I think they did."

"I'm so sorry. So very, very sorry."

"Well, yes. Thank you. It's okay."

"It's not at all okay."

"I stayed with my aunt and uncle until I was eighteen."

"Why didn't you ever say anything?"

"I don't like people giving me the look you're giving me right now."

He put his hand on his beard, like he meant to sculpt a new expression. He rubbed it a bit and lowered his hand back to his desk. "I'm sorry."

"It can't be helped. But I don't like people treating me differently, I don't like people pitying me."

"I'm sure they don't pity you."

"They do. Some do. It seems like you are."

"I'm not. I'm sad. I'm grieving for you. Losing your parents at that young age was bad enough, and both of them at once . . . you're a very strong woman."

"They never even arrested anyone. I've talked to the detective a few times over the years. I think he should be passionate about trying to find out who did it, driven to solve the case, but he's kind of casual about it. He's all, *oh well, we talked to everyone, we don't have leads, nothing we can do.* So now, they made it inactive."

"I'm sure he wasn't casual about it. Maybe you don't remember what it was like immediately after . . ."

"Joe. Stop," Kate said.

He actually looked guilty, and remorseful, if you can look both of those at the same time.

"Kate suggested I tell them I want to look at all the files."

"But the photographs . . ."

"I already saw everything."

"I suppose," he said. He closed his eyes for a moment.

"Anyway . . ." I stood. "Now you know."

"Thank you for telling me."

"No problem."

"I still can't . . ." he said.

"I know," I said. I walked to the doorway. Kate stepped back and I went to my desk. I didn't feel like working, but maybe that was the best thing to do.

Kate gave me another hug and went back to her office. Joe's door remained open, but I couldn't hear him typing or even moving books around. It was like he wasn't in there at all.

I sat at my computer, opened the newsletter template, and started working on the next issue, even though I'd mailed the last issue less than a week ago. I had to do something.

THAT NIGHT, JD came over again. He cooked dinner while I sat at the table and surfed the web, *Googling* my parents' names, as if that would do anything. *Googling* murders in Marin County and Detective Smith, which of course was fruitless. I *Googled* my parents plus crime, my parents plus Gloria and Paul, my parents plus their address, plus every single thing I could think of. Nothing came of it, but it kept me busy while he cooked.

We sat down to a dinner of spaghetti with meatballs, fresh Parmesan cheese, garlic bread he'd made himself, and a small salad. I was starving.

He got up, turned out the light and lit the big, barely burned candle in the center of my table. He sat down, then he got up again and carried the fishbowl to the table. He went upstairs and returned with the birdcage. Sierra, Sara, and Simon were a little annoyed, but once he put the cage on the coffee table, they settled down and made nice background sounds while we ate our salads.

"Delicious," I said after my first forkful of spaghetti.

"You always say that."

"Because it always is." I put down my fork, leaned over, and kissed him.

While we ate, I told him everything. I couldn't believe all that had happened in the past eighteen hours. I started with the ghost. I'd already told him a lot about the ghost and Cindee in the email, but I went over it all again, adding quite a few additional details. Then, I worked my way around to the most awful part. Although, when I explained Kate's viewpoint, the news seemed less awful and I felt I might have over-reacted.

After I told him about the mess I made with my latte, JD said, "I'm glad she made you feel better, but shoving it aside is still really shitty. You're right, you'd think they'd feel some moral obligation to keep trying, no matter how pointless it seems."

I put down my fork and looked at him. His hair was

so dark and soft I wanted to touch it. I wanted to touch his face, put my finger on his lips. It was such an amazing thing to feel like he was inside my head, in my heart, actually, feeling the things I felt. I wasn't sure how I'd gotten so lucky. It seems like a cliché to walk into a bar and meet a guy and hit it off, although maybe less so because he was the bartender, not a patron. Somehow, I'd managed to find a guy who believed in ghosts, liked birds — all animals, really — taught me to surf, smoked but wanted to quit, made me laugh, and loved me. A guy who listened when I rambled on and didn't make me feel worse when I did something stupid, or wrong.

"You should really look at those files sooner rather than later," he said.

"Well I'm not sure they'd let me have time off again so soon."

"Now that Joe knows they were murdered, I'm sure he'd view your request differently."

"Maybe."

"And with all that's going on with him and Cindee . . ."

"That's even more reason for him to not let me go."

"Well he can't, actually, not *let* you go." He stood. "Let's sit outside."

I stood and picked up the plates.

He took the plates out of my hands and put them on the table. "We can get these later."

He went into the living room and got his cigarettes and went out the screen door. I got two bottles of iced coffee drinks from the fridge, grabbed my cigarettes, and followed him.

When we were settled, cigarettes lit and glowing in the twilight, he said. "I've been thinking."

"Yes?"

"About our conversation on the way home from Marin. About renting the house."

"Oh." My heart felt like it had earlier that day, as if someone was inside, thrashing around, pounding their fists against the walls. I didn't know if it could keep taking all this. Maybe I was going to have a heart attack.

"I called Jan. She pretty much backed away from her ridiculous offer to just get rid of Kevin and Gwen."

"I thought that didn't seem as easy as she made it sound."

"It wasn't just that it was hard, she almost acted as if that wasn't what she'd said. That she had no interest in trying to remove them as tenants," he said.

"Maybe that's better. After how I felt inside the house, I'm not sure I could take living there, always hoping, feeling let down and alone."

"The apartment complex where Karen and Roseanne lived was kind of cool. Unpretentious."

My heart beat even harder, if that was possible, trying to shove its way out of my chest.

"I think you should ask for a leave of absence. I'm thinking I can quit my job. I've wanted to do something different anyway. And if I don't do it soon, I'm going to be too old and too settled."

"What different thing?"

"I don't know yet. I thought we could both take three months off, move up there, figure things out, and all that . . ."

I knew what he meant. He didn't have to explain. Now my heart felt like it was turning into a big puddle of melted chocolate.

"So, what do you think?"

"I think I fall in love with you more every single day. And if I never see my parents' ghosts and I really can't ever know why they were murdered, it might be okay."

JD smiled. He reached over and took my hand. We sat there watching the sun slip down below the horizon, smoking, not talking, and not counting the number of cigarettes we were consuming.

AS A TEMPORARY farewell, and Joe kept emphasizing the word *temporary*, he and Cindee took JD and me to Carpaccio's. It's a small, elegantly casual Italian restaurant in Menlo Park. We sat at a table near the front window, surrounded by soft lights and wood as dark as chocolate. A small vase holding a spray of freesia was in the center of the white tablecloth.

The change in Cindee's face was remarkable and inexplicable. The wound had been so deep I'd expected to be repulsed. The puckered skin which had made it look burned, was completely smooth. The gash itself was more of a thin line, pale pink, and almost invisible in the dim light. I'd had paper cuts that took longer to heal.

Stranger still, was that she seemed oblivious to the almost miraculous aspect of how quickly it was disappearing. During the first few minutes after we were seated, she didn't touch it as most people do when they have a fresh or serious wound.

She and I hadn't talked since the night we'd seen the spirit, and Joe still hadn't coughed up his view of the situation. But something had changed — there was a very pleasant, tender vibe between them. They didn't touch or look at each other more than usual, but there was a glow of being newly in love.

It was probably my last time with them for a very long time, depending on where the next step in our lives took me and JD, and I was not going to let them escape without revealing what they were thinking.

During the appetizer course of calamari and bruschetta, we talked about how much they were going to miss my bright and sunny personality. Rather, Joe and Cindee talked. I blushed. JD poked my leg under the table, and I wondered how on earth they could consider me and my entourage of ghosts bright and sunny. It was almost as if they'd crossed out half of who I am.

When the salads came, I let them get started eating. When all three of them were chewing, I dove in. "Your face looks amazing." I smiled at Cindee.

She didn't touch the scar as most people would have. She gave me a beatific smile.

"Are you going to tell me what happened?"

She put down her fork and took a drink of water.

"Joe and I talked."

"That's always good."

"I'm sure you can imagine what that was like." She glanced at JD. "Madison told you about it? The . . . what we did?" Despite the awful things behind her words, and her hesitant speech, her face maintained that calm, unearthly expression.

JD nodded. He plucked the anchovy off his caesar salad and put it in his mouth. Joe, Cindee, and I shuddered. I turned away, trying to remove the imagined sensation of the slimy strip of fish and the nasty taste.

"I guess I owe you an apology, Madison," Joe said.

"Me? I think you owe Diane an apology, but I suppose it's too late for that."

"I'm human," Joe said. He put his hand on the back of Cindee's neck. "Cindee is human. We all make mistakes, we all fail."

Cindee continued smiling gently, barely moving a muscle as she put small bites of lettuce that she'd cut into tiny pieces into her mouth.

JD and I both nodded, keeping our own little secrets. I suppose until a ghost returned to punish us, we could keep my failure between us. And really, what I'd done still paled in comparison. I know how to keep my mouth shut.

"I betrayed the trust I've been given. I know that. It's hard listening to so much pain. You sit there and provide relief for the person talking, and then there's no relief for your own soul," Joe said.

"Not that we're excusing it," Cindee said.

"But that's what you signed up for," I said.

"Did I?" Joe gave me a hard, cold look.

"Isn't it part of the job?"

"Sometimes it's too much."

"But people look to you for guidance," I said. "And to listen without judging them. They trust you."

"They do. I failed. I think I'm being given a second chance. I'm just saying it's hard. Very, very hard."

"You hired me because I was an outsider and their secrets would be safe. I guess the leak was closer to home."

"That's harsh," Cindee said.

I looked at her. Her words were sharp and slightly defensive, but her expression was still kind and peaceful.

"Is it?"

"No, you're right," she said. "And I have to live with that. I *have* been living with it." She touched the nearly invisible scar.

"It's healing so fast," I said.

"Maybe because I'm forgiven," she said. She looked at Joe. He leaned over and kissed her lips, then he pulled her closer and kissed the scar.

"He does that every day. Kisses it. I think it's therapeutic."

I nodded. It sounded kind of magical to me, but I suppose ghosts have a magical quality.

"Are you scared? That she's still there, that she'll do more?"

"I was at first," Cindee said.

Joe moved his hand away from her neck. He put his arm around her shoulders and pulled her toward him.

"But the rapid healing. And the way things are between us." She looked at Joe. Still facing him, she said, "Something good came out of this."

"But she was so angry." I ate a slice of avocado. "She wanted Joe to resign."

"Well I don't know what will happen, but I like to think that she's realized, now that she's vented on me, that what she did to her daughter was what damaged their relationship. And killing herself was the solution she wanted. And really, all I did was bring something out in the open. I didn't personally hurt her daughter."

"I guess." I busied myself with my salad, finishing off the last cherry tomato and the last tiny crumb of feta cheese. It sounded heartless, the way she said it. I couldn't argue with where the responsibility belonged. But I still felt the spirit's despair. All that was true, but still, Cindee and Joe had betrayed her.

"You think I'm wrong?" Cindee said.

"I don't want to spoil our farewell dinner."

"It's not farewell forever. And I want to know what you think. I really do."

"I see that Diane had some fault. But I can still feel her pain over what happened. If you hadn't revealed her secret, it wouldn't have been so tragic. Maybe she knows what her blame is. I'm sure she does. But still . . ."

Cindee's eyes filled with tears. "I'm not excusing myself. I just . . . I feel forgiven. But I guess I'll find out.

If she tries to drive us out of the church."

"I really don't think that will happen," Joe said. "But we're open."

"You're right about one thing," I said. "Something strange is going on, with it healing so fast. I thought you were scarred for life."

"Inside, I am."

"We both are," Joe said. "But I also want to apologize to you, Madison."

"Okay."

The server returned and asked for our dinner orders. I got the mushroom risotto. Joe and Cindee asked to split a pizza, and JD ordered linguini with clams. I hoped he'd share a bite or two with me. I looked at him and he winked, so I guess he knew I was, not for the first time, stretching my meal beyond the boundaries of my own plate.

The minute the server turned away from the table, Joe said, "I didn't mean to imply you weren't truthful. You have more integrity than most people I know."

I swallowed. Thinking about the correct status of my integrity made my stomach clench, and I wondered if I wasn't going to want a clam after all.

"I've felt uncomfortable with the ghost thing. Sure there's a story in the Bible, but I always interpreted that as the individuals *believing* they were contacting a ghost. We're also told not to get involved with the occult, and I've been worried about your interest, the depth of your involvement with . . . them."

"Okay."

"After my experience, I can see that it's a very difficult thing . . . to avoid talking about. And either way, even if I still prefer you not discuss it in the office, I'm so sorry for implying you were lying about what you'd seen, and heard."

"And felt," I said.

"Yes."

"Thank you for that," I said.

JD's hand was still on my leg. I felt his fingers tighten. I don't think he liked me giving Joe a pass, but what was the point? I'd proved I wasn't the integrity queen of California. Besides that, we were saying good-bye. Even though they assumed I'd return in three months, I wasn't so sure. There were lots of possibilities, and it wasn't as if my dream in life was to be an administrative assistant, and certainly not in a church office. If I could get things settled with my past, I might want to go to school. I'd told Gloria and Paul I didn't want to waste money going to school when I had no clear goal, but maybe going to school would cause a goal to emerge. I'd never considered that until right that minute, eating creamy, delicious risotto and a generous portion of linguini and clams.

We didn't talk about ghosts again. I still wondered if Diane would return. But watching Joe and Cindee, my view of marriage had definitely taken a turn for the better.

Eleven

ONE GOOD THING about moving, even temporarily, or possibly not temporarily, was I had to go through all my stuff. I did not find any diaries.

I packed up all my clothes, and the dishes and cooking things I couldn't live without, but most everything else I was leaving. My condo would remain empty for the time being. Since JD was renting out his place, we were taking all of his furniture. We rented a truck, and he and I did all the lifting and carrying. The last thing into the truck was the cage with Sierra, Sara, and Simon. The truck had a bench seat, so I put the cage between us. I wrapped the third seatbelt around the cage and buckled it in place. I still planned to keep my hand on the top when we went around curves. The fishbowl was in a pot between my feet, secured by dishtowels. The still unnamed fish were swimming in slightly less water so it wouldn't splash out if we hit a bump.

Two weeks before, we'd gone up to Marin County for

the day to look for an apartment. Not surprisingly, both Roseanne's and Karen's units were vacant. Since it was a small complex, every potential renter asked the neighbors what it was like to live there. No one wanted to live in an apartment inhabited by a murderer, or her victim. We chose Karen's unit. JD and I were obviously not intimidated by a potentially haunted apartment.

I didn't tell Paul and Gloria we were moving to the area, and I didn't say a word to my old buddy, Detective Smith. They'd all find out soon enough.

Lugging all that furniture up the stairs was not fun. And it was hot. When we were finished, we laughed that we should have found an apartment with a swimming pool. Still, it felt good to be in a place with such a lush, peaceful garden. I didn't sense even a whisper of Karen's presence, not that I would have minded. She'd been a rather mellow spirit, compared to most.

We spent two days shopping for new things — bedding, a kitchen table and chairs, patio furniture for the balcony, and an espresso machine.

Although I had plenty of savings, and JD also had quite a lot stashed away, he'd come up with the idea that he'd offer pet sitting services so we'd have a bit of money coming in. He figured that people living in a rather expensive area like Marin county vacationed more than average, and most people prefer having their pets cared for in their own homes rather than taking them to a kennel. He started up a blog about animals. He printed business cards and fliers and went to veterinarians in the area to let them know he was available for their furry, feathery, and even scaly clients. He took out an ad in the weekly paper. Even though he didn't have references, he got two dog-walking jobs fairly quickly — one for a woman who'd broken her hip and couldn't go out, and another for a guy who was dependent on a walker. His dog was too rambunctious for him to handle alone, so he and JD walked together. Those two wrote reviews for him, and then other jobs started to trickle in.

ON FRIDAY, AFTER we'd finished with our shopping and first round of settling in, I called Gloria. Paul answered the phone. He sounded unsurprised to hear my voice and said, "It's nice of you to call."

I ignored his stiff greeting. "How are things?"

"Good, good. It's good to hear from you. What's new with you?"

"Not a lot. I just wanted to do a better job of staying in touch."

"Nothing new here, either. We're busy with church."

"I suppose you heard they abandoned my parents' case?"

"Yes, we did."

"What do you think about that?"

"Of course, it would have been preferable if they'd made an arrest."

That was the word he chose? *Preferable?* Maybe it wasn't just Detective Smith, maybe everyone in Marin county lacked passion. They were all too low-key from that weird blend of a New Age belief system and never having to worry about money. Of course, I don't worry much about money and I'm sort of New Age as well, so maybe it wasn't that at all.

"Is Gloria home?"

"I'll get her."

He almost sounded disappointed. Maybe I'd misread him. After all, he was my mom's brother. It was possible he felt more for me than Gloria did. Blood is thicker than water and all that. And especially since Gloria had such a prickly relationship with my mother.

It took several minutes before Gloria came on the line. "Hello, Madison. How are you?"

"I'm doing okay. A little upset about them giving up on my parents."

"That's understandable."

Wow. *Preferable* and *understandable.* They were just burning with rage over it, I could tell.

"I was wondering if you'd like to meet for lunch. I'm in the area."

"Oh. Well. That's a surprise."

"I know. I thought it would be nice to see each other a bit more than once every two years."

"How thoughtful."

"I guess."

"Well that would be nice. How long are you here for?"

"Does tomorrow work?"

"Let me check with Paul. There's nothing on the

calendar, but I'll just make sure he didn't have something in mind."

"Okay."

She was gone for less than ten seconds. It seemed as if he might have been standing right there, listening, possibly able to hear my voice, nodding his approval before she spoke.

"That would be fine. It's nice of you to ask. You aren't inviting Paul?"

"No, just us girls."

She laughed softly, nervously. "Okay. Where should we meet?"

"Do you have a favorite restaurant?" All I knew of was the burger place and the deli where I'd eaten when I stayed up there a month or so earlier. Since we'd arrived, JD and I had cooked all our meals at home.

"There's a Bistro on Chestnut. Do you know where that is?"

"I don't, but I can look it up."

"It's called *Jackie's*. Twelve-fifteen tomorrow?"

That was very precise of her. "Sure. Should I make a reservation?"

"I'll do it."

"Okay. Good. See you then."

"Thank you for inviting me."

She sounded so prim. I wasn't sure if it was the stiffness she'd displayed during our visits earlier that summer and through the whole phone conversation, or if it was something new — hinting I had invited her, and so

I should understand that I would be paying. I'd planned to treat her anyway, so I decided to put that thought out of my mind and not start off by thinking she was being rude before I even walked into the bistro.

JACKIE'S WAS DECORATED more like a tea room than a bistro, and I didn't see bistro on the sign, so I had no idea how Gloria came to the conclusion it was a bistro. Not that I really knew what defined one, but it seemed as if it should be funkier and have nice soups. This place didn't have any soup. Of course, it was eighty-seven degrees outside, so I didn't need soup.

According to an old fashioned clock in the entry area, it was ten past twelve when I stepped up to the hostess stand. "I'm waiting to meet Gloria . . ."

"Oh, yes. Follow me," the hostess said.

When I reached the table, a menu was open in front of the empty chair that was waiting for me. Gloria's menu was closed. She didn't stand up to give me a hug which was probably just as well since I didn't want to hug her. The hostess walked away and I sat down. We greeted each other with genuine smiles and a few casual words.

Gloria lifted the pot of tea sitting at the center of the table and filled my cup. "Why don't you look at the menu while your tea cools?"

I opened the menu. At the top left it said, *Jackie's*. I looked up. "I was wondering, this seems like a tea room. Why did you call it a bistro?"

"Bistro means small restaurant."

"Oh. I didn't know that."

She smiled, and not in a condescending way.

I read the menu while she sipped tea, leaving her own menu closed on the table. Either she came here a lot or she'd been busy. Maybe she'd arrived at noon, despite her very precise suggestion of twelve-fifteen.

Finally I decided on flatbread with tabouli, feta, and hummus with a side of red beans and rice. Gloria ordered the same thing, so I guess I did good. Or maybe having her as my pseudo parent for three years had put us more in sync than I'd realized.

"I'd also like a glass of Chenin Blanc," Gloria said.

We handed our menus to the server.

When the server retreated, Gloria said, "What brings you up this way again?"

"It's home." I smiled. I picked up my teacup and took a sip. Tea isn't really my cup of tea, so to speak, but it wasn't bad. It didn't taste like anything familiar, but it was soothing and since the room was well air-conditioned, it was pleasant.

"Are you here to try to talk with Detective Smith? Even though the case is inactive?"

"I don't know yet."

"Is JD here with you?"

I nodded and took another sip of tea. Her wine arrived and she smiled at the glass as if she was greeting an old friend. She didn't dive right for it, but drank some tea first, then pushed her cup and saucer aside. We made small talk about my job and her church activities, which fit together quite well, and then the food arrived.

"I was wondering . . ." I said.

"Of course you have a reason for lunch. Not just catching up after all."

"Can't we do both?"

"It's kind of insulting to be invited as if there's no agenda. But I'm constantly reminded, you're blunt, like your mother."

"I didn't intend to be insulting, but you weren't exactly welcoming the last time I was here."

"That's fair." She took a sip of wine and started eating.

"What I was wondering was — you still have my boxes, right?"

"What boxes?"

"When I moved out. I left three or four boxes with things from when I was a kid."

"I'm not sure . . ."

"I assume you took them when you moved to your new house?"

"I'm sure we must have. I just don't remember."

"I should get them." The minute I said that I remembered that I'd just moved into a smallish apartment with another person, three birds, and two fish. I wasn't sure where I was going to put these boxes, but I'd figure that out later.

"I'll have to ask Paul where they might be. What's your sudden need for them, after all this time?"

"I think I have some diaries in there. I wanted to

revisit my teenaged self."

"Oh, really?"

I nodded. I filled my teacup. I aimed the spout toward her cup and looked at her. She shook her head and pushed her cup further away. I put the pot down near my teacup.

"You did this after your mother and father died?"

"Yes."

"I didn't know that."

"I remember writing in diaries when I was about thirteen, maybe twelve."

"It's a good thing to do."

I picked one of the beans out of the beans and rice and put it in my mouth.

"I've kept journals all my life." Her voice was almost a whisper.

"Wow. That's impressive. Since you were a child?"

"Since I was ten years old."

"Do you ever go back and read them?"

"No."

"Why not?"

She shrugged. "I just enjoy working through my thoughts. Once they're written down, there's no need."

"I guess I can see that."

"And I write prayers in them."

"Oh. That's different."

"Not really. A lot of women in my groups at church do the same."

I picked a few red beans out of the rice and ate them

with my fingers. I almost didn't want to take a breath. It felt like we were having an actual friendly conversation and I didn't want to break the spell. The feelings I'd had when I found out Paul and Gloria didn't really want me were fading somewhat. Maybe there were too many other feelings taking their place. You can only be upset about so many things at a time.

"Well, would you like to come over after lunch and look for the boxes? Or at least ask Paul about them? I'm sure he remembers. He remembers where everything is." She smiled.

"That would be great."

"Are you hoping you'll find out more about yourself, about Annie's and Dave's death?"

"I don't know. I just . . . some things happened at work that made me remember them. I'd forgotten about them."

"I'm sure we have them somewhere." She sipped her wine.

Immediately, my mind flipped from thinking we were connecting, to considering again that she knew exactly where the boxes were and she knew all about the diaries, because she *had* read them. But after what I'd done, maybe I didn't have a right to be upset about that. If she had.

GLORIA WAS RIGHT, Paul knew exactly where the boxes were — in a separate storage room at the back of their garage. He pulled them out and I could see right away from the tape that they hadn't been opened and re-sealed. I'd been too eager to project my guilt onto Gloria. Seeing the secured boxes made me feel worse, knowing that I'd gone through the private parts of people's lives and was so critical of Gloria and Paul for their failures — for behaving as if they didn't want me, for giving me mixed messages. Maybe most of all, for not being passionate about the lack of progress on my parents' case. I felt judgmental toward them and upset with myself at the same time.

Paul handed me a box cutter.

"Do you want to go through them alone?" Gloria said.

"I think so. Thank you."

She unfolded a beach chair and set it next to the boxes. They walked to the front of the garage and disappeared from sight.

I sat down and stared at the boxes. My name was printed in thick block letters on the top and one side of each box. I sliced open the first one and pulled back the flaps.

Ten children's books stood spine up. A few of them, *The Very Hungry Caterpillar, Good Night Moon,* and *If You Give A Mouse A Cookie,* I remembered immediately in great detail, as if I'd just read them the day before. Some of the others, I didn't remember at all. Pushed up against the books, wrapped in a plastic bag, were four or five beanie babies — soft, flopping animals that I'd collected for a year or so. I picked up the coffee-colored cat with white markings and held it against my cheek. There was also a lamb, a cow, and a puppy.

The rest of the contents were baby clothes, a pair of toddler sandals, and a few framed photographs of me as a child. Buried beneath the clothes was a small white box. I opened it. Inside was a tarnished ID bracelet engraved with the name *Francine*. Even though it was mostly black and the name was difficult to read, I clipped it around my left wrist. It looked even grubbier next to my tattoo. I had no idea who Francine was. I felt like I should know. There was something about the bracelet, or the name, that tickled the back of my mind. It was the kind of thing that makes you crazy, feeling like you should know, but nothing is there except black tarnish covering a spot in your brain.

I put everything else back in the box. I tucked the flaps under each other, picked up the box cutter, and sliced open the second box. It was much heavier than the first, so I was hopeful my diaries were inside. Sure enough, it was filled with notebooks. As I pulled out each notebook, I could see my younger self growing up. The first few notebooks had thick cardboard covers with drawings of unicorns, followed by books decorated with photographs of real animals, then mystical images of fairies and tangled gardens. The last few were soft red leather journals.

I pushed the flaps back on top of each other. My chest felt tight. I tried to take a deep breath but couldn't seem to get air inside my lungs. I stood so my body wouldn't be so compressed, and stretched my head back, gasping for oxygen. Everything inside me wanted to start with the first one and read every single book right that minute, but it would take me all night, judging from the miles of ink I saw when I flipped through a few of them. And I didn't want to read them and have all those memories and all those feelings sitting on Gloria and Paul's garage floor.

I went out of the storage room into the main garage and found a roll of duct tape on Paul's workbench. I dug around in his toolbox but couldn't find any scissors. I peeled off a section of tape, placed it over the flaps, and used the box cutter to make a ragged cut.

After I carried the boxes to the driveway and loaded them into my trunk, I went into the house. Gloria and Paul were in the living room, staring at the entryway as if they had nothing to do but wait for me to finish looking through my things. They each had a glass of wine.

Paul stood. "Do you want something to drink?"

"Any chance I could get coffee?"

"Sure. I can make a pot easily enough." He picked up his wine glass and went into the kitchen.

I held out my left arm toward Gloria. "Who's Francine?"

"Your Grandmother. On your mother's side."

"Oh. I knew I had some sort of memory for that name, even though she died before I was born. I just couldn't figure out where it fit in my mind. I remember . . ."

"No she didn't."

"What?"

"As far as I know, she's still alive."

"That can't be right."

"But it is."

"Why would my mother tell me she was dead? Are you sure?"

"I'm sure."

My head was spinning. She was so definite, but that was not what I remembered. Had the subject never come up in the three years I lived with Gloria and Paul? "I'm going to ask Paul."

Gloria sipped her wine. "I wouldn't do that."

"Why not?"

"He gets very upset. He never mentions her."

"I need to know what's going on."

"He won't tell you anything. He refuses to talk about her."

"He'll talk to me."

"Why would you think that?" She took another sip of wine.

I heard the coffee maker start up, bubbling and rumbling. I wondered if Paul could hear us. The kitchen was on the opposite side of the house and the dining room and wide, open hallway were between it and us. Probably he heard nothing.

"I deserve to know."

"Maybe you do. And maybe I'm wrong. But whenever I've asked about her, he refuses to say a word. He doesn't show any feeling about why he won't speak about it. He just shuts down."

"How can you be married to someone and not know about their mother? Especially if there's a problem with their mother?"

"You can be married and not know a lot of things."

"You're sure she's not dead?" I sounded like an idiot, asking the same question when Gloria had clearly told me my grandmother was not dead. But I couldn't seem to get my brain to accept that what I'd *known* all my life was not true.

I was still standing when Paul returned with my coffee on a tray, a bowl of sugar, and a pitcher of cream. He put the tray on the coffee table. I walked over and picked up the mug. I sat down and placed it on the coaster to my left.

"Gloria told me my grandmother — my mom's mom — is still alive. Is that true?"

Paul nodded. He took a sip of wine, turned and walked back toward the main hallway.

"Wait," I said. "Why did I think she was dead? I mean, I know why. My mother told me she was dead. That both her parents were dead. Why would she do that?"

"It's ancient history. I have no idea what your mother's line of thinking was."

"But you know something?"

He disappeared around the corner into the dining room.

I turned to Gloria.

She put her glass on the table and settled back in the chair, tipping her head sideways to stretch her neck. "That's more than he's said to me."

"He has to tell me."

"Good luck."

I stood and picked up my mug. I went into the kitchen. "What happened?"

He stood near the sink, looking out the window. "I told you, it's ancient history. It has nothing to do with you, and I'm not going to discuss it."

"You have to."

"No I don't."

He turned, but stared past me, as if someone had entered the room behind me. I glanced over my shoulder. No one was there. "Why won't you tell me?"

He poured his wine down the drain, rinsed the glass, and said, "I'm going to go lie down. It was nice seeing you." He gave me a loose hug and walked out of the room.

I took a few sips of coffee and copied his move, pouring the rest down the drain. I went back to the living room. "You were right. But keeping me in the dark is unacceptable. I'm not giving up."

"I didn't think you would," Gloria said.

"Thanks for keeping my boxes all these years."

"No worries. Thank you for lunch."

I said good-bye and left. As I drove back to the apartment, I felt like my brain was on fire.

JD AND I sat on the balcony, listening to the fountain. The dinner dishes were still piled on the kitchen counter. It was so late, we would probably end up washing them in the morning. After we'd eaten, we'd gone for a short walk and stopped in the park to have a cigarette. When winter came, maybe we'd give up smoking since we'd be less inclined to take evening walks. Of course, who knew what would happen or whether we'd still be here.

"How am I going to make Paul tell me what's going on?"

"I don't think you can."

I appreciated his patient answer — I'd asked him that same question about fifteen times since I'd returned to our apartment and he'd helped carry my boxes up the stairs. He'd studied the bracelet and said it looked nice on me and asked if I was going to get it cleaned up.

After a few minutes of silence, he said, "What's the plan?"

"I thought we could watch a movie, to take my mind off this."

"I meant the plan for everything." He swept his arm toward the railing. "The detective, your grandmother, Paul and Gloria."

I held up my hand in a fist and released a finger with each sentence — "Read my diaries. Go to the police station and tell them I want to look at the files. Go back to my house."

"I see you've given it a lot of thought."

"Yes."

"What are you looking for at the house? Aside from the obvious."

"Maybe I'll know after I read my diaries."

"Don't get your hopes up."

"My hopes are always up."

He stood, took a few steps, and turned to face me. I stood and he put his arms around me. I pressed my face against his chest, and breathed in his good, clean smell and his strength. Then we kissed. For quite a long time, and I forgot about my plans for everything.

Cathryn Grant

BELOVED GHOSTS

A Suburban Noir Ghost Story

DC
Published by D2C Perspectives

One

THERE WERE A lot of things in my diaries — pieces of my heart. After I'd taken them from Gloria and Paul's garage, they'd remained in the box, standing on their ends, cover to back, as they had for all of my adult life. It took me three weeks to get the courage to read them. I was beyond curious to know what was inside, to peer back into the past, find out what I'd forgotten. I lay awake at night thinking about them. Some nights, I threw back the blankets and sat on the edge of the bed, considering whether I should read them while JD slept. Then, I'd creep back under the blankets and pull the sheet over my head. I was afraid of what I'd find and anxious to find it all, at the same time.

Every morning when I woke, before I even had coffee, I'd open the tiny closet in the entryway and look at the box. The duct tape I'd used to reseal the box was tight and forbidding. I'd think about peeling it off, randomly pulling out one of the journals. Perhaps I'd open it in the middle and read one sentence. But then, it all seemed like too much work and I closed the closet door.

It was a hot, sunny Saturday when I decided, for whatever arbitrary reason, this was the day. JD was out taking care of clients for his new, and quickly growing, pet care business. That morning, he was walking two pugs and a German shepherd. On the surface, it was an odd combination of dogs for one family, but the father loved his shepherd and the twin daughters had wanted matching pugs. I guess they hadn't hit that age where twins go out of their way to avoid being too similar. The mother was dog-less, although she probably ended up with more dog care than all the others. She was a stay-at-home mom, so you know who exercised them when the family wasn't on vacation.

I walked to the coffee shop, bought the largest iced latte they had, and carried it home, limiting myself to three sips along the way. I dragged the box of diaries close to the door that opened onto the balcony and settled myself and the latte at the table for two.

It took me four hours to read them. In the middle, JD came home, saw what I was doing, kissed the top of my head, and left me alone. He didn't return home again until dinner time, carrying a large box containing pizza with garlic chicken, spinach, and mushrooms. The apartment was overheated, so he joined me on the balcony with paper plates and icy cold water. Each of us pulled a slice of pizza out of the box sitting between us.

"Are you glad you read them?" he said.

I chewed and nodded.

"I hope I stayed away long enough for you to finish them all."

"You did." I took a bite of pizza. He'd stayed away long enough, but I hadn't read every single one. As I'd made my way through the years, I reached the book that would have contained entries from the time leading up to and right after my parents were murdered. I couldn't read it. Not yet.

I thought about what I had read. So many years of thoughts and comments, feelings written down, some events that were mentioned but not described enough for me to get a complete picture. Still, a lot of pictures *had* formed in my mind. Sometimes there were long gaps, months, when I'd written nothing. I went quickly through the elementary school diaries with animal photographs on thick cardboard covers. When I was twelve, the journal covers changed to drawings of fairies and tangled gardens. As an early teenager I wrote a few sentences a day, mostly lists of what I'd done and comments about things I'd seen in the garden or learned in my science or history lessons. I wrote about my ballet classes and piano lessons. I wrote that I was annoyed with my piano teacher because she made me replay a piece just because my posture was poor. There were so many thoughts and events that seemed as if they'd happened to another person. Why had I forgotten all these things? It wasn't as if I was a small child and they'd been lost in an undeveloped mind. I guess memory is a tricky thing.

Maybe it's because I remembered events and things I'd done, but until I read the journals, I didn't remember what I'd thought about them at the time.

Out of all those years of my life, the most interesting things I learned about the old me was that during my senior year of high school, I'd had a crush on a different boy every week. You'd think I'd crushed on every single guy in my class. I'd never had a boyfriend, but that didn't stop me from dreaming in my journals. I wrote in big, sprawling words about this good-looking guy, and that funny guy, and the guy who rides a motorcycle and how much I'd like to ride on it with him. I never did. Or if I did, I didn't write about it in my journal.

In the years before my parents died, Gloria and Paul were hardly mentioned. I wrote about them coming for dinner once. There was an entry about my parents and I going to their house, but that was about having a boring evening, and my disappointment that they hadn't provided me with cousins. A few weeks after that entry, there were a few paragraphs about my mom having a long conversation with me regarding alcohol — although it was mostly her talking, so not really a conversation. As I related the incident, she'd gone on and on about how she didn't like what alcohol did to people and how she really hated that some people didn't even realize it was doing anything to them. They thought a few glasses of wine didn't change their behavior at all, but it did.

Reading it now, knowing what I knew about my mom's criticism of Gloria's love for wine, I realized the conversation was a result of that visit to Gloria and Paul's, but I hadn't made that connection at the time. There was no mention of Paul and Gloria being my guardians, no mention of not seeing them for a long time, they just weren't there. They'd appeared on the stage of my life for two family dinners and then disappeared.

When I'd finished reading that journal, I stared out at the garden below for a while. All I could figure out was that my parents had chosen them as guardians and never got around to changing things when their relationship grew cold. I'm sure they thought the odds of dying at the same time were somewhat remote. And maybe by the time I was a pre-teen, I was pretty self-sufficient, so assigning alternate guardians wasn't at the top of their minds. There were lots of comments about my parents telling me they liked how independent I was.

"Are you re-living the past?" JD said. He was halfway through his second slice of pizza.

"It's strange because it doesn't feel like re-living. It's like seeing part of my life for the first time. There were a lot of things I'd forgotten. Nothing important, but it almost felt like reading about someone else's life."

"Do you still keep a journal?"

"No."

"Why not? I'd like to read what you wrote when you met me." He grinned and took a huge bite of pizza. Because he was still grinning, the tomato sauce and strings of cheese gave his mouth a bloody appearance.

"I got out of the habit, or got bored with it. I don't know."

"Did you figure anything out?"

"Not really."

"Nothing new, nothing about Gloria and Paul, nothing about . . . ?"

"I wrote about being upset with Detective Smith. I felt like he wasn't listening to me. He questioned me seven or eight times. Reading it made me angry all over again."

"Because he wasn't aggressive with the investigation?"

"No, because he seemed so uncreative in the way he went about it."

He laughed. "Uncreative?"

"Well that's what it was. I'd completely forgotten how he asked me over and over about my friends. He had this idea that since I was new at the high school, because I'd been home-schooled, that I was an odd duck — his word, not mine. He thought maybe I'd attracted some kind of bullying or gang interest. He was working on the theory that kids from my school had murdered them. He asked me about kids coming to the house and kept pressing me, asking me if I was *sure* I didn't let some friends inside. Was I *sure* I didn't bring home a boy who invited friends over later, stuff like that."

"Wow. That's cold."

Tears pushed against the back of my eyes. I hadn't cried when I'd read about it. My skin had gotten cold, I was angry, but I didn't even *feel* like crying. I put down my half-eaten pizza slice.

"Not hungry?"

"I am. I can see that they have to pursue every possibility, but to keep after me like that, so many times, to not believe me. And with my parents dead. You'd think he'd feel sorry for me."

"Did you have a lawyer?"

"I seem to remember there was a woman with me, but I don't think she was a lawyer. I wasn't a suspect. They just thought I was protecting a bunch of loser friends. If I did have a lawyer, I didn't write about it."

He picked up a third slice of pizza.

I sipped my water and finished my first slice in four bites. "I wonder what they missed, putting all their attention on me and my supposed ability to attract gangs."

He smiled.

"It's not funny."

"I was smiling at the way you said it not that they might have missed other possibilities. Are you disappointed?"

"About not finding the key to my aunt and uncle or some other amazing fact?"

"Yup."

"A little. I'd hoped I would discover some forgotten secret, but I know that's completely unrealistic. If I knew something important back then, it would have come out back then, don't you think?"

"Your lens has changed."

"At this point, I'm mostly disappointed that I made such a big deal out of reading them. I shouldn't have waited. Now I've done nothing else all this time." I gnawed on my pizza crust. It had turned cold, making it stiff and doughy. I felt like a dog gnawing on a chew toy. Still, it was soothing. I guess that's why dogs like chew toys. "Mostly I was a kid and I wrote about kid things. The things I think would be important now are barely mentioned. But it was fun reading."

I was glad I'd diverted him from asking what I'd written immediately after my parents' deaths. I didn't want to tell him, not yet, that I'd skipped one of the books. No matter whether he pushed me to read it, completely clueless about how I felt, or was too sympathetic, making me feel like a needy child, I knew I'd be disappointed with his response. Being disappointed in *him* would have been more disappointing than not finding a key to the past.

Two

DETECTIVE SMITH HAD made a point of saying he wouldn't be taking my calls anymore — that my parents' case was no longer active. But I figured he might not be so firm if he had to see me face to face. Of course, that wasn't exactly easy with the desk sergeant insisting on pre-scheduled appointments.

Still, it was obvious to the casual visitor where the officers parked their cars, and it was easy to hang around and wait for Detective Smith to leave the building. It might be a long wait, but I'm a patient person.

The parking lot was behind and slightly below the building. In front of the main doors was a large lawn that had been allowed to turn brown. In the center was a self-important sign announcing they were conserving water.

If they really wanted to conserve, they should have torn out the dead grass and planted something pleasing rather than using their dead lawn to pat themselves on the back.

But I suppose it wasn't the officers' fault, probably some city bureaucrat.

A ten-foot-wide sidewalk ran in front of the station and there were a few mature oak trees between it and the street. They'd nicely provided benches in the shade of the trees. I couldn't imagine anyone besides me who would want to sit on a bench outside a police station, but what did I know. Maybe there were other victims' families stalking the detectives.

I settled back, sipped icy cold latte through the straw in my plastic cup, and waited. I hoped he'd leave on official business before it got too hot, but that was like hoping someone would be kidnapped or assaulted or murdered, so I tried to focus on enjoying the tree, and not judging the sign in the middle of the dead grass.

Forty-five minutes later, I saw Detective Smith walking down the sloping path toward the parking lot. His partner wasn't with him, which I took as a sign that things would go in my favor. I jumped up and hurried across the lawn, brown grass crunching under my sandals like someone chewing ice cubes. As if they wanted to echo the sound, the remaining cubes in my cup rattled against the sides. I took a long sip so the drink was lower and wouldn't splash out, and started running.

Just as he reached the parking lot, I caught up with him. I walked fast until I passed him, then turned and stopped. He looked less tired than when I'd seem him at the beginning of the summer. His white shirt looked new.

It was more up to date, made of softer-looking

cotton. He wore black slacks and he seemed a little thinner, in a good way.

"Madison."

He didn't sound at all surprised to see me. It made me wonder if he'd regretted his sharp words, telling me not to get hysterical, telling me he wouldn't talk to me, telling me there was nothing he could do.

"Hi."

He glanced at his watch. "I really can't . . ."

"This is quick. I want to look at the files from my parents' case."

"Oh, okay." He pulled a business card out of his shirt pocket and a pen out of his pants' pocket. He wrote a note on the back of the card and handed it to me. "Take this to the officer at the front desk. He'll set you up."

"Really? Just like that?"

He raised his eyebrows. "Did you think it wasn't allowed?"

"I don't know what I thought."

"I'm surprised you never asked before."

"Then why didn't you offer?"

He laughed. "Do you think you're going to find something we missed?"

I didn't answer.

"Okay, well, maybe you will. Stranger things have happened." He raised his hand in a half wave. "Gotta go."

"Bye. And, thanks."

He nodded and hurried toward the line of white

government cars.

I stared at the card in my hand. I turned it over. He'd written — *Okay for Madison Keith to access files for David and Annie Keith.* — *Smith*.

For a moment, I couldn't make myself move. He didn't think I'd find anything interesting, and maybe I wouldn't. Still, I felt disoriented because it was so easy, because he was so nice, because everything seemed so different. And I had no idea why.

I walked slowly up the hill, around to the front of the building, and went inside. The officer at the desk took the card. He made a phone call. He asked to see my driver's license, filled out a small card, and put it in a plastic holder to attach to my shirt.

A few minutes later, another officer came out from the double doors to my left. He led me in the opposite direction, through a door with a window, and down a corridor to a small room with two tables outside a huge filing room. He asked me to sit at a table and wait for him. About ten minutes later he was back with five boxes riding on a dolly. He left the boxes, took the dolly back into the filing room, came out, and locked the door behind him. He told me to take my time, but that I had to leave by five o'clock. It was only ten-thirty in the morning, and I knew I'd get hungry long before five. The granola bar and box of milk duds in my purse wouldn't carry me that far.

"Can I come back tomorrow if I don't get through all of this today?"

"Of course. Can I get you some water?"

"That would be great. Thanks."

He returned a few minutes later with a Styrofoam cup of water and left me alone.

Two of the boxes contained clothes — my father's, my mother's, and mine. All from the day of their murder. I pulled out each piece of clothing and pressed it to my face but all they smelled of was cardboard, dust, and fabric.

The next box was filled with file folders stuffed with photographs. I spent the next two hours looking at them — every image imaginable of our house and yard, all in brilliant, shimmering color. It looked exactly like I remembered. Some of the pictures of my parents' bodies were hard to take. The first few shots of them lying in their bed were exactly as I remembered finding them. After I looked at those, I stood and walked to the other side of the room. I wanted a smoke, but I didn't want to leave. It was hard to figure out why there were some things that had stayed crisp in my memory all this time, like my parents lying on their backs in their bed, and other things, like being questioned about kids from school, and the constant repetition, that I'd completely forgotten. Memory is a strange thing, and I know visual experiences stick with you more, or at least they're supposed to, but still . . . I couldn't understand why the things I'd written in my journals were a complete surprise to me. In a way, they were visual because I wrote the words on paper.

I returned to the table and looked at all the pictures of the house again — such agonizing detail of every room, every object, the floors, the walls. There were more pictures — the bed after my parents were taken away, their bodies in the morgue, which I only glanced at and quickly turned upside down.

The next box had three shell casings and one bullet, each tucked inside a small clear plastic box. There had been photographs of the spots where the shell casings were found, and a photograph of a bullet they'd pulled out of the wall above the nightstand on my mother's side of the bed. It seemed odd that the killer was such a wild shot he, or she, missed by that much, and then managed to put a bullet through the center of my mother's forehead and my father's forehead. I shivered, thinking about it in that way.

I swallowed and wished more desperately for a cigarette. Instead, I finished the last of my iced latte. It was mostly melted ice. I sipped some of the water, ate two Milk Duds, and looked through the rest of the box. There were sheets of fingerprints, two cell phones which presumably belonged to my parents, loose photographs of the driveway, some photos showing tire impressions and footprints, and some boxes with threads and dirt samples.

The last box contained all the notes — interviews, and Detective Smith's observations.

I packed up the other boxes and went back to the front desk. I told the officer I was going outside for a while and he said that was fine, but not to leave the area or they'd need to pack up the boxes again.

I returned to the bench under the oak tree and smoked two cigarettes, letting my mind go blank, trying to focus on the smoke going in and out, the shrinking of the cigarette, cars moving in and out of the parking lot, and a lone blue jay hopping around above my head.

When I returned to the room, the white walls and ceiling, off-white floor, and off-white tabletop made me feel as if I was going in for surgery. And maybe I was. Smoking two cigarettes in quick succession had made me lightheaded. I was used to one every six or seven hours. When I binged like I just had, I didn't normally jump up and walk in midday heat.

I drank the rest of the water in the Styrofoam cup. I wished for more, but didn't want to waste any more time avoiding the box that offered the most hope and the most likely disappointment.

I was trying not to hope, not to expect anything. Police officers and detectives with decades of experience investigating crimes had conducted all the interviews and studied the evidence, of which there was precious little. The box was half filled with file folders of typed notes. It also contained a stack of small notebooks used during informal talks with witnesses, if you could call them that, since no one actually witnessed anything. At least not that I was aware of.

By the time I was finished reading, I wanted to cry. There'd been more information in my journals than there was in the pages and pages of notes. Most of them were so boring, I skimmed —

Q: How did you know Dave and Annie Keith?
A: They lived down the street from us for five years.
Q: How often did you talk?
A: We said hello when we were out in the yard at the same time.

My interviews read as if they'd been talking to a make-believe twin sister of mine. Like me but not like me. It gave me the same disconnected, distant feelings I'd had reading my journal. Most of my answers were three or four words, and many of them simple *yeses* and *noes*. As I'd complained about in my journal, they'd asked me the same things over and over and *over* again. There were interviews of kids from my high school and their answers had even fewer words.

The whole thing left me with a feeling that the detective was absolutely convinced a bunch of kids, or one kid, had shot my parents and they were going to repeat the questions until a *no* turned to a *yes*.

Q: Have you ever been inside the Keith home?
A: No.
Q: Madison never invited you over?
A: No.
Q: So you're sure you were never inside the house?
A: Yes.

Q: How well did you know Mr. and Mrs. Keith?
A: I never met them.

I wasn't sure if Detective Smith was supremely stupid, stubborn, or defeated. There were no fingerprints in the house but mine, my parents, and some friends of my parents. I'd only been going to the public high school for a few months, so I hadn't had time to find a friend I might want to bring home. I had friends in the home school group my mother had belonged to, but we played at parks and went to the beach and took educational trips to Alcatraz Island and Año Nuevo beach to observe the sea elephants. They weren't in my house that often.

There were interviews with men on parole for violent crimes, and interviews with local drug dealers. Yes, they actually had a theory that one or both of my parents used drugs and had gotten into a bad relationship with their supplier.

The interview with Gloria and Paul gave a bit of their background, which I already knew, and information about their church. That was followed by pages of questions and *noes*.

The only new and interesting information was the bullet that they'd dug out of the wall over the nightstand. And since I'd already seen the bullet and the photo of its location, there was nothing all that interesting to add to it in the notes. Just some comments that it might have been a warning shot, but a warning of what, they had no idea. It was an open question — how someone could miss so badly and then aim so precisely. There were notes about gunpowder and blood. I skimmed the blood parts.

When I was finished, I had an inexplicable surge of anger at Kate. Maybe not so inexplicable. She'd mentioned it so casually — suggesting I go through the files. But the idea had been startling to me, and it had filled me with hope, even though I told myself it hadn't. After so much time with no new leads, no ideas, no suspects, a new idea all on its own seemed like progress. And although I'd told myself I had no expectation, I now realized I'd had huge expectations. I'd thought the only thing preventing me from finding a goldmine of information would be an iron gate blocking my access to the evidence and notes themselves. I thought that if I could manage to get access, I'd see through lies and find meaning where Detective Smith had not. I thought my genetic connection to my parents and my instincts and sensitivity would reveal something surprising and profound — a clue to turn the investigation in a whole new direction. Detective Smith would be compelled to haul all those boxes out of that dusty, forgotten back room and stack them beside his desk, where he'd have easy access to the information needed to locate and prosecute the person who did such a horrible thing.

I put the notebooks and files back in the box, replaced the lid, and left all the boxes stacked on the floor. I picked up my bag, dropped the Styrofoam cup in the trashcan near the door, and returned to the front desk. I thanked the officer and told him I was finished.

It crossed my mind that I should contact Detective Smith, but what was the point? To admit my failure? To admit he was right?

I SAT INSIDE the air-conditioned deli, holding my phone, trying to decide if I should text JD. But then he'd ask why I wasn't coming back to the apartment. I wasn't there because I'd decided to visit Paul and Gloria and tell them about the files. I wanted to know if they'd ever looked at those files. I wanted to know more about my grandmother, whose tarnished bracelet was still on my left wrist. The grandmother I'd been told was dead. It seems I'm a person who can't stop banging her fists against the same walls, always thinking that this time, a previously unseen door will appear and someone will open it, ushering me into a world filled with answers and peace of mind.

I took a bite of my sandwich — dark rye bread, avocado, shredded carrots, cucumber, jack cheese, and alfalfa sprouts. The crunching felt good, and the cool, crisp vegetables soothed the inside of me where heat from the sun and heat from my frenzied thoughts had turned my esophagus into a furnace.

The phone now sat on the table. Its blank face stared at me. If I called Gloria and Paul, they might say they were busy, or make excuses that another time would be better. But I didn't want to wait until the next day, or the day after that. I had to talk to them. Even if I drove over there and they weren't home, it was worth the effort. And driving has a tendency to shake my brain like a kaleidoscope, moving things around into different patterns.

If I texted JD, he might want to go with me.

I turned my phone face down and finished my sandwich. I bought another bottle of water and went outside. The parking lot was baking under a ninety-degree sun. I stood with my car door open for five minutes, trying to get a small breeze to cool off the seat. I finally gave up, got a beach towel out of the trunk and got in.

When I pulled into their driveway twenty minutes later, I was thrilled to see the garage door open and their SUV and Jaguar sitting inside.

They seemed genuinely happy to see me. Even more shocking, they offered me flavored water and both of them had a bottle of the same, rather than their usual glasses of white wine.

I told them about the files. "Did you ever look at any of that stuff?"

Paul shook his head. "No point."

Gloria stood and walked across the room. She sat beside me on the couch. She put her cool fingers on my wrist, gently touching the bracelet. "Don't you think you'd be happier if you let go? There's nothing that can be done. It's been too long."

I swallowed. "I can't just give up."

"There might not be an answer."

"Why does everyone keep saying that?"

"Because it's the truth," Paul said.

"Someone killed them, and that someone is still out there."

"Yes," Gloria said. She touched the bracelet again. "But I think it's too late."

"Old murder cases get solved all the time."

"I don't think it's all the time," she said. "When something like that happens, there's a lot of attention, so it seems more significant. But if you think about the hundreds, thousands of murders . . ."

"It had to be someone they knew."

"Why?" Paul said.

"They looked so peaceful." The image I'd carried for years filled my head, enhanced by the photographs I'd seen for the first time.

"You can't know that," Paul said.

"Yes I can. That's how I remember their faces, and the photographs proved it."

Gloria snatched her hand off my wrist. "You saw the photographs?"

"Yes."

"Why? Why would they allow that?" she said.

"I'm an adult."

"But they were your parents."

"I saw them when they were dead. The pictures weren't any worse than what's been inside my head all these years."

She squeezed my arm, just above my wrist, moving it gently up and down, as if she were trying to soothe herself more than me.

"It's okay. I'm fine." I carefully pulled my arm away from her fingers. "Did you push the detective at all? Try to get him to work harder, to think outside the box?"

"It seemed to me, to us, they were putting a lot of effort into it," Paul said.

"But what about over the years, once I was an adult and moved away?"

"There wasn't anything we could do," he said.

"There's always something."

"You didn't find anything new by looking through their files, it doesn't change the outcome," he said.

"Why did you lie to him? I still don't understand."

"We didn't lie," Paul said.

I waited, my mouth in a slight frown, staring and trying not to blink, forcing him to back down from such a ridiculous statement.

After several minutes of silence, Gloria said, "It wasn't about anything important."

"It was important to me!"

"No one knew but the detective."

"It still wasn't right, making my parents look bad for not paying a debt."

"I suppose. But I was upset with her — Annie, your mother, I . . . I was upset that she called me a drunk. It was cruel, and not true. And to be honest, I was a little upset that she didn't even bother to let us know we were still your guardians. It was a huge responsibility, taking you on. And your parents, your mother especially, had very grand ideas about how you should be raised. You did whatever you wanted because she taught you to think you should make all of your own decisions. From a very young age. It was difficult to care for a teenager who thought she was an adult."

"Well I turned out okay."

"Yes, you did. But you were a challenge, just having a teenager in our house when we'd never had a child. Listening to you tell us you were going to smoke no matter what we said."

"That's all? Smoking?"

"Thankfully, yes. But we didn't know that at the time. And then all those questions about whether kids you knew had murdered Annie and Dave . . ."

"I read about that in my journals. I'd forgotten all of it. Or maybe I didn't want to remember. Why didn't you remind me?"

"What's the point of all this?"

I glanced back and forth at their faces. They wore matching beige linen shirts, and their skin tone was nearly identical. Their weak, tired smiles had the same sagging quality. "I want to know who killed them. I want to know why."

"Why now?" Gloria said. "That's what we're asking."

"It's not a new desire."

"You never talked about it much, you didn't push so hard. It's like you're picking at a scab, making something that was almost healed start bleeding again."

"It wasn't almost healed."

"You might never know. You'll probably never know,"

Paul said. He looked sad, almost ready to cry.

"Why do people keep saying that? Why does everyone give up, why do they want me to give up? Don't you care about justice?"

"Of course we do."

I stood and walked to the window that looked out on the front garden. I stood there for a few minutes, trying to answer those questions for myself. It was as if I'd been asleep for a long time. Or maybe I just felt helpless when I was a teenager, and when I was first on my own. Maybe I didn't think I could do anything, so I didn't try. I don't even know. It's not like we have to know why we do every single thing in life. I turned. "What about my grandmother?" I held up my arm and let the heavy bracelet slide along until it couldn't go any further. "Why did my mother tell me she was dead? Why is there nothing about her in the interview notes?"

Paul stood. "She doesn't live around here. She has nothing to do with it."

"Then why did my mother . . ."

"She probably wished your grandmother was dead," Paul said.

I stared at him. He stared back, as if he dared me to ask more questions. Then, he walked out of the room, toward the wing where the bedrooms were.

I waited for Gloria to say something. She just looked at me with a huge *I told you so* expression. I folded my arms.

"Would you like some coffee?" she said.

"Sure. Where does my grandmother live?"

"In New York, if she's still there."

"When was the last time you saw her?"

Gloria stood and smoothed her jeans even though they weren't wrinkled or crumpled up. "She has nothing to do with their murder. She won't be any help."

"How do you know that?"

"Paul hasn't had contact with her in thirty-five years."

"Why?"

"He won't discuss it, I already told you that."

"You don't know anything about where she is now, or what happened between them?"

"I really don't."

"Do you have her address? Or a phone number?"

"I'm not sure. I'd have to ask Paul, and he . . ."

"Yes. I know."

"I'll make the coffee."

As she headed toward the kitchen, I knew I had to find a way to reach this woman I'd thought was dead.

Three

JD DIDN'T SEEM to mind that I'd been flitting about town, going through files and visiting Gloria and Paul without him. He was happy to be home base. I liked that too. Mostly. A small part of me wanted him to be thinking about it all the time, angry about it all the time, like I was. I wanted someone else on the merry-go-round with me, and I felt as if he was sitting at a picnic table, waving each time my wooden horse passed by. But it was also something I knew I had to do by myself. This was between me and my parents and their killer.

JD wasn't thrilled about the next step in my plan — a return visit to Gwen and Kevin, the couple living in my old house.

"After the things Jan said about them, I don't know. His weird friends, the fact that they shut themselves up in there and no one knows anything about them. If it bothered her enough to want to evict them, that concerns me."

"Those are just her opinions."

"It sounded as if there's something off about them."

"Maybe there is. Maybe they're so off, they'll reverse their position on letting me inside the house."

"You've already been inside." He turned sideways on the couch and put his feet in my lap. He leaned sideways and picked up his beer off the coffee table.

"I want to find out if they've had any unusual experiences. Maybe that's why Jan's disturbed. Maybe *she* saw something over there and she's hiding behind all these petty criticisms of Gwen and Kevin. Maybe she's scared."

"Fair enough. I didn't think of that. It would be interesting to know." He sipped his beer.

I smiled.

"I'll go with you." He took his legs off my lap. He got up and went to the kitchen, dumped the rest of the beer down the drain, and stepped back into the dining. "I shouldn't have dumped my beer, should I."

"It's like we've said before. Another person changes the dynamic."

"You didn't get very far with them last time, doesn't the dynamic *need* changing?"

"Next time. I just want to see what happens, talking to them by myself. Now that a little time has passed. And you're a big guy, I don't want Kevin to get drunk on testosterone."

He laughed. He bent his elbows, flexed his biceps, and leaned forward slightly. "That's me. A big guy."

I stood up. "Don't make fun of me."

"I'm not." He lifted his arms out to the sides more and turned, bending one knee like a bodybuilder.

"That's enough."

"I'm trying to make you laugh."

"Ha ha."

He stood normally. "I won't get in the way of your plan."

"You're not in the way."

"You know what I mean." He walked back to where I was standing, put his arms around me, and kissed me. "Are you going now?"

I nodded, rubbing my cheek against his collarbone. It was just after seven. It was probably the best time to catch them both at home. Finding Gwen there by herself wouldn't get me anywhere, and I sort of didn't want to see Kevin alone. It seemed much more likely things could go wrong, that I'd push him into a corner, he'd become more stubborn, and that would be the end of it. Gwen was more malleable, and she seemed to have a softening effect on him.

KEVIN'S MOTORCYCLE AND Gwen's minivan were parked in the driveway of 1701 Whitewood Way. It wasn't any easier than the other times — seeing that little house and feeling like it was mine, but not, a huge part of my life and at the same time, something foreign. A place I loved and a place I hated. But mostly loved and missed.

I parked in front of Jan's house and sat in the car for

quite a few minutes, looking at 1701, trying to figure out what I was feeling. I suppose fear. I was afraid that nothing would come of another visit, afraid I'd never get inside the house again, afraid that if I did, I wouldn't encounter my parents' ghosts. It was difficult to decide whether I should come right out and ask Gwen and Kevin if they'd experienced any supernatural phenomenon, or try to find out more about them first. Or maybe I should try to find out more about where they'd gotten my mother's sunflower picture that was hanging in their living room.

The longer I sat there, the more I risked them looking out the window, seeing my car, and putting up psychological defenses against me. Maybe they wouldn't even answer the door. I got out of the car, walked to the front porch, and rang the bell.

Kevin immediately opened the door, as if he'd been standing at the window watching me after all. His hair was wet which made it dark, turning the reddish highlights to brown. There was a wet spot on his t-shirt near his collarbone as if he'd put it on before he was completely dried off. The t-shirt was black with a white, faded image of Che Guevara. His jeans had a big hole near the left knee, but it wasn't a stylish, manufactured tear.

"You," he said.

"Yes, me."

"What do you want?"

Gwen called from the other room. "Is it Jerry?"

Kevin turned and yelled — "No, it's that tattooed girl.

The one who used to live here."

Gwen didn't respond. I heard water running and dishes clanking against tile.

Kevin turned back. "What do you want?"

He acted as if I was intruding, but at the same time, I had the odd feeling he didn't want me to leave. There was something about the way he leaned against the doorframe and the challenge in his eyes, that made me think he wanted to talk to me. He acted so combative, so put out, but still gave off the vibe that he wanted to get me talking, keep me standing there, as if getting me riled up was his entertainment for the evening.

"I was wondering . . ."

"Yeeees?"

"That print of the sunflowers behind you . . . where did you get it?"

"Are you looking for new artwork?"

"No. It's familiar. I mean . . . I, my parents had one like it. With the same frame."

"Are you accusing me of stealing it?"

"No."

"Then what's your interest?"

"I just told you. My parents had one like it."

"And you think this is the same one?"

"It's a big coincidence, don't you think?"

He grinned. "It was in the attic. Okay? And you drove all the way here from wherever you came from to ask where I got a cheap print?"

Gwen appeared behind him. Her hair was also wet,

plastered to her head, making her look even more delicate than I remembered. She seemed annoyed but said nothing. She wasn't looking at me, directing her steady gaze and the twist of her lips in Kevin's direction. He couldn't see her, and seemed to have no idea she was not happy.

"Were there other things in the attic? Maybe from my parents?"

"Just some boxes of toys."

"Where are they now?"

"In the attic. I'll sell them to you, if you want. But they're pretty beat up from what I saw." He grinned.

My throat tightened, partially at the thought of toys that had belonged to me, and partially at the further proof that he seemed to be enjoying making me suffer. I didn't want to admit I thought he was cruel. I didn't want him to see he'd upset me, to give him that power over my feelings. But I think he noticed, because his grin became more firmly etched on his face.

"You don't think that's fair, do you?" he said.

"I don't know what I'm thinking, so you surely can't know."

"You look like the type that is extremely concerned about fairness."

"What type is that?"

"Someone who has rules about how people should behave. Rules about how life should operate, and you've never experienced the fact that life is astronomically unfair."

I smiled. The tight, fragile sensation in my throat was gone. There's nothing like a little anger to get rid of weak, powerless feelings. Maybe he was trying to make me angry. Maybe he knew the previous owners of the house had been murdered and he'd figured out why I was so eager to get inside to say good-bye to the ghosts of my childhood, even if he didn't literally think I was looking for ghosts inside his house.

"Am I right?" he said.

"Don't be an ass, Kev." Gwen folded her arms across her middle. Her tanned skin was almost the same color as her beige t-shirt, making her look as if she didn't have any arms.

"Not talking to you, Gwen." He moved the door, trying to fit himself in the opening to block her from seeing me.

The conversation was slipping out of my control, if it had ever been in my control. I had no idea what I'd hoped to accomplish by showing up at their house. I had to get inside, but if they followed me around, what good was that going to do me? If being there alone, or semi-alone, at least alone in my room, had done nothing a month earlier, what good would it do to prowl through the rooms while Kev made snide comments? The toys sitting up in the attic could get me inside. Offering to pay for them might open the door to asking for time alone inside their house. But the cost was any shred of pride or justice. If I had to humble myself to offer to pay for my own childhood possessions, I might as well go all in.

"Have you heard any stories about this house?" I said.

He pinched himself more tightly in the door. "Stories?"

"Do you know anything about the previous owners?"

"I don't care about the previous owners. I'm not the owner. We rent."

"Have you . . . do you mind if I come in? Have a glass of water and talk? It's awkward standing here."

"Why is it awkward?"

"It would just be easier sitting down."

"Sure. Why not." He opened the door so I could step inside. "Gwen, get us some sodas."

"Water's fine," I said. "I'd rather have water."

Gwen disappeared. I was surprised he'd invited me in, but tried to remind myself that it might be another piece of his game. Maybe he was bored. Maybe he was weak and any chance he had to show power over someone was a welcome diversion from the rest of his powerless life.

We sat in the living room. The backyard was cloaked with shadows as the sun lowered itself behind the trees. The grayish rooftops of the nearby houses glowed as if they were metal, throwing back reflections into the sky. Gwen came in carrying a small round tray with two cans of cola and a bottle of spring water. I picked up the water bottle, opened it, and took a sip. She sat next to Kevin, leaning against him, as if his sharp words were forgotten, or didn't matter.

"What's your proposal?" Kevin said.

"My proposal?"

"The price. For the boxes." He pointed at the ceiling. "I guess you want to see them before you make an offer."

"That's not why I wanted to come inside."

"Then why? What's wrong with you? There's something weird, like you're obsessed with this place. Next thing I know, I'll wake up in the morning and you'll be standing in the bedroom, watching us sleep."

Gwen glanced toward the hallway, then jerked her head back toward me.

Have you ever . . ." I took a long swallow of water. I screwed the cap back on the bottle. "Have you felt anything strange here? Seen anything . . . frightening?" The minute I spoke, I regretted it.

A mixture of ridicule and amusement spread across Kevin's face. Gwen remained serious, and I wondered if they'd had different experiences of the house. Or was she on an entirely different planet, hardly hearing what either of us said or noticing how Kevin treated her? But Kevin was going to laugh at me and continue taunting me, like he was a tomcat who'd found a mouse he wanted to bat around until he got bored, or it died.

"Do you mean is the house haunted? It's nothing like a haunted house. It's a cottage. In a sunny, bland suburban town. Or maybe that's the same thing — bland suburban." He laughed.

"Being a suburban cottage doesn't mean it can't be haunted."

"Why does it seem like there's something you're not telling me?" he said. "Something big."

I shrugged.

"It's not haunted," he said.

"You've never felt like you were being watched, or . . . ?"

"I have," Gwen said. She sipped her soda.

Kevin patted her leg. "That's because you're paranoid."

She took another sip of soda.

"What happened?" I said.

"Nothing *happened*," Kevin said.

"I felt I was being watched." She spoke more loudly, as if to silence Kevin. She glanced toward the hallway.

"Did you see anything or hear anything? Were you scared?" I said.

"What's all this about." Kevin took his hand off Gwen's leg. "I thought you wanted stuff out of the attic. Why would this place be haunted? Why would someone be watching us?"

"Just curious," I said.

"Why'd you ask me if I'd seen a ghost when you were here the last time?" Gwen said. "Did you see one when you were a kid?"

"Kids see all kinds of things. They *think* they see all kinds of things. They have crazy imaginations," Kevin said. "I bet you were a nutty kid, because you sure are batshit crazy now."

"That's not nice." Gwen moved away from him. He reached over and patted her leg again and she wriggled back until she was pressed against him.

It's true," he said.

"I'm not crazy."

"Then why are you here? You're giving me the creeps. Are you casing the place? Because if you are, we don't have anything worth taking. Look around." He waved his arm over his head.

I looked up at the sunflowers. I wanted the print, but if he was going to make me pay for my own toys, something he couldn't even use, there was no way he'd let me have the print.

He stood suddenly, bumping Gwen's shoulder. Soda splashed out of his can and landed on her leg. She tugged on her shirt and patted at the damp spot. "I thought you wanted to make an offer on the crap in the attic. Instead you're consuming our beverages and giving Gwen the creeps. She doesn't need someone feeding her over-anxious imagination." He stepped around the coffee table.

"What I really want," I said. "I was wondering if I could stay here some time, when you're out for the evening, or something like that."

"Are you kidding? What for?" he said.

"I just feel like I never got to say good-bye."

"To a house?"

"I understand what she means," Gwen said.

She didn't look at me, but I remembered my visits earlier in the summer, when I'd started to feel a spider thread of connection with her. Then Kevin bulldozed in and there was nothing more.

"That's 'cuz you're nuts, too," he said.

"I know it must sound weird. Maybe you don't want a stranger staying in your house, I can understand, but you did say there's nothing worth stealing."

"That doesn't mean I want you in my house. Do you want that stuff in the attic or not? If you don't, I think it's time for you to move along to your next stop."

Asking to stay alone in their house had been pointless, but what other choice was there? I should have known he'd refuse. I knew how crazy it sounded, he was right about that. It seemed as if Gwen understood. Couldn't he listen to his girlfriend, couldn't he understand the desire to close a door on your past life?

"Let's go." Kevin moved toward the door, keeping his eyes on me.

I inched to the edge of my chair, then picked up the water bottle and took a sip.

"No stalling."

I screwed the cap on the bottle. "What if I still want the toys? I might change my mind."

"I doubt it," he said.

"How do you know?"

"I'm not stupid. I can see you have an agenda that you aren't being upfront about. You had your chance with the toys, now I just think you should leave."

I stood. I held up the water bottle. "Can I keep this?"

"There's nothing I can do with it," he said.

Gwen remained on the couch. I couldn't tell whether she was looking at me or Kevin, embarrassed by his pettiness, or something else. Her eyes shifted more in my direction, then back to Kevin.

"I don't understand why you find me so irritating. I was just curious about your house. Buildings can have different moods, don't you think?"

"No."

"Doesn't this place feel like home to you?"

He stared at me as if he hated my guts.

"What's wrong?" I said.

"Were you raised to think you're the center of the universe? I bet you were. You were never told you couldn't have something, never heard the word *no* throughout your entire childhood."

"That's not true."

"Then where do you get the chutzpah to walk into a house and ask if you can have it back, even it's only for an evening?"

"I didn't ask for it back. I just wanted . . ."

"It's the same thing." He opened the door wider. "This time you're going to hear the word *no*. Like I did my entire life."

I took a few steps toward him. "You sound like you're angry at me. I was just asking a favor."

"No more talking."

I went to the door. As soon as I passed the spot where he was standing, he reached around me and pushed open the screen. I stepped onto the front porch.

"Don't come back," he said.

"But . . ."

"The house isn't haunted. The things inside belong to me now. If you want my opinion, I think you should get a grip and let go of the past, like most people are forced to do. They don't get to run around trying to recreate their lost childhoods. Some of us never even got a childhood, so be thankful for what you had and move on."

"I don't need your advice."

"You come into my house and act like it still belongs to you, then you get my advice. For free. Lucky you."

"Lucky me," I said.

The screen slammed, followed quickly by the front door. I walked to my car and drove home, replaying the conversation and trying to figure out what I did to make him so angry. Finally, I decided he was one of those people who's just angry and takes it out on anyone who crosses their path.

THE APARTMENT WAS dark and JD was sitting on the balcony when I walked in the front door. The balcony doors were closed because he was sneaking a smoke out there. The birdcage was on the table next to him and he had the ashtray on the ground to his left, keeping the smoke away from the birds. Still, I didn't think it was good for them to be that close to it. I dropped my bag on the couch, kicked off my sandals, and went out to the balcony. I kissed the top of his head, tugged gently on his ponytail, and picked up the cage.

"What are you doing?" he said.

"The smoke isn't good for them."

"One time won't hurt. I was lonely."

"Well I'm here now. We aren't supposed to smoke."

"I just took a few puffs."

I carried the birds inside and put the cage on the stand in the dining area. I grabbed my cigarettes out of my bag and joined him on the balcony. Below, the fountain burbled. From the balcony on the opposite side of the courtyard, I heard voices, softer than the fountain. There was something about the sound of water and the lush, overgrown garden that seemed to make all the residents keep their voices low.

"I hope no one complains about us smoking," I said.

"No one seems to be around, except those two women across the way."

"Still, I don't want to get kicked out."

He put out his cigarette. "Like I said, just a few quick puffs."

I held up my package. "I guess I'll do the same. Half?"

He flicked his lighter and I leaned in. The flame caught and I walked around and sat down.

"How'd it go?"

"I pissed them off. Mostly Kevin."

"What happened?"

I related the conversation, took two more puffs, then handed my cigarette to him so he could smash it in the ashtray.

"Do you think I blew it?" I said.

"Gwen might have been more open, but maybe not.

Remember how she had to run everything past him?"

"Yeah. I know it's a weird request. I get that. I'm sure they think I'm some kind of stalker or thief, or just an out and out freak."

"Could be." He patted my shoulder. He moved his hand to my neck and twisted my hair around his fingers.

"I still might go back. Wait around for him to leave."

"You're sure doing a lot of flitting about — the police station, your relatives, your old house. You're like one of the parakeets."

"I thought you were on my side?"

"Just making a comment about how it is watching you. It's good to try every option."

"Well if I'm a bird, I'm not finding any worms."

"You will."

"Do you think so?"

"I hope so. You have to keep hoping or else finally figure out a way to let go of it."

"I'm scared — I'm almost out of ideas. But there is one last thing. Well, two things. Like I said, I'm going back to my house when Gwen's alone. I have to know more about her feeling as if she's being watched."

"Yeah, that's pretty interesting. Do you think she's a little nutty, or that she really picked up on something?"

"I prefer to think she picked up on something. People think I'm nutty, too."

He tightened his grip on my hair. "Not all people. What's the other last thing?"

I held up my arm. He was looking out toward the

courtyard and didn't seem to notice. I moved it closer to him, lowering it slightly so the ID bracelet slid toward my wrist bone and the small porch light glinted on the silver.

"Your grandmother?"

I lowered my arm and put my hand over the bracelet. It felt cold, as if I'd just dug it out of the ground.

"How will you get her contact information?"

"I don't know."

"I guess Google wouldn't work."

I squeezed the bracelet, pressing the thick links into my skin. "I don't even know what city she lives in. Paul might not even know where she is. Thirty-five years is a long time. I wonder what makes someone cut their mother out of their life completely. Both their lives. I still can't believe my mother lied to me about her being dead."

"Paul must know something."

"But he walks out of the room if I even mention her. And Gloria probably can't find out without asking him."

"Maybe you could get Detective Smith to do it."

"You mean the guy who said he's not putting any more resources into the case? The guy who said he wouldn't take my calls? The guy who . . ."

"He let you look through the files."

"I guess he didn't have a choice."

"But he could have stonewalled you, and he didn't. Maybe his superiors told him to stop spending time on it, and that's not how he feels."

I'd never thought of that. Lately, it had seemed like the detective was fighting against me, but maybe that was only in my mind — *me* fighting him. I never thought about him having a boss, being frustrated, even trying to push for an answer when some other person above him cared only about expenses and win rates, or whatever they call their success statistics — their hours per case.

"What are you thinking?" JD said.

"I never looked at it that way."

"Should we go over there tomorrow?"

"Yes." I smiled into the darkness.

INSTEAD OF ASKING us to set an appointment as he had on our other visits, the desk officer picked up his phone and called Detective Smith. The detective appeared in the lobby two minutes after that. He walked toward us, smiling. He shook my hand, then JD's. I felt I was in the twilight zone. Had he completely forgotten about his phone calls a few weeks earlier? His words had sounded like utter rejection — *I won't be able to take your calls. Stop being hysterical. Move on. Let go. You're becoming dangerously obsessive.* He didn't say all of that, especially the last part, but he sure hinted at it.

"Should we walk around outside?" Detective Smith said. "It's a gorgeous day, but in a few hours we'll all be plastered against the AC vents."

We crossed the lobby and he held the door for us. The dry lawn still had its boastful sign. The dirt beneath the stubs of dead grass was as hard as concrete. We cut across the deadness toward the sidewalk that ran around the buildings. One pathway lead to the parking lot, another lead toward a picnic table under an oak tree as old and impressive as the one I'd sat beneath the previous time. He walked toward the table and we followed. He sat on one side and we climbed onto the bench facing him.

Detective Smith settled down with perfect posture and folded his arms. "Was it helpful going through the evidence and notes?"

I nodded. "There wasn't anything that struck me. It was disappointing."

He managed to keep his expression from saying *I told you so.*

"I think Madison's a little surprised you're talking to us," JD said.

"After the phone calls . . . telling me you've stopped work on their case," I said.

Detective Smith nodded and gave me a small, sympathetic smile. "I've always understood how it must be for you, Madison. But we ran out of leads. That's it. It's a waste of resources to keep spinning our wheels."

"Then why did you say you wouldn't take my calls?"

"To be completely honest, that was a bit of an over-reaction on my part. I'm sorry."

I turned my head and looked at the building, glass and white concrete glittering in the morning sun. I didn't want him to notice I was laughing at him. People sound ridiculous when they add pointless phrases like *on my part.* Whose part would it be on? It sounds as if they're stalling, or creating a wall of words to prevent them from being completely *honest,* despite his insistence that he was being honest.

"You've pushed so hard, you've been so certain there was something we missed. And there wasn't. I thought I was doing you a disservice to keep talking to you, because it gives the impression there are other avenues to pursue."

"Well I have something. And it's nothing for you, but I hope you can help. Sort of officially."

"What's that?"

"My grandmother."

"I understood all of your extended family was on the east coast, and more or less estranged."

"Yes. And my grandmother is so estranged I thought she was dead."

Detective Smith laughed, then looked uncomfortable as if he realized it wasn't at all funny, either that she was estranged or dead. Or maybe it occurred to him I'd been lied to. That was the first time that word had passed through my mind. Thinking of my mother lying to me was like a fist slamming into the softest part of my belly. I couldn't breathe for a moment. I don't think Detective Smith noticed, but JD put his arm around my waist. I took a few shallow breaths. I felt guilty, thinking of my mother as a liar, criticizing her when I didn't know anything about *her* mother, and she wasn't there to explain. But it didn't stop her from being a liar. It wasn't as if she'd simply managed to avoid the subject my entire life. She flat out told me my grandparents were dead. Unless Paul was the liar. And Gloria. But Gloria sounded genuinely surprised that I'd thought the woman was dead.

Detective Smith seemed to be waiting for me to provide more information. When I didn't, he said, "What does that have to do with me?"

"My mother obviously didn't want me to know she existed, and when I tried to talk to my uncle, he refused to discuss her."

"And that involves me, how . . . ?"

"She probably knows nothing about what happened, if she's even alive at this point. But neither is there any information that she's dead. I'd like to try to get in touch with her. I don't even know why. I guess to try to understand my mother better."

"And if you understand her better, you'll figure out a new angle?" Detective Smith said.

"Maybe. I just want to talk to her. I've asked Paul twice, and he shuts me out."

"Okay."

"I thought you could talk to him. Tell him you want the contact information. Officially, or something."

"For what reason?"

I felt like hugging him, hugging JD for giving me the idea, climbing up on the table and dancing. He hadn't said no, he didn't think it was unethical!

JD took his arm away from me. "Do you have to give a reason? Can't you tell him you're aware of her existence and you want to talk to her."

"The case is inactive."

"Then tell him it's reactivated," JD said.

"That's not true."

"Do you have to explain it? You're the law enforcement official. Do you really go around explaining yourself to Jack Public?"

Detective Smith leaned his elbows on the table, then immediately pulled them back and inspected them for dirt. "I'll give him a call."

Since I'd already imagined myself hugging and dancing, there were no more exhibitions of elation to consider. Instead. I just felt everything inside me glowing, excited. I was eager for something to do that didn't feel as if I was banging my head against a concrete wall.

"Don't get your hopes up," Detective Smith said.

"Of course not," I said. "You're very good at reminding me."

He grimaced, but there was a genuine smile underneath.

Four

ACCORDING TO DETECTIVE Smith, Paul gave over my grandmother's name — Eileen Manchester — and her address and telephone number without any argument. He'd asked why it was needed and Detective Smith had said he was dotting all of his *i*'s. Paul didn't question that the case was supposed to be inactive. Of course, the information on Eileen Manchester's location was thirty-five years stale, but it was a start.

When Detective Smith called, I wrote the information down in the red notebook where I make lists of things to do or things I'm thinking of. Lists of things I want in my life, such as a macaw, and more birds in general, an aviary, in fact. I picture a house with a room at the center, featuring a glass ceiling that slides open beneath a screen so the birds can have the feeling of living outside. The rest of the rooms in the house would look into the aviary through sliding glass doors. I don't know if macaws can live with parakeets, and other kinds of birds, so I guess I have a bit of research to do before I go too far in imagining this bird-centric house.

I think JD expected me to immediately call the number with the 315 area code — Utica, New York. He kept glancing at the red notebook, staring at me when I was watching a movie or cleaning the kitchen, or feeding the birds and fish. He didn't say anything, but curiosity was plastered all over his face, wondering why, after pushing so hard to get the information, I was letting it sit unused. I'd assumed he would realize I had a completely different, bolder plan. But maybe he thought I was scared, maybe he thought I was still in shock from learning about a formerly dead relative who had come back larger than life.

"WE SHOULD GO to the grocery store," JD said. It was Wednesday morning, and cooler than it had been outside, but hot in the apartment. The doors were closed because the birds were out of their cage. While I rinsed scrambled egg residue off the plates and lined them up in the dishwasher, he was on the couch, playing a game on his tablet. Sierra was perched on his shoulder. Simon and Sara hopped around the coffee table, acting like they were looking for food, even though they'd just come out of a cage with two full tubes of seed.

"I'll make a list." I dropped a cube of soap in the dishwasher tray, pushed the heavy duty option and the start button, and closed the door. It began to rumble, forcing me out of the kitchen so I could make myself heard. "I need to do something else, first."

He tapped his tablet a few times, then put it on the table. "Call your grandmother?"

"Hearing that word — grandmother — sounds awkward."

"Because she's a stranger?"

"Not just a stranger, someone who didn't exist."

"You should turn off the dishwasher while you call, it's hard to hear."

I walked over and sat next to him. I put my feet on the table. Sara nudged my big toe with her beak. I giggled and leaned my head on JD's shoulder. "I'm not going to call her."

"Why not?"

"I need to visit her in person."

"You're flying to New York?"

"Yes."

His bicep tightened and he shifted his position. Sierra flew off his shoulder to the top of the TV. "You don't even know if she still lives there. That's a lot of money to look for a person who could have moved three or four times. But aside from the money, she might not even know you exist. You can't just show up."

"I think it's the best way."

"Why?"

"If I call, she might hang up. And if I tried again, she might not pick up, she might . . ."

"And she might slam the door in your face after you spend seven hundred bucks on a ticket. If she even lives there. If she's even alive."

"Either way, there are a lot of *ifs*."

My mother was thirty-eight when she was murdered. Now, she'd be fifty-three. That meant my grandmother was in the ballpark of seventy-five years old. The odds were decent that she was alive. And the thing about most people that age, most people any age that settled down with kids, they tend to stay in one place. She wasn't so old that I'd worry she was in a care home. If she didn't live at the same address, maybe neighbors would have information about where she'd gone, something I wouldn't be able to get over the phone.

It was a lot of money, but it seemed like something I should do before she died. Even though she probably knew nothing about my mother's adult life, or me, as JD pointed out, it felt like she was my last hope. Well, except for my parents' ghosts, but right then, I figured someone still alive might be able to help. So I should have called her my last breathing hope.

There's something about showing up and delivering a shock with your actual personhood that seems more compelling than an unfamiliar voice through a piece of plastic.

"You've made up your mind," he said.

"I have."

"I wondered why you were letting the number sit there, burning a hole in your notebook."

"Please don't tell me I'm setting myself up for disappointment."

"I didn't."

"I'm just planning ahead for when you might say that."

"Fair enough. It is a lot of money."

"It is. But it's money I have and I have to know why my mother told me she was dead. What is so awful that she'd lie to me? For my entire life? I never thought of her doing anything immoral. What kind of woman lies to her daughter?"

He put his arm around me. "Wait until you know more. Maybe she was protecting you. Maybe that's why Paul won't talk about it."

"Maybe. But everything I remember about my mother's approach to parenthood was giving me too *much* information. She wanted to discuss everything and know what I thought about every little detail, even if I was too young to have an opinion. I just don't understand."

"And . . ."

I put up my hand. "I know. I might not understand after I meet Eileen Manchester. And I might not meet her at all. Or I might meet her and we won't exchange more than five words."

"But you're doing it."

Sierra had joined the other birds on the coffee table. I put my finger on the table and touched it gently against her belly. She climbed on and I lifted her close to my face. Sierra is the bird I rescued from the open space preserve behind my condo. She's a wild, willful little creature, just like me, I like to think. She tipped her head and I was absolutely sure she was nodding in agreement, her eyes shining through to my soul, assuring me I would get some answers. It might be some time, but they were out there, and I'd find them, just like I'd found her.

FORTY-EIGHT WARREN Avenue, Utica, New York, was a large Victorian house. The chocolate brown siding with black window and roof trim gave it a gothic appearance. The crow sitting on the peak of one of three dormer windows added to that impression. So many windows faced the street, I didn't bother to count them. All the drapes were closed. The house stood three stories high, with a balcony running past several windows and two sets of French doors on the second floor. The dormers provided the windows of the third floor. There were two chimneys and a weather vane with a lion standing at the cross point of the arrows. Based on information from the weather vane, there was no breeze. The air was muggy and silent.

The name Manchester was on the mailbox near the front gate. I unlatched the gate and walked up the path. Withered, faded wildflowers that must have looked spectacular in April or May filled the front yard, surrounded by tangled shrubs and vines. It seemed no one had sat on the rotting bench under the barren apple tree, sprinkled a can of water, or pulled out a bramble in years.

The front door was dark green with a window that was so high a footstool would be required for anyone to see out of it.

The street was lined with older homes, most of them with moderately kept yards, but none as large and dark and closed off as the Manchester place. I couldn't think of it as having anything to do with me or anyone I knew. The minute that thought crossed my mind, I realized that if Eileen Manchester was anything like her son, her immediate reaction might be an assumption that I was there looking for a place in her will. I sighed. Before I could get my mind in a tangle of worry over that, I pushed the bell. It let out a loud, deep chime.

The sound of wood heels echoed down a corridor, growing louder. The door opened and I was facing a thin woman with long gray hair in a gray ponytail that was tied at several spots along the length of hair. She stared past me as if she were more interested in my rental car parked at the curb. She wore a blue tailored shirt, a skirt to her knees, and ankle-high boots with low heels.

"Who are you?" she said.

She was still staring at the street. I turned to see what had her attention. The car wasn't even visible, obscured by the tangled yard. I turned back and looked at her face again. I realized she wasn't staring at anything. She was blind.

"My name's Madison. I think I'm a relative of yours."

"Not likely."

"Why not?"

"I know all my relatives." She started to close the door.

"Wait. I . . . I came all the way from California."

She blinked and pressed her lips together. Her fingers, ringless except for a very thin, almost flimsy platinum wedding band, tightened on the edge of the door.

"I'm Annie's daughter."

Her face didn't have a lot of color to begin with, but it lost even that, turning almost as pale as the whites of her eyes. Her throat moved as she swallowed. She put her hand to her neck, pressing against her collarbone. In a low voice, she said, "What do you want?"

"May I come inside? I won't stay long. Unless you want me to."

"Definitely not."

"I can't come in or you don't want me to stay?"

"You can come in for fifteen minutes. I suppose I owe you that, if I owe you anything, which is doubtful. And if you're here to circle around the hole they've dug for my grave, definitely not."

"It's nothing like that."

She opened the door wider, but not by much. I stepped inside and she closed it behind me. She turned and walked down a long hallway with empty cream-colored walls and dark oak baseboard. The hall ended at a small room that looked out on a backyard, more overgrown than the front. The room was a semi-circle, lined with sparkling clean windows. There were two armchairs facing the windows. A small table sat between them, and on that, a fragile teacup with dark, cloudy liquid in the bottom. Next to the cup was a black leather

Bible. She sat in the chair on the left and I took the one on the right.

"So what is it about? If it's not about money."

She was blunt, which was definitely emerging as a family trait. I decided to be equally blunt. "I thought you were dead. Until I found this." I held up my arm before I remembered she wasn't looking out the windows, she was looking at nothing, except possibly her future. "I found an ID bracelet with your name engraved on it."

"Who told you I was dead?"

"My mother."

She nodded. "That's not surprising. As far as I'm concerned, she's dead."

I gasped. Tears that I didn't know were there spilled out of my eyes. My bluntness faded. I swallowed and it dissolved even more, as if it had slid down my throat and was being digested while the tears swam around my eyes.

"Is there anything else?" she said.

"Of course there is." My voice was a whisper. "I just don't know where to start, to be honest."

"At the beginning."

"I don't know where that is."

She said nothing. I waited a few more minutes. My tears dried and I remembered I was on a time limit so I'd better not waste any more of it. "My mother is dead. She and my father were murdered."

"By whom?"

"They haven't found the killer."

"I see. Well, your sins come back to haunt you."

Her expression didn't shift even slightly. She felt my mother had died a long time ago, so the news was nothing to her. The coldness coming from her words, her face was bone-chilling.

"I don't understand why my mother told me you were dead."

"Not surprising." She nodded her head, although she did look a little surprised.

"Did you know about me?" I said.

"Never heard of you."

"I don't understand. Why did both of you act as if the other was dead?"

"I have no idea what your mother thought or what she did."

"How can you be so cold to your own child? Your little girl. Your . . ."

She picked up her Bible and held it on her lap. It didn't look like it was written in Braille, so she must have liked holding it for what she remembered reading in it. I wondered how she lived inside a huge house, how she took care of things if she couldn't see. But only for a moment. There wasn't anything about her that moved me to care about her problems.

"I did what I was told." She tapped the Bible. "I raised her to follow the Lord and she turned her back on Him. So I turned my back on her." She lowered her voice but increased the volume, the sound so harsh, I flinched. *"I've come to turn a man against his father, a daughter against her mother. He who is not with me is against me."*

"What do you mean?"

"Ann was a sinner. She hardened her heart, and we put her out of our house. But your sins come back to haunt you."

"What did she do that was so awful?"

"She broke the commands of the Lord. She became defiant and cursed the name of the Lord. She drove herself out. All I did was close the door behind her."

"Didn't you love her?"

"Love is action, not cheap emotions."

"But . . ."

She was hugging her Bible, pressing it so hard against her ribs she was short of breath. "*Anyone arrogant enough to reject the verdict of the judge or of the priest who represents the Lord your God must be put to death. Such evil must be purged.*"

I closed my eyes. The room was cool but the air circulation was poor so it was hard to breathe. Around me, inside the walls, and in the rooms above us, the house creaked. Something knocked against metal — a sound like a hammer on a cast iron pipe. This was followed by a whistling that seemed to come from inside the walls. I felt something brush against my face and opened my eyes. Nothing was there, but the whistling continued, a moaning, wailing, more like wind than air escaping from pipes. I felt something brush my face again. I sat up straighter. If there was a spirit in this house, I didn't want to know. It couldn't be anything good. Not if it was a being lingering here with this horrid woman, a woman who should have pulled me into her arms.

"Doesn't God forgive?" I said.

"When you repent. His blood was spilled for Ann, for Paul, and they trampled on it like it was pigs' blood. They're the spawn of the devil, darkness itself. And they'll pay with an eternity in the flames of hell."

"That's horrible!"

"It's the Word of the Lord!" She waved the Bible in my direction.

"I can't imagine she did anything so terrible. She was sweet and good. She laughed a lot. She was an amazing cook and she taught me so much. She did everything for me — took me to ballet and piano lessons. She showed me how to grow vegetables and bake cookies. She read to me when I was little and talked to me about books and science when I was older. I don't believe that she . . ."

"Those things are vanity and chasing after the wind." She lifted the Bible higher. "This is the source of life. Not those things. She was silly and childish."

"And you treated her like she was dead because of that?"

"Oh, no. So much more."

"What is it?"

"I'm a godly woman. I can't speak of things that defile my lips and my heart. And if you're here to argue, then you've chosen the same lot as her. You can die with her and burn with her."

I stood. "You're a horrible person."

"I'm a righteous woman. I'll have my reward."

I undid the clasp on the ID bracelet. I held it out and

let it touch her wrist. "This bracelet has your name. She kept it, so I don't think she truly considered you to be dead."

"She told you I was."

"To protect me. I think."

"Protect you from what? To lead you astray is more like it. Straight into the jaws of hell."

"Should I put the bracelet on your wrist?"

"I don't want it. Take it out of here. Your sins come back to haunt you."

"Why do you keep saying that?" I waited for several minutes, but she didn't speak. I guess she was done. I walked around the chair and went to the doorway leading to the long, empty hall. "Good-bye, Grandmother."

I wanted to ask about my grandfather. And Paul. I wanted to know what my mother had done that was so terrible, although I was pretty sure it wasn't all that terrible. To that woman, sitting blind in her cold room, facing glass she couldn't see through, life itself was a terrible sin. I wanted to escape more than I wanted to know any more of her thoughts.

There was a block of wood with three brass hooks on the wall near the front door. I fastened the clasp on the bracelet and looped it over one of the hooks. I opened the door and stepped outside.

It seemed I wasn't meant to have a family. A grandmother filled with self-righteous wrath, an uncle who wouldn't tell me any of the secrets from my past, and parents who'd been ripped out of my life. I hadn't done too badly on my own. Maybe being alone wasn't such a bad thing. Better than being connected to someone like that.

Five

JD PICKED ME up at the San Francisco airport and the minute he looked at my face, he could see it hadn't been what I'd hoped. He put his arms around me and held me close for quite a long time. The noise of people walking and talking and dragging suitcases on little wheels roared around us. He kissed me.

"The apartment was too quiet without you."

"The birds didn't make up for it?"

"You're more interesting." He kissed my earlobe then pressed his nose against my head. "Your hair smells like coffee."

"I'm probably sweating coffee. I drank at least five cups on the plane."

We let go of each other and started walking toward the exit to the parking garage. "So," he said, "What's the Twitter version of your grandmother?"

"My grandmother is blind, and apparently deaf to anything but what's written in the Bible. And she's even missed half of that. At least the good parts."

"Sounds like a fun grandma."

I laughed. My throat tightened and I stopped. "I guess I understand why my mother told me she was dead. You were right that she wanted to protect me. According to grandma, my mom did something so awful, she considered my mom dead before she was killed. But she wouldn't say what this terrible sin was. And she seemed uninterested in the fact that my mom is really gone."

"Does it matter?"

"No. Unless what my mother did would cause someone to hunt her down and shoot her in her bed."

"If it's so awful, it's strange she wouldn't tell you. Usually people can't wait to outline someone else's sins."

"She's too pure to mention the awful deeds."

He patted my hip.

Once we were in the car, he asked me to tell him the conversation word for word. Of course, that's impossible. No conversation can be repeated like that. I tried to remember the things she'd said, mostly words lifted out of the Bible, or at least they had that Biblical cadence. Parts of the Bible are familiar to me, some of the stories, but I certainly haven't read the whole thing. For all I knew, the things she'd said came out of her own unseeing mind and she'd arranged the words to make them sound Biblical.

I couldn't imagine the woman who'd raised me growing up under the hand of that woman inside that dark, echoing house. It seemed as if my mother must have invented her own persona after she got out from the grip of that monster. And I don't think monster was too strong a word. Hate spilled out of her lips and even her blankly staring eyes seemed incapable of seeing anything but destruction and self-righteous pride. Had she ever loved my mother? Based on what I'd seen, I couldn't imagine it. At least not the way I think of love. I pictured my grandmother doing her job — providing childcare, setting rules, and cooking meals. In her mind, doing those things meant love. I get that love is shown in your actions, but there's more to it. So much more. Something magical and unseeable that's far beyond just checking tasks or duties off a list.

Neither of my parents mentioned religion very often when I was growing up. I realized now, my mother had had her fill of that by the time I came into the world.

WE WENT TO dinner at an Italian place. Spaghetti with meatballs and three pieces of garlic bread were very comforting. On the way home, JD asked the inevitable question — *What's next?*

I felt as if I was making daily forays out to dark caves buried in the side of a mountain where I expected to find gold, diamonds. All I had was a bunch of coal, if that. Mostly I was just tired.

"I want to talk to Paul," I said. "I sort of hope he'll be so shocked that I went to see her, he'll stop being so evasive. But I don't know. Maybe he's not evading anything. Maybe he just doesn't want anything to do with her. Which is understandable."

"It is."

"He must know what my mother did to warrant being flung out onto the street. Maybe Paul invited God's wrath too. The more I learn, the less I know."

"Some people say that's the theme of life."

"Whatever. I don't like it."

"You should try talking to Paul without Gloria."

"Why?"

"I was thinking . . . the coldness between your parents and your aunt and uncle was really your mother and Gloria. Paul probably took up Gloria's defense against your mother — standing by his wife. Protecting her."

"Okay. Why would he do that?"

"It's what men do. It's what couples do, most of the time. Stick with each other and close ranks against outsiders who hurt them."

"That sounds extreme. Besides, my mother wasn't an outsider."

We were climbing the stairs to our apartment. He paused and stuck his key in the lock. He opened the door and we went inside. Without discussing it, we walked across the living room and opened the balcony doors. We sat down and breathed in the scent of flowers, not quite as sweet as they'd been earlier in the summer. I wanted a cigarette but I'd forgotten to say something when we left the restaurant. Now, I was too lazy to want to go back out for a walk to the park. My ritual of three a day was all out of order. It could be a good thing, helping me break the habit, but I was still smoking three, even if sometimes it was half at one time and half of a new one an hour later. Overall, I hadn't made any progress in cutting down. I'd been stuck at three for years. Sometimes I wondered if I really wanted to quit.

JD put his hand on my wrist. "It's possible Paul doesn't want Gloria to know anything unflattering about your mother, doesn't want to aggravate her negative feelings. Now that your mother's gone, it might be hard for him that Gloria is so antagonistic. Maybe he feels caught in the middle."

"Caught in the middle of what? My mother's not here."

"Caught in the middle between loving his wife and protecting her feelings, and loving his sister, holding onto his memories, and not wanting his wife to dislike her even more."

I thought about this for a few minutes while he continued gripping my wrist as if he wanted to hold me to the chair so I wouldn't drift up into the night like a helium balloon that had slipped out of a child's fingers. I had no idea how I was going to talk to Paul alone. It shouldn't have been any different from when I'd called Gloria and invited her to a girls' lunch. But I expected Gloria wouldn't be as willing to step out of the picture.

I DECIDED I was making something out of nothing. I'd ask Paul to lunch and if Gloria objected, I simply wouldn't back down. She couldn't lock him in the house, could she? And why did I think she'd want to? I called and got their voicemail. He didn't call back, so I called the next day. I got voicemail again. This time I left a message.

JD was gone most of the day taking care of his mushrooming list of clients who wanted him to feed birds, look in on their cats, walk their dogs, and even feed and water their horses. While he was out, I spent a few hours staring at the one journal I hadn't read. I still couldn't bring myself to face the inky words and sentences that had dried nearly fifteen years ago. After lunch — leftover spaghetti — I walked to the park and sat on the bench looking at the spot where the man-made creek fed into the duck pond. It rippled sluggishly, water trapped by rocks that were thickly coated with moss. Ducks drifted, hardly paddling in the midday heat. Occasionally one quacked, but it didn't seem to really mean what it was saying.

I lit a cigarette and smoked slowly, watching the smoke drift lazily away from me. Some of the people walking past didn't look as if they enjoyed following the movement of the smoke as much as I did. In fact, they looked annoyed that it was hanging in the branches above me. I know it's an unhealthy, smelly habit, but it's oh so relaxing. People who have never tried it have no idea. I love it when my mind drifts as casually as the smoke, no real direction, just waiting to see which way the breeze will take it.

Over a stir fry dinner, I told JD I was going back to my house that evening. Alone. Again.

He shrugged.

"It's not that I don't want you around, it's just . . ."

He looked at me. Dark brown eyes seeming not to mind, yet a questioning look around the corners, as if he wasn't sure why I kept running off without him.

We'd done nothing to figure out the next steps in our lives. I think we both knew that was on hold while I did everything I could regarding my parents. But it was feeling more and more as if I kept taking steps toward a possible answer, and falling off a cliff into nothingness. I was sure he was wondering when it was going to end. When I was going to give up. But as long as little thoughts kept presenting themselves, I couldn't walk away. It was as if I needed a giant sign to tell me — *Enough. You need to stop and move on with a normal life.* I hadn't seen that sign yet.

WHEN IT WAS dark, I left the apartment. The street was empty of people, despite the lines of cars parked on both sides. I stood by my car for a moment, smoking a cigarette. I thought about my fractured family and how exhausting it was, chasing people, trying to find out things they didn't want me to know. I realized Detective Smith's job was harder than it looked. It wasn't that I wanted to give up, or thought I should quit looking for answers, I hadn't seen that sign. But I wondered, for the hundredth time, when that moment would come. How would I know? Kate could say all she wanted about never giving up, but she'd done exactly that. She thought if I didn't quit, things might turn out differently for me. But not really. Her never-quit attitude was because she thought she might have prevented her brother's death. I wasn't preventing anything. Just trying to fill a hole inside of me. I wanted them to have justice, but what does that even mean? If the killer were arrested and locked up for life, that wouldn't help my parents at all, and it wouldn't help me either. But still, what about justice?

But I couldn't stop. Something drove me like I was possessed with another force. Maybe it was their spirits pulling me toward them. I couldn't stop looking for crevices where I might find a way to crawl inside of their lives, make my way into the past.

I drove slowly to Whitewood Way. The house was dark. I got out of my car and walked along the side yard. I heard music coming from an open window — a rock song that had been redone as instrumental only. The tune was familiar but I couldn't think of the words.

I walked further and stepped onto the edge of the back lawn. The grass was dry, but damp underneath, as if someone had watered it, expecting it to come back to life. It was a bit slippery. A single light shone from the master bedroom window. The music was louder now.

Kevin and Gwen were talking rather loudly themselves, but the music obscured their words. I crossed the yard, headed toward the swing as if drawn by my former self, a little girl clutching the ropes, pumping her legs, flying into the sky, thinking life is perfect and beautiful. A little girl who seemed like a different person entirely — a stranger, now. The swing tugged at me. I tried to ignore the soft dirt in the bare patches of the lawn. It crept over the tops of my sandals, working its way beneath the soles of my feet, covering them with grit and making me long to kick them off. My practical side won out. If Kevin or Gwen looked out the window and saw me, I wouldn't want to run and leave my sandals behind. They were almost new. And my favorites.

I reached the swing and sat down. The wood was smooth and soft, almost warm through my jeans. I pushed slightly. The branch creaked, but in a friendly way. I knew it wouldn't let me go — it was thicker than I remembered, at least ten inches in diameter. I pushed harder and felt myself gliding, starting to fly.

The voices inside the house were getting louder. When I was a child, I don't recall a single moment when there was a raised voice inside my house. That's unrealistic, I know, to believe that a married couple never argued, that they never lost their patience with their demanding daughter, but it's what I remember. Certainly not harsh, ugly voices like I was hearing now.

When JD and I met Jan, the landlord next door, she'd complained the house was too quiet. Had things changed? Or was this arguing a first-time event? If it was a first, could it be they were arguing about me? It had seemed as if Gwen welcomed me inside of their house. Maybe on some level she knew something wasn't right and she felt my restlessness, even if she didn't attribute her feeling of being watched to any unseen restless souls.

Any moment, their voices were going to rise above the music and then I'd know if they were talking about me. It was rather self-absorbed of me to think two strangers had no other areas of disagreement, but I couldn't help the thought. It appeared in my head and lingered, hoping for their volume to increase or the music to come to an end.

Gwen's voice became more distinct. She'd moved closer to the window. "I hate it. I don't understand why you're obsessed with it."

"I'm not obsessed." Kevin's voice was much louder now.

Suddenly, the music stopped.

"Don't shout at me," Gwen said.

I slowed the swing. They were so close to the window, the night air so fluid, I didn't want them to hear the creak of the branch or the movement of rope across bark.

"I want to be out of here," Gwen said. "This street is full of old people and kids. We don't fit."

"Maybe I want kids."

"I'm not gonna talk about that now."

"Well it's a nice house, the rent is doable, and we're close to everything we want."

"I don't like it anymore. It gives me the creeps when I'm here by myself."

Something thudded on the floor.

"Sorry," Gwen said.

"No worries. We're not moving. Not right now. You're imagining things because of what she said."

"Madison?"

"Yeah."

"I felt things before she mentioned it."

"All imagination."

"How do you know?"

"I just know. She's trying to spook you. She wants us out so she can have her old house back."

"No she doesn't. She wants to say good-bye."

"Who says good-bye to a house? She's a nut. She wants something she can't have."

"It seems like you just want to torment her."

"Maybe I do," Kevin said.

"Why?"

"She's asking for it."

The music started up again and their conversation was lost among the notes.

I didn't think I was asking to be tormented. He had to have the upper hand. I was sort of done with him. Gwen was my way in, if there was any way in at all. I pushed my feet against the ground. The swing carried me back and forth for quite a long time. I didn't stop and return to my car until their bedroom light was turned out.

Six

AFTER TWO AND A HALF cigarettes in the park near our apartment, a delicious chicken taco with fresh guacamole, and a quick stop for an iced latte, I returned to Whitewood Way at three o'clock. The van was in the carport and the motorcycle was gone.

At her front door, although really my own front door, I pulled open the screen and knocked hard. Gwen answered immediately. Her face was half angry, half surprised. Her nose and her eyes were red.

"Are you okay?" I said.

She shrugged. "What do you want? I'm not letting you inside the house or giving you the toys behind Kevin's back."

"That's not why I'm here."

"Then why?"

I shoved my hands in my pockets. I laced my fingers over my cigarette lighter, then poked it into the inside of the seam. "You said you had a feeling of someone watching you."

"It's nothing. I have an active imagination."

"That's not how it sounded yesterday."

"Well that's how it is."

"You can't help what you feel, even if other people think you're a bit off."

"No one thinks I'm off."

I turned my smirk into a sympathetic smile. "What's it like? The feeling of being watched by something you can't see?"

"Why are you doing this?"

"Because I'm curious about how that feels. I'm wondering if . . ."

"Why do you keep coming over? I know what you said, but it seems like you want something more. Kevin is right. It seems like you have an agenda. I'm sure that's why he plays games with you."

"I told you why."

"I saw you on the swing last night. I didn't tell him I saw you, and I didn't make you leave. You were there for at least an hour. Wasn't that enough time with your memories?"

I shifted my feet. My legs were getting tired, but I wasn't about to ask if could go inside and sit down and risk her closing the door. "Thanks for not mentioning it to him."

"You're welcome."

"I know you've felt something and I want to understand."

"Fine. It's a feeling that someone is following me around the house when I'm cleaning. Okay? And sometimes when I'm sitting at the kitchen table having a cup of tea, it seems like someone is there with me. And . . ." She took a deep breath. She closed her mouth and folded her lips inward. She looked over her shoulder, staring behind her for several seconds, as if Kevin were somewhere else in the house, despite the missing motorcycle.

"What else?" I said.

"I wake at night and feel that someone has been watching me sleep. I have the nightlight on all the time now. I know there's no one in the room, but the feeling is very intense."

I wanted to cry. I wanted to hug her and rush inside the house no matter what she said or did. It was too amazingly wonderful. What I'd hoped for more than anything in the world was happening. While I stood on the front porch, my legs aching, my knees stiff, the cigarette lighter digging into my hipbone, and the August sun trying to burn a hole in my back, she was telling me my parents' ghosts were lingering inside our home.

"What's wrong?" she said.

I swallowed and tried to breathe. My voice sounded like I was being strangled. "Nothing."

"What do you really want?"

I started crying. I didn't mean to and I didn't even realize it was coming. In less than three breaths, I was sobbing. Tears poured down my face and terrible sounds came out of my chest.

Gwen pulled the door open wider and stepped back. "Come inside."

I walked into the entryway and headed down the hall without an invitation. I opened the door to my old bedroom and stepped inside the vacant room. I went to the same corner where I'd sat when Jan let JD and I into the house. I slumped down with my back dragging along the wall. I pulled my knees up close, crossed my arms on top, and leaned my head forward. I was crying, but already feeling calmer, just being there. I was aware of Gwen standing in the doorway. After a minute or two, I looked up.

"I understand about being attached to a place," she said. "But this is way over the top. I'm a little worried. What's wrong with you?" She looked regretful that she'd invited me inside. She glanced down the hallway, nervous about a sudden appearance from Kevin, I'm sure.

"My parents died here. They were murdered." Saying it made my tears dry suddenly. I took a deep breath and tried to snuff all the mucous back in my head.

"I know," she said. "Do you want a tissue?"

"You know?"

She nodded. She disappeared from the doorway and returned a moment later with a pink box of tissues. She crossed the room and handed it to me.

"This was my room."

"It's obvious."

"Why don't you use it?"

"No need."

"It makes me sad that it's sitting empty."

"Well we don't need an office. I'm not a computer person. I keep all my business records in notebooks in the kitchen so I can work at the table."

I nodded.

"Besides, this room feels sad. I understood why that was, after the first time I met you."

I managed a smile and blew my nose. I pulled out another tissue and blew again. I pulled out a third and patted around my eyes. "How did you know they were murdered?"

"Everyone on the street knows. And the house was empty forever."

"Oh."

"We got a good deal on the rent."

"It doesn't bother you? That people were killed here?"

"It does. I want to move."

"But it didn't bother you until now?"

"It did, but I tried not to think about it. It's such a cute house. It's so light and even the slightest breeze passes through. I try to focus on that," she said.

I straightened my legs in front of me. "Tell me more about being watched."

"There's nothing more to tell you."

"Does it scare you?"

"It's not scary, but it doesn't make me feel great. It distracts me. I feel unsettled, I guess is the way to describe it."

"Do you feel it all the time?"

"No."

"Every day?"

"I'm not sure. I'd say no, but sometimes I wake at night and I've had strange dreams, so I don't know if I felt it while I was asleep."

"Everyone has strange dreams."

"These are vivid, it's like . . . I know that I'm dreaming *while* I'm dreaming. The dreams are always about Kevin — scenes from his life, stories he's told me. But they happen as if I'm him."

"I don't think I've ever dreamt I'm someone else."

"That's why I think they're strange."

"Is it lucid dreaming?"

"I don't know what that is. Although I can guess — dreaming with clear thoughts?"

"Not exactly. It's knowing that you're dreaming. Some people think you can direct your dreams in a different direction, because you're aware."

"Oh. That sounds tiring. What's the point?"

"To explore your subconscious, I guess, or understand yourself better. Or maybe to not have bad dreams."

"My dreams about him aren't nightmares. Some are upsetting, but not terrifying."

"And you think that's related to being watched?"

"I don't know. All I know is I don't want to be here anymore. If Kevin won't move, I'm going by myself."

"Breaking up with him?"

"Nothing so dramatic. But I can't stay here."

"Have you ever seen anything? Heard anything?"

She shivered. She hugged herself and rubbed her hands on her upper arms.

"If that happened, I wouldn't even pack, I'd be gone so fast." She laughed. The sound was more hysterical than amused. "Do you think it's haunted? By your parents?" She looked like she was going to cry.

"I hope so."

"What?"

"I'd give anything to see their ghosts."

"Is that what you mean by saying good-bye? I thought you meant the house, your memories." She backed up toward the doorway. "What's wrong with you?"

"Don't be scared."

"Are you kidding? I think you should go."

"Wait. Just listen."

I remained where I was, slumped against the wall. I didn't think she'd grab my ankles and drag me out. Not yet, anyway. "I've seen ghosts before, they're not horrible."

"I don't like it. I don't want anything to do with it. Feeling like someone is watching me — I hate it. I feel like I can never relax. I thought it was in my mind, maybe, that I was over-sensitive, not that there were really things, spirits inside my house. I don't want to die." She began whimpering.

I pushed myself up to my feet and took a few steps toward her. Even though she wasn't looking directly at me, she must have felt my approach. She shrank into the hallway.

"They won't hurt you. Seeing a ghost doesn't mean you're going to die."

"What are you? Some kind of expert? Are you a medium or a witch or a . . .?"

"I'm none of those things. I'm just a normal person who's seen ghosts. A lot of people have, you know. More than you'd think."

She shook her head. Her short, fine hair flew across her face like a feather duster. "I don't want to hear anything about it."

"But don't you want to understand what you've felt?"

"No."

"It's not scary. They truly won't hurt you." The minute I said that, I remembered the ghost that came after JD. But that was different. That ghost mistook JD for his twin brother, and she wanted him back. It was nothing like this. My parents — if they were my parents, and I knew with all my heart they must be my parents — wouldn't want anything to do with Gwen. Maybe they liked being around a girl who was about the same age as me.

"How do you know?" she said.

"In my experience, which isn't huge, but I have a bit, ghosts are lingering because they can't separate from the living world. There are people and situations they've left behind that they want resolved, or settled in some way."

"Kev is right, you're a whack job."

"I'm really not."

"All whack jobs think they're sane."

"Maybe, but then does that make you crazy? Ghosts don't reveal themselves to everyone, you know."

"How would I know that?"

"There's nothing to be afraid of."

"There absolutely is."

"My parents were kind, friendly people. I don't think . . ."

"Then why are they watching me? It's creepy. They don't even know me and they have no business in my house." She laughed, shrieking almost. "I can't believe I'm saying these things."

"Can I come back at night? Stay here with you?"

"I told you, I'm leaving. And now you're giving me an even better reason to get out of here. I'm not wasting any more time thinking it over."

"Don't you love Kevin?"

"He needs to love *me* more. If he loves me, he can leave this damn house. I think he likes the macabre feeling of living in a house no one else wants. It's sick. And I hate it. He likes that people died here. He thinks it's cool. He likes the dark feeling, knowing death is always nearby, or something sick like that. If that's more important to him than me, he can have his haunted house."

I took a few steps closer. "Can't you stay a bit longer? You've felt their presence. I want to feel that so badly it hurts."

"Don't come near me."

"I'm not going to hurt you."

"You need to go."

"Please."

"It wouldn't even matter. Kevin isn't going to let you in the house. And now that you've told me all this, there's no way I'm staying here alone at night, if he's out with his friends. Even if he's home, I can't stay. I'm out of here today."

"I'd be with you."

"What good would that do? You'd probably stir things up. Who knows what could happen. I really want you to go now. I need to pack. I need to be gone before he gets home."

"Why? Is he going to stop you from going? Are you afraid he'd do something to you?"

"I just can't be here. And I don't want him to influence me."

"How can you walk out on someone you love?"

"Easy. Love isn't a one-way street. I don't want to be with him if he doesn't love me enough to leave this place. I'm done." She turned and walked down the hall.

The house was silent. I knew she was waiting for me near the front door, but I couldn't leave. Maybe I would force her to grab my ankles and drag me out after all.

After a few minutes, I felt I could hear her breathing. She didn't know I was more stubborn than her. As much as she wanted to leave, her desire was nothing next to my desire to be in this place, wanting to stand in my old bedroom until I felt them watching me, felt their breaths on the back of my neck. I'd stay until Kevin came home and grabbed my hair and carried me down the hall and threw me out the door. Maybe even then I wouldn't leave, I'd fight with every ounce of strength, scratching his face and kicking him.

All this time I'd hoped their ghosts were still walking around on the earth, and now I knew for sure, or at least as sure as I was going to, that they were here. Nothing could make me leave.

I desperately wished I'd asked JD to come with me. If he'd been there, it would be much more difficult for Gwen, or Kevin, to get rid of me. But then, if he'd been there, she might not have let me inside the house to begin with.

"Madison! You need to leave!"

I didn't speak.

"I mean it!"

I wanted to laugh, but it was too serious. It felt as if I was a child in my bedroom, my mother calling from the living room that it was time to go.

Gwen reappeared in the doorway. "Please don't do this to me."

"Please don't do this to *me*. I need to be here."

"Not going to happen." She charged at me, grabbed my arm and yanked, hard. It was surprising that such a small, delicate-boned woman could be so strong. I tried to resist, but she pulled me, stumbling and tripping along the hallway. I thought about kicking her, grabbing at her hair, but if I did something violent, there'd never be a way back in. If she were gone, I'd bring JD. Maybe I'd even bring Detective Smith. Surely he had some authority, although telling him about the presence of ghosts might be tricky.

As she pushed and dragged me down the hallway, I glanced into the kitchen. The cactus in the yellow ceramic pot that I'd brought for her the last time I visited was sitting in the center of the table. I wondered if Kevin knew where it had come from.

She shoved me onto the front porch and yanked the screen closed. She locked it and started to close the door.

"Please don't do this," I whispered.

She shut the door.

Seven

MY UNCLE PAUL sat across from me in a coffee shop that was the most utilitarian place I'd seen in a long time. I was used to cozy coffee shops with sofas and groupings of chairs, coffee tables that are used to actually hold cups of coffee. This place was like a diner from the 1950s, but without the retro charm. The tables had Formica tops and the benches were a sickly turquoise Naugahyde. Weak coffee was served in thick white cups with saucers. There were no lattes, and they didn't even offer an espresso.

I sipped the watery coffee and wondered how I was going to make it through a 30-minute conversation. Paul had agreed to go out for coffee easily enough, but I never should have let him pick the meeting place. He didn't ask why I wanted to get together without Gloria and he didn't ask why I wanted to get together at all. He acted as if we'd been meeting up for weekly cups of coffee all our lives. Maybe he wished we had.

He ripped the edges off two bags of sugar at once

and poured the granules into his cup. He stirred vigorously and dribbled in a splash of milk. "Have you had any more thoughts on college?" He stirred faster.

"No. It's hard to think about anything but my parents."

"It's a dead end." Even though his words were matter-of-fact and harsh, his voice had an undercurrent of kindness.

"Is it?"

"I think so. Hard as that is, I think so."

"I didn't mention it to Gloria, but JD and I are living here now."

"Here? In Marin County?"

I nodded. I sipped the coffee and tried to keep from puckering my lips at the bland taste. "I thought it would be easier to stay on top of things. With the investigation."

"There is no more investigation. The detective said . . ."

"I know what he said. But there are still a few little things that might lead to something new."

"Such as?"

The door opened with a clanking of bells that were hooked to the top edge. Two police officers walked inside and headed straight toward the back on the opposite side from where Paul and I were seated. The second one glanced our way. He seemed to hesitate, as if he was trying to figure out where he'd seen me. I caught his gaze and held it. He didn't change his expression and then he turned and followed his buddy, so maybe I imagined it.

The place was filling up even though it was two in the afternoon. People were apparently willing to drink weak coffee just to escape the heat and have a place to sit. It was expected to get to one hundred degrees by four o'clock.

I turned back to Paul. "I was hoping my grandmother might give me a new perspective. But all she did was create more confusion."

He stared at me, looking slightly sick to his stomach. He picked up two sugar bags, tore off the tops, and emptied them into his cup. I wasn't sure if he was in shock and had forgotten he'd already sweetened it, or if he'd decided more sugar would make it tastier. I didn't think it would help.

"I went to see her," I said.

"How did you . . ." He closed his eyes. "Oh, yes. Detective Smith. I should have wondered why he wanted her contact information at this point in time. I'm so used to doing what the police ask, I didn't think about what it meant."

"If you're so used to doing what the police ask, why didn't it to bother you to mislead them? Saying bad things about my mother just because Gloria was embarrassed?"

"Supporting the person you love is more important."

"You don't think it was lying?"

"I don't."

"I thought you were so religious."

"It wouldn't have helped anything. Your mother's opinion of Gloria wasn't relevant."

"It's still a lie."

"Did you invite me to coffee to berate me?"

"No. I just want to clear the air, about a few things."

"Including your grandmother?"

"Why won't you talk about her? Why haven't you spoken to her all these years?"

"I didn't want you to know what a terrible person she is. I thought you had enough to deal with. What's the good in finding out your only grandmother wouldn't want to know you?"

"It wasn't your decision."

"I suppose not. But it seemed . . . I'm sure you saw how she is."

"I did."

"She's devoted her life to portraying God as a monster," he said.

"Why?"

"I have no idea. She was like that as far back as I can remember."

"What did my mom do that was so awful? To make her own mother never speak to her again? To make her tell me my grandmother was dead."

He stirred his coffee, rattling the spoon against the sides of the cup, going in circles, then back and forth across the center. He stared down into his cup. "Why do you want to dig up the past?"

"I'm not digging it up, I'm trying to put it to rest."

"You can't."

"What do you mean, I can't?"

He looked up. Behind his glasses, his eyes were shadowy, as if he weren't really looking at me. As if he were seeing another world entirely, his past life with his mother and his sister — a life I'd never catch even a glimpse of.

"It's impossible to feel at peace over your parents' deaths. They were murdered. It's ugly and terrible and tragic and unjust. No matter what you do, it will always be ugly and terrible and tragic and unjust. Finding out who did it, trying to understand why it happened, won't give you peace of mind."

"How do you know?"

"You're hurting because it happened. Not because you don't know who or why. Knowing who or why will just cause more pain."

"How can you possibly know that?"

"Because right now, you're diverting all kinds of emotional energy into your search. If you find an answer, and you don't need that energy for searching, then where will it go?"

"Then I'll feel like I did everything I could for them."

"Is it for them? Or for you? It doesn't matter to them."

"That's not fair! Of course it's also for me. There's nothing wrong with that."

"Knowing is not going to satisfy you."

"Crimes are supposed to be solved. Criminals are supposed to be punished. That's how it is. Do you think people should just get away with murder?"

"That's not what I'm saying. I'm talking about you. It's not going to help *you*. It's not going to make you feel better."

"Why is everyone else such an expert in what's going to make me feel better or worse?"

"I'm not trying to be condescending."

"Good. Then don't be."

"You're wasting a good piece of your life trying to fix something that can't be fixed. What if you never find out and you'll have lost all these years? You could be putting all this energy and time into your education. When are you going to say it's enough? There is no answer?"

"I'm not wasting my life. It's what I want to do."

"I just think you should seriously consider how you'll feel about all of this in five years. How you'll feel if there's a person, or several people, that you can hate for murdering your parents. It won't be good for you."

"People want to see justice for their loved ones. It's natural and normal."

"Yes, it is."

He drank his coffee and turned to his right. He tried to catch the eye of a teenaged boy who stood behind the counter, carefully wiping the glass even though it looked clean. Paul waved at him. The boy dropped the rag and hurried to our table with a coffee pot and two menus. "Did you want something to eat?"

"No." Paul shook his head. "Just a refill."

The boy filled Paul's cup and added a splash to mine.

When he was gone, Paul resumed the ritual with the

bags of sugar. "How was it? Meeting your grandmother."

"She felt like a total stranger. No one related to me."

"What did you talk about?" he said.

"We didn't really have a conversation. She wasn't thrilled to see me. She talked at me, told me that my mother turned her back on god. She acted like I didn't matter."

"That's how she treats everyone," he said.

"Did she kick you out of the house too?"

"Not really. I left home for college and never went back. I was lucky. I had solid scholarships, so I didn't need her money."

"What about my grandfather?"

"He died of cancer when I was twelve. Your mother was eight."

"I didn't know that either."

"I guess not," he said.

"So what did my mother do that was so terrible?"

"Not following your grandmother's vicious version of God is grounds for shunning."

"So that's it? She made it sound like there was something specific."

"Your grandmother has manufactured a harsh god in her mind. She hates the world and hates most of the people in it. If she makes God a tyrant, then she can hate Him as well."

I drank all the coffee in my cup, trying not to think about the taste, just letting the lukewarm liquid fill my mouth and provide some moisture. Outside, the sun beat down on the cars parked with their noses facing the restaurant windows, hot metal glistening like liquid. I dreaded going back outside, but I didn't think I could handle much more of the coffee. "What was my mother like when she was a child?"

"Calm. Cheerful most of the time. She liked to read a lot. She liked to hide and jump out and try to scare me."

"What else?"

"She was a good listener, although she talked quite a lot too. It's not a combination you see very often. Most talkers are talking inside their own heads even when their mouths aren't moving."

I laughed. "That's a good way to describe it." I hoped I wasn't like that. I do talk a lot, but I can be quiet. I vowed to pay attention to that, to start making sure I was listening instead of chatting up myself when other people were talking. Especially JD. But really, all other people. Even Paul and Gloria.

"What kind of mother was she? Gloria said I was already pretty much raised when I went to live with you. I wonder if I turned out the way my parents hoped."

"It's the eternal puzzle — nature or nurture."

I picked up the menu the server had left on our table. The coffee was making me queasy, like tainted water.

"Are you hungry?" He waved at the server.

I ordered a small glass of tomato juice and a side order of fries. The thought of fries must have made Paul hungry because he ordered apple pie.

"Are you avoiding my question?" I said.

"What question is that?"

"Did I turn out the way they'd hoped?"

"I can't really answer that because I'm not entirely sure what they hoped. But any parents would be proud of you."

I felt teary and wished the fries were there to divert me.

"They, Annie especially, had a vision for some kind of model child."

"What do you mean?"

"As if they could shape your life and it would turn out exactly as they'd planned. Which of course is impossible. That's why they homeschooled you, so your education would be custom-shaped to your interests and personality. And that's why the piano and ballet, the art and all the other things they offered you."

"I don't feel perfect." It seemed strange, saying something like that to a guy I hadn't really talked to beyond an occasional casual conversations for the past ten years, and I'm not sure how much I talked to him when they were raising me. From what I'd read in my journals, it seemed as if I'd spent more time talking to myself, via those pages, than I had to my guardians.

"I suppose there are reasons for her wanting a perfect kid, wanting to be a perfect mother," he said.

The image of my grandmother hugging her Bible formed in my mind. I could imagine the reasons my mother wanted to be a perfect mother to me.

"I suppose that's why she said those harsh things to

Gloria, about not wanting you to spend time with us, because she thought we drank too much. Because she thought Gloria drank too much. It was very upsetting."

"I'm sure."

The fries, tomato juice, and pie arrived. Paul got a coffee refill and asked for a refill of the sugar container. I ate a fry, not caring if it burned my tongue.

"Do we like wine?" Paul said. "Sure. Do we drink it fairly often? Sure. But do we drink it every day? Not even close. Do we binge drink? No."

It sounded as if he wanted to persuade himself. Whether they did or didn't drink too much wine was between them.

"Maybe those sound like excuses to you," he said. "But they're not. I'm sure you go through the same thought process with your smoking decisions. Although frankly, a few glasses of wine are a lot less dangerous than a steady inhalation of nicotine and tar."

"I know it's bad for me."

"Then I guess the parallel isn't there after all. I don't think wine is bad for us and I don't think we overindulge."

"Well my parents aren't here to debate that point."

He was quiet, cutting off small pieces of pie and eating them, his over-sugared coffee forgotten for the moment. "Anyway, it was off-putting. Having her make that accusation, behave as if she was a goddess for creating you. Gloria never even had that chance. Annie seemed a little callous about that, to be honest. I don't mean to tell you bad things about her, but you got me going." He smiled. Again, he seemed warm, despite the things he was saying. And his smile was genuine, a little bit sad.

"I didn't know."

"We don't talk about it. There's no point. We accepted it as God's will, but that doesn't mean the feelings of wanting a child go away. The sense of loss. The envy, at times."

There he was with the God's will thing. Even though my grandmother hadn't said those exact words, the way he viewed it seemed to echo her take on the world — some enormous, invisible hand interfering and moving us all around like we mean nothing. As if we're all just little robots, mouthing Bible verses and not wanting anything we shouldn't or doing anything questionable. Like smoking cigarettes, or drinking too much wine, I suppose. Not chasing after the identity of a killer. Maybe that's why Paul hinted that he thought it didn't matter. It's fine for society to chase criminals and punish them, but if law enforcement fails, then we should accept that as God's will too.

I guess things from our ancestors plant themselves in our lives and even though we think we're taking a different route, the things we're trying to escape are right there, living inside of us. I wondered what things I might have wanted to run away from in my parents' lives, if I'd had the chance.

I took a handful of fries and put them all in my

mouth at once. When the plate was empty, I finished the tomato juice. It was a very tasty combination. I was glad the sour coffee had been wiped off my tongue.

I was overcome by a feeling that Uncle Paul was trying to dodge telling me the truth. It seemed as if he was saying a lot of words, talking around in a huge circle to avoid getting too close to some of the things he knew about my mother, and my grandmother. The problem was, I didn't know what question to ask to get him off his track. There was something he wasn't saying and I couldn't begin to figure out what it was.

He started in about college again, as if he wanted to recruit me to his school, as if my life would be entirely and finally perfect if only I had a college education. Maybe it was his stamp on the formation of my life, to make sure there was some credit for what he and Gloria did to take care of me. I did want a college education, and I would get one, sooner or later, but I had to finish this first. Even if he was right — that it would make me feel worse to know why my parents were murdered. I still had to know. And that made me wonder if he knew who killed them. I asked, and he said *no*, very quickly, as if he'd anticipated the question. But I still wondered. It felt as if there was a huge thing that I could sort of feel but couldn't quite touch. Something he wasn't telling me, over which he'd very carefully woven a thick cover.

Eight

I FELT I'D NEGLECTED JD. We'd been in Marin County for over a month and all I'd done was talk to my aunt and uncle, hang out with unpredictable strangers who lived in my old house, and dig through written records and objects from the past. Then I'd dashed across the country for a fire and brimstone sermon from my grandmother who couldn't care less whether my mother, or I, lived or died. It was starting to feel as if I was more drawn to spend time with ghosts than with him.

It wasn't as if he was whining, acting clingy, or regretting making a new start in life with me, but we were drifting past each other, or at least I was drifting past him, spending hours talking about people who were dead. It wasn't that I'd stopped longing to encounter my parents ghosts. I wanted that more than ever, and I was so close, I could almost touch them. But I woke up in the middle of a dream and imagined myself in his position — the person you love gazing blindly at the wall behind you while eating the food you'd cooked, or steering nearly every conversation around to her relatives — good, bad, and the-jury's-still-out.

I decided to surprise him with a day away from the apartment and all my speculation. JD likes surprises. At least I thought he did. Most of the time.

There's a small, reclusive town in the southern part of Marin County, near the California coast. The town of Bolinas is so private, it's only accessible by unmarked roads. A lot of counter-culture types are drawn there, and the residents have a history of tearing down signs on the highway that point the way. Of course, that was before navigation apps and GPS. The idea had come to me from an article I'd read in a giveaway magazine about Marin County. It sounded like it might be a fun place to live, for a while, but definitely interesting for a day trip. In 2003, voters adopted an advisory ballot measure declaring Bolinas a *socially acknowledged nature-loving town.* I think that says it all.

I'd found a cafe that served seafood gumbo, fish and chips, and fish tacos. There are clusters of unique shops to wander through and we could sit and watch marsh birds and stare at the sky and think about nothing. Not that I'm all that good with thinking about nothing, but I wanted to make an effort. For his sake. I do okay quieting my thoughts during my ten minutes of meditation every day, but the other twenty-three hours and fifty minutes, my mind is buzzing. Even when I'm asleep, I'm sure it's busy digging around because I usually wake up with all kinds of new ideas. And then there are the dreams that it's busy fabricating, as if it wants to keep me either puzzled or entertained all night long.

Before I went to bed, I packed a cloth bag with a package of popcorn, sunscreen, and our swimsuits. I tucked that and two beach towels in the closet and left the cooler under the kitchen table so I could fill it with ice and beverages in the morning.

At 6 a.m. I crept out of bed, rolled out my yoga mat and did a sun salutation while the coffee brewed. I filled two mugs and carried them into the bedroom. I woke JD with a kiss on his forehead, his nose, then his lips. I felt his mouth move as he smiled. When I moved away, he took a deep breath, and opened his eyes.

"Coffee smells good," he said.

"Doesn't it smell good every morning?"

"It's better when it comes to me." He sat up, stuffed the pillows between him and the headboard, and picked up the mug. "Thanks. Nice wake-up."

"I'm kidnapping you," I said.

"From what?"

"From your four-legged, finned, and feathered friends."

"They won't pay ransom."

"That's okay. I'll have you back in time for a smoke in the park and a pizza dinner on the balcony."

He slurped his coffee. "Are you blindfolding me?"

"Good idea. But after your shower."

To enhance the surprise, I made him get into the

passenger seat of my Bug before I loaded up the trunk. Not that it would be all *that* surprising — it wasn't as if we were flying to New Zealand or Greece. I'm sure he figured we were either going to the coast or hiking, or both.

I grabbed a four-foot-long navy blue scarf out of my dresser drawer. I dumped my bag in the backseat of the car and wrapped the scarf around JD's head, looping it under his ponytail so he wouldn't have the nub of his ponytail digging into the back of his head for the next hour or so.

"Really? A blindfold? I was kidding."

"Tell me if it makes you car sick. Part of the drive is curvy."

"Thanks a lot for planting the idea in my subconscious."

"The blindfold was your idea. It'll be fun."

"If you say so."

I tried to take the curves more slowly than I normally would so he didn't feel like he was being tossed from side to side. When I stopped the car and untied the scarf, he still didn't know where we were. I handed him an overview of the town I'd printed off the web and a copy of the free magazine.

He glanced through them. "Sweet. What's the occasion?"

"The occasion is a murder-free, relative-free, ghost-free day."

He leaned over and put his hand behind my head. He

pulled me toward him and kissed me. "I like your ghosts."

"I know. But a break is good."

We walked around the town, in and out of the shops, which only took about an hour, since the whole place consists of about four streets, not counting the scattered cottages and homes.

At lunch, I ordered fish tacos and JD had an oyster dish. We used the restroom at the back to change into our swimsuits, although it was foggy and breezy so I wasn't sure I wanted to go into the water past my ankles.

I needn't have worried. We spread the blanket on the pebbly sand, stretched out on our sides with our arms around each other, and fell asleep. When we woke, the sun had broken through in parts. We waded along the short and skipped stones across the water. We talked about nothing but birds and how to identify the perfect skipping stone. I told him about my dream of a house built around an aviary and he said that would need some architectural work because a Macaw couldn't live with the parakeets. I began picturing a house with two aviaries — one for small birds and one for the Macaw. For the entire afternoon, I didn't have a single thought about ghosts.

TWO EVENINGS LATER, I drove to Whitewood Way. Alone. Again.

It was good of JD to recognize my need to do all these things alone. I knew he was waiting for me to be ready to let go of it all, but at the same time, he managed to keep hoping right alongside me. But I could feel him wondering how long we would keep hoping. It was there, just beneath his skin, almost as if there was a ghost of another kind, wanting to speak, waiting patiently for its turn.

Over the previous few months, I'd become convinced that I existed in some sort of holding pattern, waiting for my life to start. I couldn't escape the gaping hole that wouldn't be closed until I found out who had torn my life in half. I still had the mug I'd broken in the church restroom — split cleanly in two. Whenever I thought of it, I had the silly, somewhat dramatic idea that I'd glue the pieces together when I had some answers, when my life could start moving forward.

I was very lucky, I know that. Not many people can afford to spend months not working, searching for answers about their past. But I'd been careful with my money, and with what my parents had left me. Even fewer have an equally frugal boyfriend willing, eager, to do the same.

I tried not to beat myself up for waiting so long to start asking questions about my parents' murders. I tried not to think about whether answers would have come more easily if so many years hadn't passed. But there was nothing I could do about it — no way to go back in time and re-live those years when I was numb and looking all over the place for things to distract me. It wasn't until I started seeing ghosts that my mind cracked open. I think Detective Smith played a part in making me push so hard by shrugging his shoulders as if there *were* no answers, simply because he hadn't found them yet. *Yet!*

When I pulled up in front of 1701 Whitewood, the carport was empty. The house was dark. It was just after eleven-thirty at night, and I'd thought for sure Kevin would be there. Maybe he'd left for good, right after Gwen. Or maybe she'd persuaded him to go with her. Or, maybe she hadn't left him at all and they were both out for the evening. Maybe, he hadn't even come home yet.

Whatever the reason, I was thrilled they weren't home, but I felt unsure about the next step, since my plan had been a full-on push at Kevin to allow me inside, and then leave me alone. Stupid, after my experiences with him, but I'm always hoping, always expecting something new and different, always expecting things to work out. I turned off the engine. I got out of the car and shoved my keys in the pocket of my oldest, rattiest jeans, patted my back pocket to be sure my phone hadn't slipped out and buried itself between the cushion and the seat back like it sometimes does, and walked quickly around the side of the house.

In the moonlight, the backyard looked like a vacant lot with its neglected vegetable garden, weeds growing along the edges of the patio, and an expanse of dead grass under the tree, stretching out toward the shed at the back of the property. The swing moved gently, even though the breeze was faint. It seemed as if the swing was inviting me to go for a ride. I walked over and sat down.

The breeze died completely as I sat there with my hands wrapped around the thick ropes, my heels flat on the ground. Each time I'd sat down on the swing, I'd been in a wildly different mindset. The first time, I'd been overcome with feelings that I was back home after all those years, and that my swing was still there. The second time, I'd immediately set it in motion, feeling nothing but the sensation of flying up toward the branches and the sky. Now, I realized from the position of my feet that the ropes had been adjusted. I'd used it when I was a teenager, but I'd grown an inch or so since I was fifteen. The change was so slight, and the work that would be required to make a small correction in the length of the ropes, which were tied around such thick branches, made me feel as if it had been done for me.

I wasn't sure who had lived in the house before Kevin and Gwen, but Gwen was shorter than I, so it wasn't for her. Kevin certainly hadn't untied and retied the ropes for me. I pressed the soles of my sandals hard against the earth. My legs were a perfect ninety-degree angle. I tipped my head back and looked up into the branches. Even though moonlight filtered through the leaves, it was impossible to see enough detail to determine whether the rope was worn from a previous knot. I gripped the ropes, squeezing my hands until I couldn't make them any tighter. I squeezed my eyes shut as well, trying to prevent the thought from creeping through my mind that my parents' ghosts had altered the swing, inviting my return, waiting somewhere nearby to make themselves known to me.

Then, I opened my eyes, pushed off hard, and started the swing moving. The warm air flowed over my face and arms. My legs pumped, the fabric of my jeans pulling tight across my kneecaps as they bent, loosening when they straightened. I pumped harder, flying up into the night, feeling like I was trying to touch my toes to the moon. Swinging was one of my favorite things when I was little. I don't know why we give up childhood things when we grow up — no more jumping rope, unless you're in a gym, working out. There's no more climbing trees and playing hide-and-seek. Why do those things become unimportant? Maybe adults need more complicated games, we want to play sports with more intricate rules than simply closing your eyes and counting to one hundred.

I kept the swing going for a while. I can't say how long, whether it was ten minutes or more like half an hour. The moon didn't seem to change position and the air remained the same bathwater temperature, with a whisper of something cooler coming soon.

I half expected Kevin to arrive home, his motorcycle rumbling into the driveway, lights in the house turning on, Kevin opening the bedroom window and catching sight of me on his property, using his swing.

I stopped pumping my legs and let the momentum fade, finally simply drifting back and forth. As I studied the house, a dim light appeared. The only sounds were crickets and some far off voices coming from another house on the street. I hadn't heard the motorcycle. Had they come home in the minivan and I was so lost in my thoughts I didn't notice the sound of wheels crunching on stray pieces of gravel and the engine purring then going silent? Doors opening and closing?

The swing moved a bit. I steadied it, tensing my quadriceps to keep it in place.

The light didn't seem to be in the master bedroom or the living room, the two rooms which faced the back of the house. I tried to think how a light from the front would be visible, but couldn't picture it, with the hallway in between. I realized it was softly glowing out all of the windows, as if the entire house was lit up, but not. It was a nonsensical thought, but that's how it was.

The light began pulsing, not like a strobe, or a bulb that's ready to burn out, but like something living. I realized I was holding my breath. I let it out slowly and tried not to blink, not wanting to miss a single thing.

Slowly, I loosened my grip on the ropes. I let go of them and stood. My body felt wobbly from the swinging, as if I were still flying through the air, gliding over the surface of the earth, not fully rooted to the spot where I stood. I took a few steps toward the house.

Through the French doors that opened from the living room into the backyard, I saw two shadowy figures. They seemed to be looking out at the tree. All I could see were the outlines of their forms. There was something insubstantial about them, and I knew immediately they weren't Kevin and Gwen. They stood silently, the beloved ghosts that I'd waited for. They looked out, but I couldn't be sure if they even saw me, much less recognized me.

They were watching. I thought about how Gwen must have felt, that sense of being observed when you can't know why or to what end. I imagined for her it was unnerving and upsetting, but for me, it felt delicious. Even if they didn't see me, or recognize me, they were watching, waiting for me to come home. Waiting to see me using my swing, picking vegetables in the garden, blowing bubbles, and all the other things I did when I was small and none of us ever imagined our lives being split apart, even in our nightmares.

I wanted to walk closer to the house, but I was terrified of scaring them away. It seemed like a foolish fear. If they were there to watch, why would they be afraid to encounter the one being they were watching for? Their only child, the girl they'd left behind through no choice of their own.

I took three more steps. The light continued to pulse. I wished desperately that I could make out some shape of the faces, the figures. I couldn't even be sure which one was my father and which one my mother. As I stared through the darkness, I began to see solid areas where the faces would be, the sockets into their heads, openings for their eyes. It wasn't gory, just the shadows that form when someone isn't in full light but the very familiar shape of a human face is still evident.

The crickets had stopped, whether it was because of the presence of the two unearthly figures or something else, I couldn't say. The voices from down the street were also silent. The figures grew less distinct and panic gripped my heart. I walked carefully toward the doors. Why wouldn't they come out of the house? Why wouldn't they speak?

As I was asking these questions inside my head, I was aware of how I always want more. I wanted them to appear and here they were, and immediately I was wanting closer contact, words, all kinds of things. I moved up close to the patio and stepped onto the hard surface. The moonlight was behind me now, blocked by the awning, and although the light still pulsed inside the house, the interior looked much darker from where I stood.

I opened my mouth, unsure what to say, but trusting the most important thing would emerge without me making a conscious effort. "It's Madison," I said.

The figures remained where they were, their faces still obscured. I walked closer and tried the door handle. It was locked. I touched the glass. I took my hand away and gestured for them to open the door. They didn't move. I wanted to cry. It was exactly what I'd wanted, what I'd hoped for all this time, yet so wrong and so painful to be standing nearby and have no way of reaching them, no way of hearing their voices.

"Can you hear me?"

The night remained silent.

"Can you come outside?" I raised my voice, not wanting to shout, but wanting to be sure I could be heard through the glass. "Can you hear me?"

They remained unmoving. I stood there for a very long time, not saying anything more. After a while, they faded to nothing. I sat on the patio and leaned my face against the glass. The strip of wood outlining the pane pressed into my forehead and I cried.

Nine

JD WOKE ME the next morning the same way I'd woken him before our trip to Bolinas — a kiss on my lips and a mug of coffee on my nightstand. Of course, that's how he wakes me whenever he's up before me, but it never stops being awesome.

He'd been asleep when I got home the night before and I'd been guiltily pleased that I didn't have to talk about my experience. It was too much — trying to describe what had happened, trying to figure out what I was feeling. Even if I'd figured it out, I doubted I'd be able to wrap words around those thoughts. It was too huge, too . . . everything.

I sat up and scooted over and he sat on the edge of the bed. He put his hand on my shin which was nice. I picked up my coffee and blew on the surface.

"Why didn't you wake me up last night? You were gone a long time."

I put my mug on the nightstand again. "I saw them."

"Why didn't you wake me?!"

"It was just too much, I was upset. I didn't know what to say."

"It sounds like you figured it out now."

He looked so sad and so disappointed I wanted to cry. Tears seemed to be my default lately. But maybe it comes from nearly fifteen years of hardly crying at all, at least as far as I could remember.

"I'm sorry. I was just . . . I needed to sleep. I didn't want to think about it, or make it fade by talking too much."

"So what happened?"

"Kevin and Gwen weren't there. I stayed in the backyard, swinging for a while. Then, when I stopped, there they were. Inside the house. Well, I saw two figures. It had to be them. I know it was them. But they couldn't seem to hear me and they didn't speak."

He nodded.

"It was so wonderful and so awful I didn't think I could talk to you about it. I'm sorry."

He squeezed my leg. "How many times do I have to remind you — I'm with you in this."

"I know, and I don't mean to keep leaving you behind."

"It's not that. It seems like you don't think I'm all in."

I tugged on his arm and he moved up next to me. I hugged him. He put his head under my chin and I rested my head on his. "I know you are. I just couldn't talk. I couldn't."

He nodded. His head pushed against my chin, rattling my teeth. I laughed. He sat up. "But you saw them! It's almost unbelievable."

"I know. After all this time, all this hoping, and being afraid to hope too much, but then hoping even more."

"Do you think Gwen and Kevin are gone for good? Maybe that's why they showed up."

"It makes sense. I didn't think of that."

He stood. "I have to head out. I'm walking the Zyglers' and the Changs' dogs. And then I have to make the rounds on cat care. I'll stop at the store on the way back."

"Sounds good, I need shampoo. How about burritos for dinner?"

He nodded and went into the bathroom, and turned on the shower water. I settled back against my pillows. I picked up my mug and started my promised thinking. Everything had changed and nothing had changed. I *still* had to get inside that house. But I was more desperate. Nothing was going to stop me. I wasn't ruling out breaking in.

JD left without me revealing my thoughts, although I'm sure he'd guessed.

I showered, put on a comfy t-shirt dress, and drank two more cups of coffee. I painted my toenails blue to match my dress and then made scrambled eggs with cheddar cheese, tomatoes, onions, and chunks of avocado. I topped it with salsa JD had made and ate it on the balcony with another cup of coffee.

The night before had been so intense, and I felt so close to thinking it was going to be possible to communicate with my parents, I decided I was finally ready to read the journal I'd skipped. If my next visit to the house allowed me access, one way or another, it was important to go into it with as much recollected memory as possible.

I washed the breakfast dishes and went to the hall closet. I opened the door and poked my toe at the box full of journals. My heart started thudding hard, as if some cellular part of me remembered what was in that book, even if my brain didn't have any memories. I pulled out the box, opened the flaps, and lifted out the journal. It was the same red leather as the others from my teenage years, but the pristine edges of the unused pages made it easy to pick out from the others. I closed the box, pushed it back into the closet, and carried the book out to the balcony. I sat down, then changed my mind. If I had another bout of crying, I didn't want to be sitting out on the balcony on display to the neighbors. Even though eighty percent of our neighbors were at work during the day, I still felt exposed. I went into the living room and curled up on the couch. Then I decided a beverage would be nice. I went back to the kitchen, got a glass of water, and returned to my seat.

I opened the book on my lap and let my eyes drift over the words without focusing. After a few minutes, I took a deep breath and started to read.

The days before my parents' murder were filled with

short entries about my new experiences going to high school. I'd found some girls to eat lunch with. I loved my art teacher. Most of the classes were beyond easy — I guess homeschooling had put me ahead of my peers in a lot of ways. Although I was a bit behind in understanding slang and in navigating all the groupings of jocks and geeks and free spirits, techies and surfers and A-students.

There was a gap of two days, which wasn't unusual, but I knew this was a significant gap. On the Thursday after their deaths, instead of the date, I wrote this — *Thursday. I'm an orphan.*

It was awful. Horrifying. My life has been blown apart. Tuesday night and Wednesday night I only slept for a few hours, but it wasn't real sleep. A doctor gave me some pills but I still woke at three in the morning, my dream as real as if it, IT, the awful thing, had just happened. I had the same dream both nights and I'm scared I'll have this dream for the rest of my life.

In my dream, I walk into the house and it's quiet. I know right away . . . even though I act like I don't . . . I pretend to myself it's not . . . but I know something is wrong. It's quieter than I've ever known. Quieter than midnight, so quiet it feels as if someone has punctured my eardrums and I can no longer hear anything. I call out for Mom, using a loud whisper because it's so quiet. I know she'll never hear me, my voice is too soft, and a tiny ping inside my heart tells me she'll never hear me at all, ever again, but my legs and eyes and hands and the top of my brain keeps acting like everything is fine.

I go into the kitchen and it's empty, the counters are clean, and it smells like nothing. I walk down the hall and whisper her name. I whisper for my Dad. I look in my bedroom and it's all normal. I don't know why I'm looking because why would my parents be in there? I look in the hall bathroom with the same question in my mind — why am I looking in here? It's dim and empty and if they were inside, the door would be closed. I even pull back the shower curtain and look in the bathtub. Maybe I'm afraid someone is hiding in there, although the house feels very, very empty.

Their bedroom door is closed. That is so very wrong. It's never closed during the day.

I knock and silence answers. I knock harder. I'm afraid to open it. I've never opened their door without a parental voice saying — come on in. I knock harder. Then, I'm pounding, shouting, are you there? Where are you? Where are you? Where ARE you?

My knuckles hurt and I rub them, standing in front of the closed door.

After a very long time, I turn the knob, push it open, and see them. Immediately I see them. Immediately I know they aren't sleeping.

At first, I think their faces are gone. And in the dream, they are. I can't remember what they look like, I can't remember a single thing about the color of their eyes or the shape of their smiles. But in real life, it wasn't like that. I think it's just that I didn't see their faces. All I saw were those two black, bloody holes in the centers of their foreheads. Almost identical. So much alike I wonder if two people stood in the doorway and shot them simultaneously.

I stumble into the room. I grab the iron rail at the foot of their bed and scream. I scream so loud, the image of that painting appears in my mind, a howl worse than the grave, and I'm screaming one long cry but at the same time feeling ridiculous that

I'm thinking of a painting, a painting I don't even like very much. When I'm finished screaming I feel like crying, but I can't. I can hardly breathe.

I lean over the railing and touch my mother's left foot and my father's right, I hold them and try to feel something — warmth, or movement. I squeeze tighter and tighter, expecting them to tell me to stop hurting them, but they don't. Their eyes remain closed, their mouths not moving. They look content, or at least asleep, as if sleep is content. But they also look horrible. Frozen and unreal. I let go of their feet and turn away.

I sit on the floor, leaning my back against the bed, and close my eyes. I try to think, but thoughts won't come. I see their faces and the bullet holes and I wonder if that's what I'll see every time I close my eyes. Always. I open my eyes and stare down the hallway.

I think I should call someone but I don't want to talk to anyone. I don't want anyone in my house. I wonder who was already here. Who did this awful thing? And why? WHY? My parents were wonderful people, who would kill them? Who would want to hurt them at all, much less want to see them dead?

The room gets darker. The sun is moving behind the trees and I know I need to call my Aunt and Uncle. Not any of my parents' friends. Not my friends. What would I say? I need to call the police. But I still don't want to talk to anyone. I want it all to go away. I want my parents to sit up and say, What are you doing on the floor? I stand and look, to see if they're sleeping, and just now waking up.

They aren't.

I grab the end of the bed again because I think I'm going to faint. I glance at my mother's nightstand and see something so awful

I can't breathe. I can't even write it. I can't . . .

That was all written in black ink. In blue ink, a few lines down, I wrote this.

I buried it. I buried that awful thing in the vegetable garden. I dug up one of the tomato plants. I gathered all the ripe tomatoes in a bowl, and carefully placed the plant on the dirt. I buried it deeper than the roots, put the tomato plant back in its place, and shoved the loose dirt in around it. I packed down the dirt with a shovel and dropped some dried weeds on top.

Then, I called the police. As soon as I hung up, I called my Aunt and Uncle, because there's no one else.

I can't write any more. I don't know what I feel, I don't know what I think. There are no words to describe what happened. I'm staying with my Aunt and Uncle and I guess this is where I'll be. For a long time. Until I'm grown up, I suppose.

I read the rest of the entries. Only five. And then fifty or more blank pages. Such a beautiful, expensive-looking book that was hardly used. The next time I started keeping a journal was in my senior year of high school. Those were the journals I'd read earlier, during the binge of wallowing in my past.

All those months were lost forever. I'd never know how I felt or what thoughts wormed their way through my mind. Maybe it didn't matter. Maybe it's not really good to know too much about what you thought about and cried about, what you were excited about and what plans you wrote down in the past. You don't live there anymore. It's better to be looking at where you're going.

I remembered what Gloria said about her journals — that she never returned to read them. And maybe she had that right. It's the act of thinking through your life on paper that matters, not clinging to every thought you ever had as if it's some kind of jewel that you need to take out and look at repeatedly.

During those months when I didn't write in this beautiful leather journal, leaving nothing but blank pages to mark my days, my life had truly been a blank. Surviving day to day was a full-time job. It couldn't have been easy, going to high school, going to school at all — a new experience with overwhelming feelings of its own — trying not to think about being an orphan, missing my parents. There were no more after school chats, no more games, no more hiking or trips, or praise, or encouragement from them. And all the things that hadn't happened that now would never happen — seeing their proud faces at my high school graduation, my college graduation, talking over my career goals, a wedding, having a child, and all the tiny little bits and pieces of life in between that.

I took the book back to the hall closet, opened the box, and tucked it inside. After I closed the closet door, I stood there for a moment. I opened it again and removed the journal. I carried it into the bedroom and placed it on JD's pillow.

I got my bag, went outside, and walked to the park. I

sat on the bench near the pond and wondered about the thing that I'd buried. I had no idea what it could be. As I lit my second cigarette, I closed my eyes and tried to think, tried to remember. But there was nothing. Not even a memory of digging in the backyard.

Whatever it was, it had to be there still.

THE RED LEATHER journal remained in the same spot all day, despite JD going in and out of the bedroom several times after he came home from animal care. He even sat in the bedroom and worked on the laptop that's on a small table in the corner next to the closet.

Our comforter is such a pale green it's almost white, so there was no way he hadn't seen it. I felt like I'd laid my heart out there on the bed, inviting him to read what I wrote at the worst moment of my life, and he wasn't bothering to peek inside.

When we went to bed, it was still in the same spot, the red cover pulsing like a heart ripped out of someone's chest.

He picked it up and put it on his nightstand.

I caught my breath. The inside of my throat and chest froze.

He climbed into bed, turned out his light, and propped the pillows behind him. He sat there, watching, waiting for me to join him.

I got in next to him and he put his arms around me. "Thank you for letting me read your journal."

The only response I could come up with was, "Oh!"

He squeezed me. "Why didn't you tell me about it earlier?"

"I didn't read that one when I read the others. I could see by the empty pages what it was, and I left it in the box. I didn't think I could face it. Today, I decided I needed to."

"How do you feel?"

"Kind of numb. It's like I've shifted from feeling pain to observing pain. It makes me feel hollow. I can't explain."

He didn't say anything, which made me very, *very* happy. Sometimes, you want to hear someone agree with what you're saying, hear them affirm your experience, but there are times when it's better for others to keep their mouths shut.

We lay there for a long time, staring at the ceiling. At least I was staring at the ceiling, and I think he was too, but I didn't turn my head to check. Our breathing was evenly paced.

It was starting to look like everything between the two of us had become evenly paced. The more we were together, the more I felt as if our two lives were shifting their tempo, so that everywhere we went, we moved with the same stride. That sounds fanciful, thinking your actual body rhythm is changing for another person, but it's true. I used to see older couples in restaurants or out hiking and they weren't talking. I thought how sad that was, to enjoy an amazing meal together and have nothing to talk about. But once or twice, when JD and I were eating sandwiches on the balcony, we hadn't talked. And I saw that not talking didn't mean you weren't together. Our eyes were seeing the same flowers and the same people passing by, and our ears were hearing the same dribbling of water in the fountain below. Our tongues were tasting the same cheese and toasted bread and heirloom tomatoes. Of course our thoughts weren't identical, but our minds were speaking to each other on an entirely different level, I think. Not the specific ideas and opinions, but a sense of comfort in an almost telepathic kind of communication.

It doesn't matter if that sounds crazy. That's how it was. After that, when I saw an older couple eating and glancing at each other, then looking out the window, I recognized that parts of each of their brains were melting into a very pleasant fondue. It wasn't that they were bored with each other at all.

JD took my hand.

After a few minutes, he said, "Do you have any idea what the awful thing was?"

"No."

He was quiet for quite a long time again. Voices from the garden below drifted up to the open window. A plane flew over, but it was quite high, so it was a distant, peaceful, steady sound rather than a wall-shaking racket.

"Do you think it was the gun?"

I sat up. "No. I hadn't thought of that. I don't know."

He squeezed my hand.

Like I said, some of our thoughts were starting to

speak to each other without the involvement of our mouths and vocal chords, and I know that he knew I was going to be visiting the house with a shovel. And I knew he was thinking a pick might also be necessary, because of the drought, and also how long the thing had been buried. Both of us knew we'd be doing this together.

"That would really be something, if it was the gun. They could get fingerprints," I said.

"Maybe."

I sighed. "But I don't know how that would feel. Seeing it."

"Are you thinking you should tell the detective? Let the police do the digging?"

"Absolutely not."

"Just checking."

"They would get a warrant, and then Kevin would get involved. They might search the house again, and what if all the chaos chased away my parents' ghosts? After I'm so close, so close I can almost touch them."

"So midnight gravediggers?" He coughed. "Sorry, I didn't . . ."

"That's okay."

"Sorry."

"Really, it's okay. We are like gravediggers, in a way."

"We can't dig up the entire backyard," he said.

"I know. I think once I'm out there, I can remember where the tomatoes were planted. So that will narrow it a bit."

"Okay. But you think you can remember where

specific plants were located, but not what was buried?"

"You know, I really doubt it would be the gun. I'm pretty sure I would have wanted the police to deal with that. And I wouldn't want to have touched it. Even though I was so shocked and so . . . outside of myself, I would have known they needed it to find the killer."

"Good point. But I wonder what could be so awful you blocked it out of your memory. Dug a hole and buried it and then shut it away entirely."

"I hope we find out," I said.

"Or not."

"What do you mean?"

"It scares me. What it might do to you."

"Maybe it just seemed awful to a teenager," I said.

"Maybe."

I snuggled up close to him. I put my head on the muscle where his shoulder joins to his chest. He put his hand on the side of my head and held it close.

We fell asleep. When I woke up a few minutes after midnight, I wanted a cigarette in the worst way. I decided to risk smoking on the balcony again. I took my journal from JD's side of the bed, kissed his forehead, and got my cigarettes and a flashlight. The tile on the balcony was cold, but it soothed my feet that were steamed up from the sheet and the blanket wrapped around them.

I went back in the house and got an empty can from the beans we had in the burritos. I rinsed it out and took it outside. I closed the door behind me and lit my cigarette. Immediately, my mind stopped scurrying around trying to think about how we'd dig up the backyard. After three or four drags, I put it out in the can. I leaned forward over the table and opened the journal. I turned on the flashlight and once again, I read everything I'd written.

Ten

JD AND I arrived at Whitewood Way just after two in the morning. We had a pick and two shiny new shovels in the back of his SUV. We pulled up across the street, one house down. Kevin's motorcycle was in the carport.

I twisted my hair, a single, fat braid, around my wrist and tried to think. I closed my eyes and pictured us digging good-sized holes throughout the remains of the vegetable garden. I imagined the pick hitting a rock, clanging like a dinner bell, the bedroom light coming on, Kevin appearing at the back door, shouting.

"What do you want to do?" JD said.

My eyes were still closed, trying to see what Kevin might do next. Would he call the police? He didn't strike me as a police-calling kind of guy. He seemed more the type to handle problems himself. But how would he handle it? I had no idea whether Gwen had left him permanently, temporarily, or was just away for a few days visiting someone. Based on the last time I'd seen her, I was pretty sure it was the first. But still, without her there to keep him in a semi-reasonable state of mind, I couldn't predict what he'd do.

The SUV engine ticked softly. Outside JD's open window, crickets were chirping. I heard an insomniac songbird. I wondered if the crickets would keep on once we started digging. Their silence might wake Kevin, even if our digging didn't.

"I have to find it," I said.

JD opened his door. We got our tools out of the back and crossed the street. Thankfully the moon was a thin sliver, although if someone were looking out a window, they would still be able to see us. My heart felt thick and slow, while my pulse raced, if that's possible. Then my heart got even thicker as I realized there probably weren't a lot of guys who would do what JD was doing for me. I tucked the shovels under one arm and hooked my finger around his belt loop as we made our way along the side of the house to the backyard. JD had a small flashlight, but he kept it turned off while we were close to the back of the house.

We crossed the yard and leaned the tools against the tree. We looked at the larger-than-I-remembered and never-thought-of-it-in-terms-of-digging-it-up vegetable garden. He turned on the flashlight and shone it in a slow arc across the area. The rows of weathered, stringless stakes that still remained where the green beans had been planted helped me eliminate one potential burial place. I remembered carrots in front of the beans. The tomatoes had been furthest from the oak tree, in order to give them the maximum hours of sunlight.

I motioned to JD and started walking across the dirt, still uneven where there'd been trenches between the rows. Once we got to the far corner, I realized there was no way to pinpoint it any more closely. We had a lot of digging to do.

I pulled JD close and spoke softly into his ear. "Let's start at the farthest corner and just loosen the top four or five inches. I can't believe I went that deep. I wanted it out of sight, but I probably wasn't thinking about it being there for fifteen years."

He turned off the flashlight, took the pick, and attacked the soil. I felt like I should be doing more than standing there as a shovel rack, but it didn't make sense to use a shovel until he'd loosened a decent section of dirt. It wasn't hard-packed clay, but it still would make the shoveling go more quickly once the pick did its job.

While he dug, I glanced at the house every two or three seconds. Finally, I stopped watching him and turned to face the house. It remained dark.

After thirty or forty minutes, he'd turned over the top layer of dirt in a section that was about eight by eight feet. In five or six spots, he'd loosened desiccated roots and the stubs of stems. I took one of the shovels and started digging around one of the tomato plant corpses, assuming I was accurate in what I'd written about re-planting a tomato on top of the thing I'd buried.

I can't be sure how long we dug. JD worked with one

shovel, I worked with the other, and with one eye on the house.

I stopped and pulled my braid to the top of my head. It was a pleasant night, about sixty degrees, but sweat was starting to pool at the back of my neck and dribble along the sides of my spine. There were two water bottles in the SUV, but I was too excited, too filled with adrenaline to want to stop searching long enough to walk back out and get them. Besides, opening and closing the door added to the risk of someone hearing or seeing us. The shoveling was strangely quiet, the metal spades slid into the soil like a knife slicing through a piece of chicken. Because the ground was relatively rock-free, even after all the years of neglect, the dirt was warm and welcoming.

"Madison." JD spoke in a normal tone.

I dropped my braid and turned.

"I hit something that sounded like glass."

I grabbed my shovel and walked to his side. He scooped way loose dirt. He inserted the shovel and stepped on the top edge, pushing it deeper, bringing up a full scoop of dirt. He tossed it to the side. Something glinted at us.

He put his shovel on the ground and pulled the flashlight out of his pocket. He directed the beam into the hole. It was the corner of a silver picture frame. A shard of glass protruded where his shovel had rammed into it.

I dropped my shovel and knelt down. I began scraping at the dirt with my hands, not caring that grit wedged beneath my fingernails. I dug faster, opening up a space around the frame. JD knelt beside me, holding the light steady. I pulled out the bent frame and picked away pieces of glass from the photograph.

JD held the light closer, and when I saw what it was, I dropped it as if a piece of glass had sliced through my fingers. I whimpered softly. JD put his arm around my shoulders and I leaned into him.

It was a photograph of me. I was about ten years old, my hair cut to my shoulders with bangs that covered my eyebrows. I was smiling and looking slightly away from the camera. Near the top of my thick bangs, surrounded by shards of glass, was a bullet hole in the photograph.

Maybe Detective Smith had been correct in his line of questioning. Maybe all of this *did* have to do with me. It was kids from my new high school, not after my parents at all, but wanting to kill me. But I wasn't there. And they never came back, as far as I knew or remembered. Did they kill my parents to hurt me? But why? How would I have made enemies when I'd only been attending the public high school for a few weeks before they were murdered? Was I so despicable that I generated that much hate in such a short period of time? Or jealousy?

"That's . . ." JD said. "It's . . . it's very disturbing. How twisted . . ."

I pressed my head against his shoulder. Did someone want to kill me, even now?

More than anything, I wished I could remember why I'd buried it. Why it seemed important to hide it from the police, from my Aunt and Uncle, from myself. It was maddening to try to put myself back in that teenaged mind, torn with grief, yet taking time to do something deliberate and private. Was I scared? Did I secretly have thoughts I was trying to bury along with the picture, suspicions about who had killed them? Unless I had some miraculous resurgence of memory, I would never know.

I shoved the picture frame back in the hole, even though I knew I wouldn't leave it there. We sat holding each other for a while. Finally, JD stood and picked up the shovels.

"I'll put these in the truck," he said softly.

I nodded. He probably couldn't see my head move, but he turned anyway. He walked to the side of the house and disappeared around the corner. He returned a moment later with the bottles of water. He drank some of his, replaced the cap, then grabbed the pick.

"Should we get going?" he said.

"Not yet." I sipped some water. I picked up the picture frame. Without looking at it, I handed it to him.

"I'm gonna sit in the truck and try to catch some sleep," he said.

"Thank you."

He walked back toward the street, carrying the pick and the photograph. I wondered if he'd look at it before he fell asleep.

I SAT ON THE FAMILIAR WOOD of my swing. I thought about JD, sitting alone in his SUV, holding that tarnished, dirt-encrusted picture frame, his fingers carefully avoiding the slivers of glass, and his eyes avoiding that black hole in my forehead. I couldn't begin to think what was on his mind. Whatever it was, he knew exactly when to leave me alone.

He knew when I needed to be held. He knew when I wanted to spill my brains out of my mouth, holding out his hands to catch all my thoughts and keep me from drowning in them. It felt so good to have someone watching out for me, taking care of me, and never, or hardly ever, stepping on my toes. I really did not know how he did it. Good instincts, or a guy who'd learned to pick up on feelings and moods after all those years as a bartender. It's possible he already had those instincts, and that's what made him a good bartender. And now, caring for animals who seemed to adore him as much as their fabulous Yelp-review-writing owners. He was a remarkably kind and sensitive and intuitive human being. He'd seen a ghost long before I ever did, so he clearly had a curious, listening soul. How did I get so lucky to find a man that brings me coffee and shares the cooking and cleaning so that we're equal partners? I have a man who makes me feel protected — as if he's a knight in shining armor and all that archaic stuff — and at the same time makes me feel like I'm a female superhero who can take on any opponent, and win.

It's not that he's perfect, but at that moment, I could not think of a single flaw. It could be he's just perfect for me.

As the night moved deeper into the darkest hours, I continued to think about him waiting for me. Maybe he could sleep, or maybe he couldn't, maybe he just wanted to, or was pretending he wanted to, but at that moment, I couldn't imagine ever sleeping again.

I stared at the house as if the sheer force of my gaze would drill into the lock mechanism and open the back door. I wondered if Kevin could feel my presence, only a few yards from his bedroom window. But there was something about the house, despite his motorcycle in the carport, that felt deserted, so maybe he didn't feel any human presence. I shivered. Maybe there was no life at all, spirit or otherwise. If my parents' ghosts were gone, would that cause the house to give off this empty feeling that was washing over me?

I moved the swing gently, keeping my feet on the ground. The longer I sat there, the emptier everything seemed. I became convinced that Kevin had indeed left his motorcycle behind. There's something about a house without inhabitants that feels colder and quieter than a house where the occupants are simply out for the evening or away on vacation.

I stood and walked toward the patio. If Kevin *were* there, if I woke him, he'd come out yelling. But if my parents appeared, that would give him a different demeanor altogether. I put my hand along the top of my brow and tried to look through the glass on the living room doors. The furniture was still there. I stepped back. I walked toward the door leading out from the master bedroom. The drapes were closed. I turned to face the yard. The holes and piles of dirt where JD and I had dug were hardly noticeable in the dark. In the daylight, it would look like a gopher on steroids had attacked the yard. Still, I didn't think it would be noticed any time soon. I was convinced the house was deserted.

I returned to the living room doors. I put my hand on the knob, and before I could register that it was unlocked, the door moved inward. It hadn't even been properly latched. I stepped inside and closed the door. The room had a slight vanilla smell, much cleaner and fresher than I remembered when I'd been sitting there with Gwen and Kevin. Not that it had smelled badly, but there hadn't been anything pleasant, maybe a suggestion of dust and a lack of fresh air from a house that rarely had its windows open.

I went to the couch and sat down. I took off my shoes and curled my feet up under me. It was comforting sitting in the room alone. As far as I could tell, I was finally alone in the house. This was what I'd wanted — the darkness and the absence of talking, thinking, moving, breathing human beings. If there was a sleeping person back in that bedroom, it was okay, but I was more and more certain that wasn't the case. Maybe I'd driven them out, by telling Gwen her feelings of being watched weren't in her imagination. I suppose I'd scared her a little bit, or quite a lot. And maybe, despite his prickly attitude, Kevin loved her more than he'd let on, and once she drew the proverbial line in the sand, he acquiesced. Or maybe she told him what I'd said and he was scared.

I settled my head against the back of the couch and tried to breathe softly. I needed to slow my pulse. It was picking up speed as my anticipation grew, certain that if my parents had appeared once, they were still so close I could feel them. I'd never tried to touch a ghost, and I wasn't sure it was a good idea. My pulse raced faster. It pounded at the sides of my eyes. My heart fluttered and leapt inside my chest, knocking against my bones, like a little kid clamoring for her parents to let her come into the living room and see the gifts under the tree on Christmas morning.

After two of the longest, slowest breaths I could manage, I felt, more than saw, the light change. As if the moon had slipped lower in the sky and was peaking its delicate finger in through the panes in the back door. On the wall slightly behind me and to my left, the print of the sunflowers glowed as if the yellow on the petals had been artificially infused with more pigment.

Rather than materializing near the doors where I'd seen them before, they were suddenly directly in front of me, almost fully formed. I gasped and held my breath for a moment. They weren't a physical presence, still vaporous and shadowy, but I could see their faces, their hair, the shapes of their bodies. "Oh," I said softly.

My mother spoke first. "Madison."

"We love you," my father said.

"We're so sorry. So very sorry," my mother said.

"Why? Why would you be sorry?"

"We never meant to leave you. We meant to give you a wonderful, amazing, perfect life. You were everything to us. You *are* everything."

I whispered, terrified I would exhale and they'd evaporate. "I love you. I've missed you."

They didn't speak. Even though they were a few feet away, it felt as if they were touching me, their hands on my hair and face. I closed my eyes, then quickly opened them. I didn't want to miss one single instant, one single sensation.

"It took you a long time," my father said.

"It did."

"But you came," he said.

"Nothing could stop me."

"We're so sorry." Their voices were whispers, yet so clear, and so familiar.

"Who did this to you?"

"It's hard to explain. There are things you don't know," my mother said.

"What things?"

She moved closer. I felt the weight of her hand grew heavier on my head. I couldn't see her face, but I felt she was enveloping me.

"Your brother."

"My . . . ?" I couldn't breathe. And then, she was next to me on the couch, her arms around me.

"We had a child. I was sixteen, and my mother . . ."

"Oh," I said.

"We were children ourselves," she said. "We gave him

to a couple who couldn't have a child of their own. It seemed like the best chance for him."

"We thought it was the right thing," my father said. "For him. A couple who had so much love to give. And then he came to the house."

"So angry. So very, very angry. And jealous of you," my mother said.

I couldn't breathe. The room was silent again. I heard my heart pounding, fighting to understand it all, the sound of thick blood pumping, as if their hearts were beating alongside mine. "But why . . . why did you let him . . . it seemed like you just laid in your bed and let him."

My father spoke. "We didn't think he'd do it."

"Even when he shot your photograph . . ." My mother's arms tightened around my shoulders. "We were trying to make him understand. We tried so hard. But he just couldn't. He still doesn't. And I suppose I understand that."

I tucked my feet more tightly beneath me, leaned into her, marveling that her appearance could be so insubstantial, but able to support the entire weight of me.

"He hated you. He'd spent his life hating you. The jealousy ate his heart. But when he asked us to lie down, we still didn't think it could happen."

"He killed you to hurt me? Is that what you're saying?"

"Partially," she said. "Yes, he did. But also out of hatred for us. Or hurt, I think."

The room was cooler. I didn't want them to leave, but I could feel their presence already growing weaker. Were they wanting me to help them get justice? To make sure my brother — even the word in my mind shocked me so that my thoughts froze for a moment — to make sure my brother was punished?

I never knew what it felt like to be hated. And to be hated for something that had nothing to do with me, was confusing and painful and frightening all in the same moment. "Where is he?"

The room became so quiet I could hear the sound of the leaves rustling outside, despite the closed doors. "Where is he?" I spoke more loudly. My voice was rough, as if it didn't belong to me.

"He was here," my father said.

"He won't hurt you," my mother said. "You're safe now."

"Where *is* he? What's his name?"

I felt alone on the couch. My mother was no longer beside me. She was near my father, moving slowly toward the opposite wall. Their forms were less distinct.

"Don't leave!" I stood.

"You'll be okay. You're perfect. We love you. We're so very sorry."

"Aren't you going to tell me where I can find him? So I can tell the Detective, so . . ."

"We don't need revenge," my mother said. "All he wanted was to torment you."

Her words shook something loose inside my head. A

sour taste filled my mouth, coating my tongue. I tried to move closer to them but it seemed as if there was a wall of ice between us, distorting their shapes, making their voices less distinct.

All he wanted was to torment me . . . his reddish hair, like mine, but darker . . . his mocking, his games.

"He was here," my father said. "He wanted us dead, but then he had to be here. As if he needed us after all."

"Kevin?"

"You're safe now." Their voices were far away and nothing remained but a shadowy image, like breath on a window. "Yes. Kevin."

And then, my beloved ghosts were gone.

I KNEW I SHOULD call the detective, but I couldn't bear the thought of talking to him, to anyone. For a few minutes longer, they belonged only to me.

I sat back down on the couch and brought my knees up to my chin, wrapping my arms around my lower legs, hugging them close. I pressed my forehead against my knees. Within the space of a few minutes, I'd learned I had a brother, lost him, found he hated me for the mere fact of my existence, and discovered the answer to who murdered my parents. It was hard to absorb the idea that I was related to a man who could take two lives so heartlessly, so easily. That he would do something so cruel and terrible, just to hurt me.

Images of my grandmother drifted through my head, reminding me that so many parts of my family were harsh and bitter. I hoped it didn't mean that was my fate as well. My parents weren't like that, so it didn't have to be. But it was hard to escape the feeling that other blood ran through me and might turn against me no matter how I tried to fight it.

I thought about Kevin lying to me, taunting me. I wondered if he'd known since the very first time I knocked on his door, the moment Gwen told him a strange woman had come by wanting to see inside the house. He must have.

For several minutes, I retraced the things my parents' ghosts had done and said, trying to plant everything firmly in my memory so I'd never forget. Later, I would write it all down in the nearly empty journal, so I'd have the whole thing in one place. And maybe I'd put the horrible photograph in there. Or maybe not. I didn't know what I'd do. I wondered what JD was doing, if he was asleep, finally, or if he was wide awake, worrying about what had happened to me.

Outside the French doors, the light had changed to a grayish, pre-dawn color. The swing hung motionless, the thick ropes and hard wood connected to a tree that was easily a hundred years old, made it look as if it would last forever. Beyond my lifetime. It was comforting. Thinking back how it had felt, raised slightly to accommodate my adult height. I knew without a fragment of disbelief that somehow, in a way I couldn't even understand, my parents had adjusted it for me. They wanted me to know there were close by and they wanted me to know they cared for me, always.

If I hadn't read my journal, if my teenaged self hadn't pointed my adult self back to the awful thing buried in the garden, would I ever have made it inside the house and seen them? I had no idea. But somehow it seemed like finding that photograph, in some way that I couldn't explain, had opened the door for them to reach me.

I stood and moved around, easing the tight spots out of my feet and joints from sitting for so long — maybe hours. I'd lost track of time.

I walked toward the hallway. The kitchen was also filled with gloomy light. It was time to leave, but I needed to walk through the house once more. It was possible I'd be able to come back, especially with Kevin and Gwen moved out . . . Kevin. A brother. It was too difficult to think of that as something real. I'd be reporting my brother to the police. I shivered. I pulled out one of the chairs and sat for a moment at the kitchen table. It was important to be in each room. This was the last time I'd be in the house when my parents had also been here. Any future times when I returned would be completely different.

I closed my eyes and tried to breathe, no longer smelling the vanilla. Now it just smelled stale. I stood and pushed the chair back to the table.

In the hallway it was still dark. All the doors were closed, as they had been when JD and I looked through the house earlier that summer. I walked down the hall to my parents' room, opened the door, and stepped inside.

The furniture was still there. The bed was made and the room looked tidier than I remembered. The image of my mother and father, lying on their backs, dead, was no longer as easy to recall. Instead when I tried to picture them, the memory of their ghosts appeared. I crossed the room and pulled the cord to open the drapes. The backyard looked beautiful in the pre-dawn light, even with the shadowy outlines of displaced earth. JD and I would fill it back in before we left.

I stepped back into the hallway, leaving their bedroom door open.

I went to my room and turned the doorknob. I pushed the door but it wouldn't open all the way. Through the narrow opening I could see the window seat I'd loved. I pushed harder. The door bumped and thudded thickly against the adjacent wall. I slipped through the narrow opening and turned to see what was blocking it.

A scream that can only be described as blood-curdling came out of somewhere deep inside me, so deep it was as if it came from some dark canyon I didn't even know existed.

Someone had installed a large hook at the top of the door. Someone . . . Kevin.

Hanging from the hook by a short piece of thick rope, was Kevin's body. I screamed again, louder, crying. I collapsed to my knees and pressed my forehead against the floor. I continued screaming, all of it coming out — my parents murdered, an aunt and uncle who were ambivalent about taking care of me, a hate-filled grandmother, a brother who loathed me, a brother who was a killer.

From far away, I heard JD.

"Madison?! Madison, what's wrong? Where are you?" He was pounding on the front door.

I knew I should go to him, but I couldn't look up, couldn't see a face that I now realized looked similar to my own.

I heard JD calling, more distant now, then heard his footsteps pounding through the living room. The bedroom door thudded open with the same thick, semi-solid noise it had made when I tried to open it. He pushed his way into the room.

"Oh my god, holy shit. Oh god. Baby, are you . . ." He knelt next to me and pulled me up toward his chest. He cradled my head and pressed my face against him.

I cried for a long time, feeling his breath gasp in the same pulsing rhythm as my own.

Eleven

WHEN THE SUN began to splash across the window seat, we slipped out of the room, careful not to move the door any more than necessary. I swallowed bile, feeling the weight of Kevin's body on the door, the soft scraping of his clothing on the wood.

We went out to the backyard. JD returned to the SUV to get a shovel while I pulled my phone out of my pocket and tried to think how I'd begin my call to Detective Smith. I was still staring at it when JD came back. He took a large scoop of dirt and dropped it into the first hole, followed by three more, whacking the shovel on the ground to pack the dirt. After he'd filled three or four holes, I was still holding my phone, studying it as if any moment, an answer would flash across the blank screen.

Finally, I pressed Detective Smith's number. It was only twenty minutes past six, so not surprisingly, I got his voicemail. I didn't tell him anything except that he should call me as soon as he listened to the message. "It's an emergency." I hung up and realized that was the wrong thing to say. He'd wonder why I hadn't called 9-1-1. He'd hear it and worry I was in trouble. He'd think that what he perceived as a pointless pursuit had led me to a killer and perhaps my life was in danger. I called again. "It's not an emergency, as in life or death. But I've found a body. A dead body, just to be clear. Call me."

I went to the car to get the other shovel and walked back around the side of the house. Kevin's distorted face played across the backs of my eyes. I'd never even had a chance to compare our features, to ask him anything about his life, about how he found our parents, about why he blamed me for his grief. Although I suppose he'd already told me when he said I was raised to think I was the center of the universe, when he told me he'd never had a childhood. He surely had a childhood, but not the one he wanted. Not the one he deserved. Now I knew why he'd always seemed so angry with me. I would have liked to ask him if he'd seen my parents' ghosts, felt their presence, or if he only liked living near the place of their deaths, like Gwen had said.

He'd gone out of his way to do everything in his power to destroy my life. But I wouldn't let him. Everything was settled. I didn't even need Detective Smith, except to take care of the physical details.

Before I could start filling holes, my phone buzzed.

"Detective Smith, what's up?" he said.

"It's a long story."

"Whose body?"

"It's . . . well, it's my brother."

"I wasn't aware you had a brother. Where are you? Where's the body?"

"I wasn't aware either. I'm at my house, my former house, on Whitewood. His body is here."

"I'll be there." He ended the call.

I started scooping loose dirt.

About ten minutes later, two cops in uniforms came walking around the side of the house. Both of them were young — my age — one tall and thin with a shaved head. The other wasn't as tall, but he was just as thin and had dark hair in a buzz cut.

"What are you doing?" the tall one said.

Before I could answer, Detective Smith walked into the yard. He glanced at the holes, but obviously realized they weren't suggesting we were burying a body. "Please show Officer Martinez and Officer Wilson where this body is located."

I dropped my shovel. JD kept working.

Detective Smith took a few steps toward JD. "What's this about?"

"It's a long story," JD said.

"Apparently everything is." He glanced at me. "Why don't we all go inside. I assume that's where the body is?"

I led them into the house. JD sat in the living room while I led the two cops and Detective Smith down the short hall. I pressed my back against the wall opposite from my bedroom door. "He's in there. On the back of the door. So be careful. He hung himself." I wasn't sure that last part was necessary, but both cops nodded, so I guessed it was an important piece of information. At least they were prepared for what they were going to see, unlike I'd been.

Officer Martinez, the tall one, opened the door too hard, and of course, Kevin's body thudded against the wall. I swallowed another stream of bile that rushed into my throat. He yanked his hand off the knob. He moved the door carefully and both of them went inside. Detective Smith followed.

I coughed. "I'll wait in the living room."

"Yes, thank you," Detective Smith said.

JD and I sat there, not talking. I yawned a few times. I thought about how long I'd been awake. "I wish we could have some coffee."

"Me too," he said.

"Or a smoke."

"Me too."

We continued to sit in silence. The dueling cravings for coffee and cigarettes swam inside me, making me yawn more. The voices of the cops and Detective Smith came down the hall but I couldn't make out what they were saying.

It seemed like half an hour went by and we were still sitting there. I went into the kitchen, found the coffee, and filled the pot with water. I started it brewing and went back to the living room. The coffee was done and we were holding mugs when Detective Smith finally came into the room. At the same time, the doorbell rang.

Detective Smith answered the door and let in a man and woman, who I assumed were from the morgue. They disappeared down the hall.

JD and I were on the couch and Detective Smith took a seat in the armchair across from us. "So, tell me the long stories."

JD took my hand. While Detective Smith jotted down notes, I explained everything — starting with my journal, including my parents' ghosts, despite the expression on Detective Smith's face that said I was obviously sleep-deprived. He stopped writing when I talked about the ghosts, and then made more notes when I explained how I'd walked through the house and finally entered my room. When I finished, he said nothing. He held his pen as if he expected more. The sounds of the cops and the morgue people moving around in the bedroom, voices rising and falling, thumps that made me feel sick to my stomach, filled the living room.

The people from the morgue went out the front door, and still Detective Smith didn't speak. They returned with a gurney that they maneuvered across the porch, into the house, and down the hall.

I stood. "I don't think I want to be here when they . . ."

Detective Smith nodded.

I took my coffee cup and went into the back yard. He and JD followed.

"So. What you're telling me is that your parents had a child before you, and he murdered them. But the only evidence you have for this, the only evidence you have that this man is related to you, is what you believe is a supernatural experience?"

"That's not how I'd put it," I said.

"How would you put it?"

"I don't *believe* it was supernatural. I know it was. I saw my parents' ghosts."

"I can't use that as evidence."

"Well I guess it's not like you can put him on trial and send him to prison anyway," I said.

"We don't have a time of death yet, but it's less than twenty-four hours. That's certain," Detective Smith said. "Given that, please tell me again what time you arrived here."

"What are you implying?" JD said.

Detective Smith pressed his lips into a line.

"He committed suicide," JD said.

The line remained across Detective Smith's face. He blinked slowly, waiting.

"I didn't kill him," I said. "If that's what you think."

Detective Smith's eyes flicked toward JD.

"*We* didn't kill him." My voice was so loud, a crow sitting at the top of the oak tree cawed and took off, beating its wings vigorously as if it couldn't wait to get away from us.

"It's an incredible story," he said.

"I know a lot of people don't believe in ghosts, but . . ."

"Not just that."

"What?"

"The journal."

"I can show it to you."

"Is there a way to authenticate the date?"

"Oh my God! Why would I make all of this up? You know how badly I've wanted to know who killed them. I don't want to just blame some dead guy. I want the truth. And now I have it."

"Well, Madison, satisfying you and satisfying the law aren't quite the same thing."

"It doesn't matter," I said. "You weren't trying to find the killer anyway. I don't even know why I called you. I should have called 9-1-1 and left."

"Calm down," he said. "Your fingerprints are likely all over the house, so it's not as if you could have just walked away. We would have come looking for you. I'm just asking what time you arrived. That's how an investigation works. I have to ask all the basic questions. You found the body. Tell me what time you arrived and what time you found the body."

"We got here around two a.m.," I said.

"She found the body about five this morning," JD said.

Detective Smith looked at JD. "You weren't there?"

"No. We told you. We looked for the thing that was buried." He gestured across the yard, "I went out to the car to try to catch some sleep and give Madison some time alone. That's when she saw the ghosts."

Detective Smith rolled his eyes.

"That's not very professional," I said.

"You're right. Sorry. I just don't know what to do with all of this. You must realize how it sounds. You dug up the yard, in the dark, and happened to stumble upon something you buried fifteen years ago, even though you had no idea what you were looking for. Two ghosts that you took to be your parents . . ."

"They were my parents," I said.

"Two ghosts appeared and told you a brother you didn't know existed had killed them. The supposed brother just happened to be renting this house and just happened to have hung himself the very day you came looking for your buried object and ran into the ghosts."

"We know how it sounds," JD said. "But you could make a lot of things sound improbable if you summarized them without all the connecting details."

"Maybe. But I'm having trouble with the ghosts, obviously. I can't put that into my report. And we have no proof this guy is related to you or knew your parents. Those are the missing *connecting details*, as you call them. Pretty big connections."

"Okay," I said. "I can see that. You didn't talk to the ghosts yourself."

He smiled but he looked slightly sick to his stomach. I don't know if it was the idea of seeing ghosts, or the fact that he had to deal with all of this that was making him ill. I moved closer to JD and put my arm around his waist. "I'm really tired. I've been up all night."

"I guess I have everything I'm going to get, for now.

I'll need the photograph."

"Why?"

"This is a crime scene. You can't remove anything. And it's the only solid item we have that gives credibility to the story that this guy knew who you were."

"Will I get it back?"

"At some point."

JD squeezed my shoulders. I didn't want to let it go, but then, what good was it going to do me? Did I really need something so filled with rage inside my house? Did I really need to be looking at something that said I was lucky to be alive? That someone — my own brother — hated my guts?

JD let go of me and walked to the side of the house. He returned a few minutes later with the photograph. Detective Smith put on plastic gloves, pinched the frame between his thumb and forefinger, and pulled out a plastic bag from his pocket. He dropped the picture inside and sealed it.

"We'll look into this guy and see what we come up with."

"Oh, I forgot. He was living here with his girlfriend. Gwen."

"And Gwen's last name is?"

"I don't know. I don't even know Kevin's last name. But Jan, next door, owns the house. She'll know."

"Thank you. Anything else?"

"Nothing I can think of."

"I'll get back in touch with your grandmother."

"I don't think she'll help."

"Talking to a detective is a little different from talking to an estranged granddaughter."

"I guess."

We said good-bye. I felt strangely disappointed. I'd found everything I'd been searching for, but all it had done was show me how more alone I was in the world. Except for JD. And my aunt and uncle, but mostly JD. I'd always been alone, and I'd known I was, so I wasn't sure why it was hitting me like I'd only now realized it.

ON THE WAY home, we stopped at the park and shared a cigarette. We slept until three in the afternoon. After a shower and a turkey sandwich and an apple, an enormous iced latte for me, and a black coffee for JD, we drove to Gloria and Paul's. I assumed Detective Smith had probably already been there to ask them questions, and I was right.

We sat in the living room, staring at each other. They didn't have any beverages or offer us any, as if the circumstances were too strange to have anything as common as a glass of wine or a cup of coffee. Neither one of them seemed to know what to say. But I did. I settled back on the couch and crossed my legs. "You probably know what I'm going to ask, don't you?"

Paul nodded. Gloria looked at him.

"Yes," he said, "Yes, I knew your mother was pregnant. Obviously that's why your grandmother exiled her."

"Exiled? That's a little extreme."

"That's the only word I know to describe it, so you can comprehend how complete it was. And final."

"What did you do?"

"I was away at school. I wasn't in a position to support her financially. I'd always thought, assumed, I guess, that she had an abortion. She never spoke to me about it, and when I asked, she said she wanted to start her life over, forget everything and everyone, except me, and your father, of course."

Gloria stood. "I'm sorry. Do you want something to drink?" She sounded like a robot, as if she hadn't absorbed everything that had happened. Because she didn't know what else to do, her lifelong habits kicked into gear despite the fact her mind was racing around, looking for something to grab onto. I wondered if Detective Smith had mentioned my parents' ghosts to them.

"Coffee. Thanks," I said.

"Me too," JD said.

"Make it three."

She left the room and Paul went on. "I didn't see her for more than a year, so it's definitely plausible she had the child."

"Why didn't you tell me?"

"I couldn't see the point. What would it have accomplished?"

"Why didn't you tell Detective Smith?"

"Same reason."

"Does he see it that way?"

"I think he's annoyed that none of this came out before. But why would it? I didn't think an unexpected pregnancy that happened to a teenager over thirty years ago was related at all. I had no reason to think it mattered. And he never asked any questions that made me think it was important. It was so long ago, it almost seemed like it never happened."

He talked about my grandmother, how harsh she was. How cruel, especially to my mother. A few minutes later, Gloria returned with a tray and four delicate china teacups with coffee.

When we were all settled back with our coffees, Gloria said, "It explains so much."

"What does it explain?"

"Why Annie was so determined to give you a perfect life. Why she was so smothering."

"She wasn't smothering. Not at all!"

I put down my cup. It clattered on the saucer. I sat forward on the couch.

"Don't be defensive," Gloria said.

"I'm not. You're wrong about her."

"Maybe smothering is the wrong word. But she thought she could control your life, protect you from anything bad, form you into a perfect human being. And there's no such thing."

"I don't think she was like that. She was a wonderful mother."

"She was," Gloria said. "But she did try very hard to make everything in your life perfect. Smothering was a poor choice of words. And controlling . . . it wasn't that, exactly. I don't know how to describe it. She was very idealistic."

No one spoke for several minutes. I think we all saw the irony of how absolutely imperfectly my life had turned out.

"You saw their ghosts?" Gloria said softly. "You talked to them? And they spoke to you?"

"Yes."

"That's incredible."

"I know."

"I don't know if I believe in ghosts," she said. "But I never thought about it."

There's no good way to respond to a comment like that. I sipped my coffee and slipped my hand into JD's. I still felt unsettled and I wasn't sure why. Maybe because, despite knowing what I wanted to find out, there was still so much I didn't know. Detective Smith would find some of it — he'd learn where Kevin was raised, how he found my parents, what had gone on in his life. Although none of that would explain why the bitterness grew in him to such a degree that he wanted them dead. That's inexplicable. Some people have terrible things happen, and they survive to be amazing human beings. Others just rot inside until they might as well be dead. Maybe Kevin figured that out.

"How did it feel?" Gloria said.

"Comforting."

"I can imagine. I guess you really never thought much of us. We could never measure up to your parents, of course. And we didn't try to. But still, we did our best. I never pretended I was your mother." Her face looked suddenly old, her lips twisted in a pained, doubtful expression. Her eyes were bleary and surrounded by shadows, as if she hadn't slept in a very long time.

"That's not true. It's not that I didn't think much of you."

"You took up smoking, you holed up in your room. You acted as if you were doing us a favor when you ate a meal with us."

"Smoking was all I had."

"We understood how hard it was, but still a little gratitude would have been nice." She sighed and looked even more tired.

"Thank you," I said.

"I'm not begging for praise."

"I know. I really mean it. Thank you."

"We had no idea what to do with you. And Annie and Dave had raised you to mostly listen to your own opinions, which I suppose is a good thing, for the most part. I see that now. It made you very strong."

JD squeezed my hand, agreeing, or maybe testing my supposed strength.

"I really do appreciate that you took care of me. I'm sure I was difficult. And upset. And angry. I'm sorry I wasn't appreciative. I really am."

She smiled, although it looked limp, and a little bit like she didn't believe me. "Thank you for saying so."

"There is one thing," Paul said. "A few months before

Annie and Dave were killed, Francine, your grandmother, called here. I'd forgotten about it. I wanted to forget about it, like I wanted to forget everything about her. She didn't want to see how I was or tell me she missed me. She ranted about how sins come back to haunt you. That's what she said, several times, then she hung up. I wonder . . . I wonder now if that's how Kevin found Annie and Dave. Maybe she'd couldn't help keeping track of them after all, and pointed Kevin in the right direction."

I got up and walked across the tiled area that joined the living room and dining room. I went through the dining room and into the kitchen. I picked up the coffee pot, returned to the living room, and gave everyone a refill.

"She said that to me — about sins haunting you," I said. "I couldn't understand why she kept repeating it. How terrible, to think of your grandson as a sin."

Gloria and Paul nodded.

"I feel like I should have seen something," Paul said. "I should have guessed. I should have . . ."

"How can you possibly take a senseless comment and infer all of that?" Gloria said. "Connecting her ranting to Annie's child and knowing the child would do something so terrible? You had nothing to do with it."

It's strange how noticing threads like that can make you feel that you could have done something. Gloria's reassurance was logical and true, but I could see the doubt on Paul's face, thinking *if only*. I could see that he thought maybe he should have told me my mother got pregnant when she was sixteen. Maybe my parents should have told me. Maybe I should have seen something in Kevin's face the first time I talked to him, and all the times after that, some glimmer of familiarity. But I didn't.

All these things that could have been different, but it's so easy to see that in the end, not when you're in the middle.

They invited us to stay for dinner. Paul grilled prawns and cherry tomatoes on skewers and Gloria made tabouli and a green salad. She served it on the patio table, along with Chardonnay. I even had half a glass of wine. It was okay.

TWO DAYS LATER, Detective Smith called. He asked if he could come to our place to give us an update. I was so surprised by the role reversal, I didn't speak for a moment. Then he asked if he could pick me up a latte. I didn't know cops were allowed to spend money on the public, and I didn't know he'd noticed the nearly constant presence of an iced latte in my hand. Possibly he was more observant than I gave him credit for. I agreed and told him I liked whole milk, no sugar, and would definitely like the largest size offered by his coffee cafe.

At one o'clock he knocked on the door.

He sat with his back to the balcony. JD and I were diagonally across from him, beside each other on the couch. I sipped my latte and waited for him to speak. I knew what he was going to say.

"Everything you told us was true," he said.

I smiled.

"Your mother had a child when she was sixteen. Your father was named on the birth certificate and the child was adopted by Miriam and John Malvek in New York state. Kevin Malvek grew up in Maryland. In his late teens, he had a few citations for vandalism and a shoplifting arrest. He moved to California the same year your parents were murdered. He rented the Whitewood Way house."

I sipped my latte through the straw, enjoying the mild brain freeze.

"None of his fingerprints were at the murder scene. But he did purchase a gun, legally. It was the same caliber as the weapon that killed your parents. And the bullets we retrieved, including the stray bullet that we now know punctured the photograph . . ." He cleared his throat, eager to avoid mentioning that the bullet had punctured an image of my head. "But there's no weapon to make a firm match. Ms. Lukeman, his partner, wasn't aware he owned a gun and of course pretty much knew nothing of any of this. She did comment that once you'd appeared at their front door, he became oddly obsessed with you."

"What else did Gwen, Ms. Lukeman, say? About the house?" I was eager, but not hopeful, that she'd mentioned her feeling of being watched. I wanted to know what Mr.-I-can't-put-ghosts-in-my-report would do with that.

"She didn't understand why Mr. Malvek got such a thrill out of living in a place where people had been murdered. It disturbed her, and she begged him multiple times to consider moving, but he became quite stubborn, refused to discuss it."

I thought it sounded like Uncle Paul, refusing to discuss my grandmother, but perhaps I was just looking for family connections because I hadn't had any in such a long time. Really, there are lots of stubborn people in the world who aren't related to each other. Half the human race is stubborn. Sometimes it's called tenacity and we praise it. When it's around a topic we don't like, it gets labeled stubbornness. "Anything else? About how she felt living there?"

He shook his head.

I took a long slurp of iced latte. It wasn't worth telling him what Gwen had told me. It wouldn't make him believe me — it was simply her story filtered through me. I wished she'd been more honest with him. I suppose she thought it wasn't important. It made me wonder how much people don't tell the police and how much longer it takes them to do their jobs if people don't mention things they've determined are irrelevant. And the police don't always know to ask the right questions. It's probably true of all relationships. Things aren't mentioned, trivia and little details of life, and sometimes those are huge things that really do matter. Like, oh, by the way, I buried an upsetting photograph with a bullet hole in the backyard. If Detective Smith had had that picture of me, would he have conducted his investigation differently? I had no idea, and it was too late. My teenaged self had been so upset, getting rid of it must have seemed like the more comforting course of action. And if he'd asked Uncle Paul about someone who might want to kill *me*, not my parents, would Paul have thought it absolutely *was* important to mention the call from my grandmother?

"So although we don't have direct physical evidence, Kevin Malvek is a likely suspect for the murder of Annie and Dave Keith."

"The only suspect," I said.

"Yes."

From everything they could determine about the time of Kevin's death, he was hanging there on the back of my bedroom door several hours before JD and I began digging holes in the backyard. I remembered how the house had felt deserted, and I guess it was. Except for ghosts.

Part of me wondered if Kevin's ghost would linger, but the moment I had the thought, I realized I didn't care. I had no desire to go back, no desire to wait to see if he appeared. He wasn't really my brother in the way you think of a brother. He was just someone who had the same DNA as me.

There's all this debate, throughout the years, regarding nature versus nurture. No one will ever really know which carries more weight, but it's definitely not just one or the other. And the nurture side has so many factors they probably can't ever be sorted out.

We want all the answers, but I wonder why. It's good to have a little mystery, to not always understand why people do what they do and feel what they feel, to have ghosts that come back from the other side to tell us we don't know everything.

WHEN DETECTIVE SMITH was gone, JD and I sat on the balcony. We had a bowl of pistachio nuts on the table between us. As we cracked the shells the rather loud snapping echoed across the courtyard. We drank lime flavored sparkling water and put our bare feet on the balcony rail.

After a while. My phone buzzed and I saw Kate's face smirking at me.

When I picked up, she wanted to know what the hell was going on since she hadn't heard a word from me in weeks, beyond a few text messages that told her absolutely nothing. I gave her the whole story, in agonizing detail, of everything that had happened since I'd quit my job. She didn't interrupt once, and when I was finished, there was silence.

"Did you fall asleep?" I said.

"I just . . . wow. That's unbelievable," she said.

"I know."

"How are you feeling?"

"I don't think I really looked at the whole picture until I explained it you just now," I said. "But I feel good. I feel happy that I got to say good-bye. I feel sad and a little confused about my parents hiding my grandmother and brother from me. I guess they weren't perfect and it seemed like the right thing at the time. I'm upset about my brother, and still numb, disbelieving, I guess, but it's not like I would have wanted a relationship with him."

"No. I guess not," she said.

"But talking to him would have been good. Maybe. I don't know. He murdered my parents. Our parents."

We were quiet for a few minutes, and then she caught me up on her life, which was mostly churchy stuff — the usual politics and complaints, but good times too. There hadn't been any ghosts in the basement. She thought Joe and Cindee seemed different. She couldn't explain how, just *different.* Maybe kinder, was the word she eventually came around to.

"Are you coming back?" she said.

"To visit?"

"No. And you know that's not what I meant. Are you coming back to work?"

"No."

"I guess I knew that," she said. "But I still wanted to ask."

We talked a bit longer and I promised I absolutely would be back to visit her. I invited her up to our place. "You could stay with Gloria and Paul. They have a magnificent house."

She laughed.

We said good-bye, and I promised to send text messages that weren't so empty of actual information.

I don't think I knew for sure, until I said it to Kate, that I wasn't going back to manage the church office. To be honest, it was a little boring working there. Editing and writing articles for the newsletter was interesting, but the rest was dull. If it hadn't been for the ghosts, I might have lost my mind. It was a good stopping point on my path through life, and if it hadn't been for the church, I never would have learned I was one of the lucky ones on the earth who gets to see ghosts, and hear their voices.

Maybe that's why I ended up at Central Avenue Church. Maybe those ghosts were leading me to the most important ghosts of all — the imperfect people who gave me a perfect start in life.

ON SUNDAY, I woke to the smell of chicken frying. I went into the kitchen where JD had three crispy looking pieces already sitting on a plate, and was finishing up the last. The sink was piled high with pots and bowls.

"Dinner already?" I kissed him and plucked a piece of crispy fried skin off one of the chicken breasts.

"No. And no free samples."

I filled a mug with coffee and sat at the kitchen table to watch him finish up.

"We're going for a drive," he said. "And a picnic."

He packed up all the food in the fridge, including his homemade potato salad. He washed the dishes while I cleaned the bathroom. We spent the rest of the morning cleaning the apartment. It wasn't as if it was that dirty, but it's a tiny place and things pile up. And we hadn't done major stuff like clean the windows or vacuum under the bed since we'd moved in.

We walked to the deli and got sandwiches for lunch,

and then went to the park. We ate, watched the ducks, and smoked without talking, just enjoying the quiet quacking and a bunch of guys playing soccer in the field on the other side of the pond.

After the SUV was loaded with the cooler and a blanket, we headed out. He turned south on the freeway. There was a lot of Sunday traffic, so it took almost forty-five minutes before we saw the Golden Gate Bridge, stretched across the San Francisco Bay, all of its orange-red glory visible in a perfectly blue sky.

He pulled off the freeway and drove up the curving road toward the Marin Headlands. We'd never been there together. The headlands are just beyond where the bridge hits land, up a small hill. From there, you can see the Pacific Ocean, back toward the bridge, the bay, and the San Francisco skyline. The Bay Bridge spans the opposite side, and Alcatraz Island sits innocently in the center of all that water.

JD spread the blanket on the ground and put the cooler near one edge. For a Sunday, you'd think there would be hordes of people taking in the view, but it was strangely empty. From where we sat, I could see lots of people walking and bicycling across the bridge, but I guess not many wanted to be up in the windy area of the headlands. We sat beside each other and put our arms around each other. I leaned into him and it was warm enough for me.

After looking out at the Pacific Ocean for a while, which can occupy an amazing amount of time, JD said,

"I have a question that's been on my mind."

I moved away slightly. "What's that?"

"Will you marry me?"

"Yes."

Just like that. It was so simple. And so very perfect. He didn't make a speech and I didn't make a speech, and he didn't slide a ring on my finger. Well, not at first.

We kissed. And then he opened the cooler and pulled out a plastic bag with a small box inside. He removed the box and opened it and took out a ring. It had a teardrop emerald, and along the platinum band were three tiny diamonds on each side.

"This was my grandmother's."

My throat tightened at the thought of grandmothers, but I swallowed and thought about how some grandmothers, most grandmothers, are wonderful. And then I shifted my attention to how beautiful, absolutely stunning, the ring was.

He took my left hand and slid it into place on my ring finger. He kissed me lightly on the lips and said, "I knew the moment I met you that you were the one for me."

"Really?"

He kissed me again. He didn't ask whether I knew.

"It fits perfectly."

"I put a strip of paper around your finger while you were asleep."

I laughed.

He opened the cooler again and took out a half bottle of champagne and two glasses. He poured a bit in each one and we toasted each other and took a sip. I liked it a lot better than the wine I'd had with Gloria and Paul. I took another sip.

After that, we couldn't stop talking about all the things we wanted to do together. The sun started to move close to the water, and for a while, the breeze calmed down.

I guess all those plans, and the sudden, or not so sudden change in direction, made us famished. Or maybe it was the endless stretch of water and sky. We gobbled down two pieces of chicken each and tons of potato salad. We sipped the rest of our champagne. We finished it off by splitting a huge chocolate chip cookie from the bakery. Then we kissed for a while, until the wind picked up and I was so cold, even the beauty of the water and the bridge couldn't keep me sitting there on a blanket.

Despite our crystal clear view of the ocean, we really had no idea where we were going. College, probably for sure, but where and when and what we'd study, whether or not there would be more ghosts in our lives, more pets, children, and how we wanted our lives to look were all out there beyond the horizon. All I knew, all we both knew, was we'd be walking or driving, or even surfing side by side as we went.

Of course, we never know where we're headed. We think we do, but until we arrive, we don't really know anything.